bird dreams, riding hope

- sometimes a fable, weaving
our connections to birds,
meandering rivers and dragons,
fermenting miso and consciousness,
wetlands, our extended kin and ancestors,
our mentors, and Wisdom.
Inspired by actual events
and a sense of place and belonging
by a woman who addresses the reader
on behalf of the earth

by freda karpf

Copyright 2021 freda karpf
All rights reserved
ISBN: 978-1-7368423-1-7

Cover: view from the bulwarks, photo by lynn cremona
Design partner: ryan borbely

dedication

what follows is dedicated to birds, the land and waters they touch and fly over; the people who help save, protect and steward the land and water; the many who have loved our home and shared its beauty and wonders. I thank you all for your dedication, for sharing your wisdom and life energy; for passing on the good and sharing the wonder.

CONTENTS

dedication

the elements of dragon ~ 1
October ~ 2
the imbolic ~ 3
    the part that is devotion
wounds and feathers ~ 4
waiting ~ 5
    the disappointing herons is one of the songs of longing
    "We look at things in their fullness."
    every river
    yearlong
murmurations ~ 6
    and another deep well
    the chick chirps back
tidal ~ 7
my kind of sacred ~ 8
chiaroscuro – ancestors ~ 9
    define the land, water, and air
    ancestor, family, continuity
turtle crossings, and Crow Women (sanctuaries) ~ 10
the miso walk ~ 11
the Old Woman and morning songs ~ 12
half dragon, half mishugana ~ 13
    half mishugana
    for Ruth, and for all our mothers - when am I not dying
mise en place ~ 14
water dragon ~ 15
the Old Woman and the fields ~ 16

no wrinkles no entry ~ 17
    the old lady's ragu
a talk with the Old Woman ~ 18
bird dreams ~ 19
the blue dragon ~ 20
a highway between realities ~ 21
    corridors
    you rock
    different realities make for different folks
    conjugating joy
    between buttonholes
    island in the stream
    a world where birds are not in peril
    Main Street
    a wind memory
    what holds us to the world
broken and holding ~ 22
    Viola's question
    you might not know
    the Great Kibbitzen
talking to the river ~ 23
the conversation ~ 24
      liminal
      like a blessing
      what must be shared, call them songs
      up the creek
      the old woman talks
      I ask all the time
      the council of all beings
      the jump
      when mrs. t leaves
      belonging
afterword/many thanks

the elements of dragon ~ 1

I went down to the river. I thought I'd do my qigong exercises there because I'd been wanting to get back to the swimming dragon exercise for months. Earlier in the week I had a reading with the astrologer who fugues language and astrology into a verbal pyrotechnics. This was also months delayed. But the first thing she says is that we are both water dragons. It was the year of the dragon. I knew that. I didn't know I was a water dragon. And I also learned that my osprey are sometimes also known as water dragons.

    One trip up to the Cape with Lynn we had a blow out on 95 in Connecticut. We stopped but traffic kept whizzing by. Heart and head were pounding. All I wanted was to get off the highway. But a trooper made us stay on the highway and made me get in the car. The car felt like a thin metal box. I was certain a car would hit me. Lynn was outside speaking to the trooper. I was bracing for impact when I noticed that a dragon had curled up on the right side of my skull. I don't know how but I could see it. Neither Lynn nor the trooper noticed when I got out of the car to ask if I could stand there. I was still scared but I felt a layer of safety between me and the highway. Curled inside my head, the dragon felt like the reassurance that you get with a friendly hand on your shoulder. This was the first time I was aware that dragon paid me a visit.

    I have since learned that there is a dragon for each element. In Chinese healing culture the elements

~1~

are metal, wood, water, fire and earth. But I'm thinking there is another element that might be locked up in our skulls. It only comes into play when a certain symmetry is met. It could be age coupled with PTSD on a cold highway in Connecticut. Or it could be that my zodiac came round to dragon time. Elemental dragons only come once in a 60-year cycle.

~ ~ ~

This small river gets more and more crowded by the phragmites, aka the common reed, as it moves under the highway. I met a man seining for bunkers near my favorite spot to sit, between the broken boards that time and weather opened in the bulwark. These fish are also known as bunker heads, menhaden, moss bunker, plain old bunker or even American sardine. Menhaden comes from the Native American word munnawhatteaug which means "that which manures." The Native Americans would use the menhaden to fertilize their crops. There's a whole lot of stink in those fish but it's a good stink and good for a lot of things.

The man told me he used to go out that way, pointing where Shark River goes under the little, local bridge, with some friends when he was a kid. The river thins even more as it moves under Route 18. He said there's some kind of beachhead out there and they'd stay for hours. He wonders, like I do, if it's still there. He liked the birds we saw on the river in front of us. A poor excuse for a river by some, we both agreed, but we also agreed it's the river we know best. He didn't know the names of the birds we saw, heron and egret. But he knew the fish he caught were less plentiful and didn't think his ration or the osprey's take, was the reason. Me neither. We're both not sure what the many likely reasons are. But we hope things get better. We were looking out on this little sand bar in the middle of this part of the river. From where we stood to across the way, I'd say it was probably less than a football field. It's a sweet spot for birds. The sand is soft like at the ocean's edge and there's thread-like grooves from the water running in miniature rivulets down the slopes of the sandbar back into the river's streaming. Depending on the time of day you're looking, but almost anytime there is sun, the water, the sky, the gulls or the osprey on the distant cell tower, the redwings swaying on the tall phragmites to the left, the river's moving song, coming in or going out back to sea, the salted air, the cypresses holding court to the right– all of these river elements, rises in your eyes, arms, and chest and fills the deep breath you're inclined to take with sweetness. I was standing there after the fisherman left. I had a thought to turn toward my car and then head home and start dinner. But I couldn't move. Something happened. Joy rose like the tide and pulled me into a place I never wanted to leave. Suddenly, these words filled my head, 'I am water dragon.'

    What follows is everything I know that led me here.

~ ~ ~

It is often said that water dragons learn to write but only after they have lived 100 years. This is something my mentor told me. Every contact I had with my mentor, no matter who initiated it, seemed at first random. But she was always so serious that even what might seem like whimsy to others felt like instruction to me. Of course, I had shared that there was a dragon in my head. But all this about water dragons seemed either unreal or like many things esoteric, esoteric. It is said that the first known water dragon wrote notes on a soft piece of paper for summer. For winter she did not write and in spring she was far too busy preparing for summer. She had no time to write. It is only through time that water dragons can appreciate the power of words. Even at 100 years, they do not understand winds or water. Imagine, being a water dragon and still not understanding currents or streams or the slicks that cool breezes draw on the surface of the back end of a river.

    Water and wind speak to each other in a language that many both see and hear. But knowing is different from seeing or hearing and together, seeing and hearing cannot produce knowing without the passage of many seasons. After many seasons however, something changes. Maybe a note from the summer plays like a fugue through the season and continues into the fall. Its presence swells in your consciousness and you finally hear what they're saying. It's so subtle, what with listening to their sounds or just watching the light of the sun or the moon or the light that clouds create, you hardly noticed the passage of time. The wind, the ways of birds, the knowing without knowing comes.

    When a water dragon becomes aware of water and wind, at first, she does not believe their language is real. Only a young water dragon thinks it is just a random joy. Yet, the day comes, and feels like it was always, that a water dragon has found a way to be who she really is among the reeds. She begins to listen in a different way and slowly she seems to think she heard the water or the wind say something, maybe even speak to each other; perhaps even include her in the conversation.

~ ~ ~

What do the winds, which have been busy lately, make of this notion that we are one with what we see? It may be unknowable. The fact is that some days the wind is stronger than others, even when they seem quiet they are very much around. This also means that the trees will be talking too. As everyone knows, their talk changes through the seasons. They have one language when their leaves are full and dancing and another that is a lot like whistles when their leaves are gone. And, of course they speak the language of colors and shadows, the words of shade and dampness, they sing the songs of night and, it is also said their whispers create the morning dew and the evening's quiet only comes when they hush. This could all be rumors. Who is to know these things really? It could be that before the last leaves fell, the water dragon took a large leaf softened by the sun and summer to write that she was leaving. And indeed she did leave as soon as she knew that summer was truly gone and the menhaden were following another stream in the ocean as well. As some report, the streams in the ocean talk to the mouths of rivers. This talk then travels down through the ripples and ripps where the river waters churn. This is how their messages are relayed to the back end of the river where the otters sometimes venture. And high above all this talk, the water dragon learns the news that summer is on the move.

~ ~ ~

I have watched wind closely for decades now. Much of my experience seems second hand. For instance, I look at Tibetan prayer flags and have read that their prayers are taken by the wind. There is no felt effect until the wind takes the words of the prayers off the cloth and off they go to be made manifest. I have seen American flags, and even flags of organizations lose their color to the wind. Does this mean that their mottos and emblems, their symbols and sense of boundary and fortitude even, become manifest in the wind? As an old woman, are my meditations also made manifest by the wind? Are all my dreams, so many already forgotten or transformed, becoming realities? Are they following another stream as well? When is it time to migrate? How do you know that you must leave? Do you follow your dreams? Or do dreams land on a nest in a warmer more welcoming climate and wait for you to join them so that they may seep into your bones and inform your feathers and wings?

October ~ 2

I have been called to the wetlands with some sense of urgency lately. Every October day is packed with the possibility of the osprey migrating or that I'll still find them there and be so happy, which I follow up on quickly with the worry about the need for them to get on with their migration. This is why I sometimes go to my wetlands several times a day in October, with hope, which I gather now has its own meaning apart from what I might think it is, sitting on the edge with me. I always look for the osprey first but I am aware that I am also taken by the whole experience of being there. You pull into a very small parking area delineated by a corral fence. The cattails and phragmites are growing faster now in the fall then they did in the summer. The cypress trees are off to the right. Past them, you can see the road over the small bridge leading from Brighton Avenue into Shark River Hills. This bridge was washed out years ago. It took a year to be replaced. The river runs under it and then also under Route 18 going west. Every time I think of the bridge, I remember the one time I saw two green herons on the west side.

There's a sense of intimacy as soon as you enter the small lot that begins the area I call the wetlands. It's dimensions are like a long isosceles triangle, stretched from the base at the small bridge on Riverside and pointing toward the wider river that is only just past the little spit of trees marked by a wreck, a platform with sailboat rigging hitched by drift and accident, stuck on the spit. The kingfishers frequently rest on the wreck between their brief zooms over the water when the river is visiting.

The area embraces you. The feeling of being in a bowl remains as the leaves thin and the fall colors warm the view. You see all the shades between white and gold, including egg yolk; and the deep red that is almost maroon but stops short to remind you of warmth more than cold. The river mirrors the sky. Warm variations of red. orange and apricot spill onto the river from the trees. A full palette of autumn green and brown emerge in the lazy days after summer's push. You take notice. Time slides along a spectrum of emotions colored by the season. Sentiment is packed into each strand of feeling then teased to consciousness by a cloud, a fog or a sundog, which is like a rainbow off the leash. It is no longer a question of birding when I go to the river, and really hasn't been. It's me going and being there, being birded.

I have found so many ways to feel at home it sometimes seems as if I never leave. It is true, that I haven't gone far. My marsh-woman friend, Mrs. Teale, wrote me that "birds are my family now." She had a hard loss of dad and brothers who won't acknowledge her or give her the birthright she feels is hers. So strange really that all this time wandering, even as I was both simultaneously connected to some family and estranged from others, I recognize her grief though I don't have it the same. Birds are my family now too. This awareness is not always in the same time frame as my day to day living. When I am touched by another's thoughts or concerns, or when I see a bird, all loneliness is erased. That is when I take notice. A tern diving in the stream along the Forsythe wildlife drive in Brigantine brings total joy. Here too. Multiple terns splashing and flying about like kids in a schoolyard, belly laughter. Lone crows or crow conventions, "What are they talking about?" are more important than the overdue electric bill. Starlings will cover the oak trees around my house like jimmies on a chocolate ice cream cone. The way any group of birds enter trees, choreographed. Pride wells. Even when my feelings are as low as a cloud could be, and I'm in a funk, birds will lift me up and take me on. You can work so many thoughts into a knot, but have it undone by an osprey swooping down to take that dried eel grass, like that loose pile of eel grass right over there on the river mud, that you didn't even notice until the osprey swooped down for it. Birds bring you to the present. William Least-Heat Moon said that "There are no yesterdays on the road." Same with birds. And the road I'm on, different as it may sound, takes me home.

  Roethke wrote in Meditations of an Old Woman, "the long light is my home." His old woman had bird bones. She says, "If the wind means me, I'm here. Here." And she wondered if she was a bird. I am home when I do the everyday, chop red onions and add capers to the tuna. I am home when I'm at the bulwarks, waiting for the osprey, hoping the eagle isn't jealous, speaking to spirit and my ancestors, tender as a thread the connections may be, across the river in time, confirming and affirming the hollow feeling filled, the peace, actually a breath not noticed, joy like a deceitful tide, slowly rising.

~ ~ ~

I went down to the river. It was low tide. Leaning a leg against the decaying wood bulwark is one of the most right feelings in the world. Low tide has the charms of a puppy; particularly sweet the way light dances on the low waters. The small streams within the stream moving between the raised mudflats creates water braids and many opportunities for the light to dance. Sometimes the light seems like someone trying to stand on a rolling log. It slides and bounces as it plays over the bars of water that flow into and out of the braids.

    I hold my peaceful trident at the bulwark. Its three prongs are hope for better days, healing from whatever ails me and guidance. A wise guide once said that part of devotion is to hold the knowing of one part even when you're in another part. I held the trident. Her word devotion became a strand in the stream's braid.

    Yesterday, a mighty egret crowned the highest lookout point on the trees to the left. Today, near that point, an osprey. Lightning white must accrue to that tree. Both the egret and the broad band of white on the osprey's chest were struck by it. A gang of swans, just past the bulwarks, continue the white. I hopped on the driest parts of the park to get to the bulwarks. Couldn't see osprey right off. Egrets don't represent the turns in the season, the goings and goodbyes and sense of loss that osprey do.

The water was oily-smooth. Could've been 'tween tides. Three times I saw a small hawk, tail feathers fanned out, attack the kingfisher. The kingfisher hunkered down low on the water as if sitting, which they're not apt to do on water, then hopped three times on the water as well. The hawk tried to strike each time it hopped. But the water wasn't a sure surface for it and it flew off after the third attempt. What a relief. There was a mature eagle eating on the osprey platform downriver. The eagles had twins this year and it was time for a break from the nest.

Fog was rolling in. You can't see past the ripps. There was a weird call but I couldn't see what was driving it closer to me until a giant blue heron came in for a landing in the middle the widest stream. Its croaking call was framed by its quiet landing.

When I first arrived I heard machine gun-rapid clicking. The kingfisher calling out from a wavy cedar branch. The trees and scrubs on the left were in the fog, It was barely possible to trace the osprey back once it landed on a bare branch before the bend by the ripps. It dove for the eighth time before it came up with a small white fish. Then it flew an arc around and over the middle streams before heading into the deepening fog with the fish.

Home at my desk with the window open, an occasional car amplified the night and the moisture still hanging in the air. I remembered the sounds I was met with, the honking and rattling of the great blue heron and the belted kingfisher. I wish I could hold onto the feelings these sounds evoke. I have two pair of binoculars. The good ones and the ones that were really good until they came along. There's nothing to see with them now. Some things are magnified by a damp night and a look back.

The next evening, Lynn and I were enchanted by the quality of the light; the sunset; the moon, nearly full. The water must have been between tides, only some movement near the ripps. Lynn says she expects to always see herons and egrets in the trees because she always does. That's where I look first for the osprey. The first time we pulled away from the Cape May Audubon store, we quietly moved through a covered grove. It was on a small, secluded road that felt like a secret passageway. All the more touching our psyches because this was our first time at one of the world's most famous migration places, the Cape May Hawk Watch. As we pulled onto this road a kettle of turkey vultures circled overhead forming a spiral staircase as they rode a thermal column. I expect to see this every time we go there. Just like I always expect to see the air filled with monarchs because it was on that same trip to Cape May State Point Park, all around the Hawk Watch platform. I had the feeling of being inside a snow globe filled with the royal black and orange migrants.

Photographers call this time of evening, magic hour. The sky to the west was a beautiful purple and the setting sun's rays peaked from under the horizon. The early dark will make these evening wetland stops impossible. As we crossed the bridge intending to pull into the lot, I go knowing that there is only mud, no signs of the river. You can pack my heart in this mud.

Mud focuses your eye on any little sliver of water and you can still see a million reflections of light in it.

There was some good water near the ripps. I nearly fell over trying to keep the bins on two osprey as one soared right overhead. Their tail feathers fan out and their heads articulate as they hunt. Both came into the same view just near the ripps. This is, as Witmer Stone writes, where the waters of the bay and ocean meet. That's exactly where our osprey and kingfishers like to fish. An eagle was flying near them. All three seemed to converge. Then one of the osprey attacked the eagle. They dispersed just as quickly in three different directions and heights. The attack was not even four feet above the mud. Weeks back, three osprey triangulated against the position of the eagle's kid, born this past March, and pinned it to a branch near the old osprey platform, across the way and just before the ripps. Each time it tried to fly off the branch to head back to its nest, one of the three osprey harassed it and forced it back. It tried every angle it could to escape and head back to its nest. It was pinned down but you had to have been there for a while to know this.

Later, I looked for the kingfisher hoping to confirm that it was safe before we left. I was ready to go after some prayers and complaints to whatever spirit was listening, It is good that I am able to report here that the osprey was still around.

The next day, on the way home, I saw osprey again. With my fall bouquet - of sadness, a sense of misgiving, and longing - I had thought they'd gone south. I missed too many opportunities to see the fledglings grow. I only got to see them hang in the trees to the left once. The dead branches afford a good spot over the water and it is near enough for them to keep their nest in view. One hunted right in front of me. Another one called out from a branch. I couldn't see that one right off. When I did I proved the notion that studies have shown, hearts can leap with joy. What a beauty. Shining and large, there was so much white on its head that at first I thought it was an adult eagle. Right below it was a giant white egret. A blue heron landed in the river to my right. The hunting osprey dove down and came up with a five inch fish. The treed osprey called out to it. The hunter wasn't sharing. A third osprey was flying around. As was a red-tailed hawk. Tree osprey had taken off when I was watching all the goings on. Then I saw it hunt. It dove and missed twice. Each time it rose about 15 feet in the air and shook off the water like a dog. It sailed across the way, circled and dove again. This time it caught a small, silver fish of its own. Was this its first catch? It flew back to a dead limb just below and to the right of where it was earlier. It held the fish for a long time before eating it as it watched the river over its own shoulder.

    When I had arrived at the wetlands and parked, an elderly man got out of his pickup truck and quietly asked if I'd mind putting my eyes on the tower to see if that was the osprey on the third rung. It wasn't. I've been fooled many times myself by the uprights that surround the cell tower platform. From the distance we were at it never fails that it catches your eye the way you'd think an osprey would.

I later found out that was Joe. When I introduced myself he put his warm hand out to greet me. Joe knew his birds but his hands, he said, were shaking badly that morning and he couldn't hold the bins steady enough.

Lots of crows were nearby. I don't remember seeing them there before. I love crows more than I can say. I was sorry that Joe left before the osprey appeared. I followed her with my bins, grateful for the steady gaze. Each time I lift the bins hope rises. The river was high and made sloshing, round sounds against the bulwarks.

The following day was Halloween. I went down to the river. I feared and guessed again that the osprey were gone for the season. As low as the water was it still had feet enough to run toward the ocean. Three or four sparrow size birds with striking black and white markings on their chest and bold markings on their heads were chirping from the phragmites.

There were a lot of gulls on the mud flats yesterday. Lynn, heading home from her office, ended up joining me. We both watched the gulls lazy descent onto the wet mud island as they left the unseen thermals that held them aloft. I lost track of the tide's schedule. Catching the osprey where I did was good fortune and good for my heart. As the tide recedes my mud flats become a very soggy, pucker hole smacking affair and the only real water for fish or the osprey to find them in is beyond the bend, past the ripps. This is where the river opens more and turns left to a greater fullness. From there you hang a right to go out toward the Belmar bridge and past that, the ocean.

    The sadness of not seeing my osprey until spring was erased again as I got to see my osprey kid, the one with the huge white chest. What a relief to see her. When they leave I curse them for being snowbirds and feel like I'm holding my breath until they return. But I was also alarmed that this one has not migrated. Apparently, I cannot be happy. I hope it has company for traveling south when it is moved to migrate.

    Every day it is easier to clearly see the eagle's nest means that it is also likely that the osprey have finally migrated. I know they're full of surprises, and my osprey have been known to stay well into November. But I am already looking toward St. Paddy's Day, or St. Gertrude's Day, calendar markers, for their return.

the imbolic ~ 3

While waiting at the bulwarks, I noticed a feather growing out of the right side of my abdominal area. Why should I find this odd enough to notice? My body has become a farm for skin tags, age spots, warts and marks of unknown origin and destiny. I've lost armpit hair and eyelashes. The wind combs my formally plush head like it was grass in an untended field. Nothing about the landscape of my skin surprises me much these days. Except the feather. For a child of the invincible summer, if I were to grow anything other than the usual crop I would have thought it would be scales.

    The time between winter solstice and the spring equinox is known as the imbolic. The between times. The shortest day of the winter is my bright day of hope because by being the darkest it promises light. When it feels like you cannot take one more day of winter and when an eager crocus gives a thumbs up through the cold ground, the imbolic. For many, St. Paddy's Day marks the equinox and my feminist mind reminds me it is also known as St. Gertie's Day. Both days are the pivot point for when the osprey might arrive. A day or so before, a day or so after. If given the task of naming calendar days, I would choose the very same day. It has worn a path in my longing. I would call it Osprey Day as the familiar name and more formally it would be Summer Coming Day. If the seasons had an alleyway it would be this time. Alleyways, particularly any I find on a summer day, call to me. I have come round to seeing all seasons centered on summer's time of fleshy, sweet fruit, penetrating sun, sleepy afternoons, inviting shadows and shade. My four seasons are Summer, Summer Leaving, Winter, and Summer Coming.

    Many cultures across all the world think of summer as the queen of the seasons and winter as her mate. Teale wrote that summer was the king. August the august and crowning glory. Mr. Teale and I would no doubt agree that autumn and spring, their children, are the minor seasons. The osprey come when summer is heading our way. I wonder if they are pulling it along the way you can draft behind a tractor trailer on the road. Or the way the lead Canadian goose guides the flock along, until it tires and another takes the lead. In flight, such a group is also known as a skein. This notion reminds me of my mother's knitting. I was a hopeless student for the knit and purl. After the last attempt at teaching me, she sent me off the porch to play instead of another try at knitting. It could be she brought me along by taking the lead toward summer. Without ever a word she made summer our season. I didn't know it then but osprey were moving in this direction during the imbolic, as they are now, in the time between here and there.

    Between here and there, half of me is attending to the world while the other half is waiting. No matter the infusion of Zen in the culture, I am not living in the moment. And I wonder how Wisdom, the oldest known wild bird, close to my age, manages. Wisdom has likely flown over six million ocean miles. The ocean's edge and the wetlands have become my boundary. When I cross the line it's usually by looking, sometimes by riding waves, but never the long way out toward the unknown.

    I don't know the exact place my osprey go for the winter. Or, if at any time, half their brains go to sleep, while they migrate. Half of Wisdom's brain goes to sleep while the other half keeps her aloft in a glide. I do not know how I stay aloft when my osprey head south in October. It is possible that half my brain is in a glide or that half my consciousness is out wandering and not reporting back to me. The truth remains, if a migrating bird is tied to your heart, your heart is tied to the calendar. They return home mid-March. This could all be a coincidence, but I seem to be most awake then as well.

    Camus wrote, "In the midst of winter, I found there was, within me, an invincible summer. And that makes me happy. For it says that no matter how hard the world pushes against me, within me, there's something stronger - something better, pushing right back." Winter pushes against me. The osprey, my water dragons, move on and then the count begins. At least five months pass before they return to the tower and all the other nests they have made around my part of the shore. My joy rises when I see them on the hunt. I have watched the certain spiraling down to the water followed by the miscalculations of young osprey's plunges. Last August, I saw an osprey take a flounder at the thin line of water with bathers only a few feet away. They did not see the plunge or the flounder rising with the osprey. I watch for osprey. And because I do I see the terns dive, the kingfishers dart head first into the water; the skimmers cruising the back end of the river like bandits, and flounder flying.

Wisdom travels the long road of waves because it is wise, of course, and because that is her way. At 64 years old, she came back to raise her 36th chick. A cowbird raises its chicks in another's nest. "Cowbirds don't know they're cowbirds until they hear their special song." My brain might be half asleep during the imbolic, and I might glide over more miles of ocean than I know in this reality. What I do know is that somehow, even though I am my mother's daughter, I am also like the cowbird. I heard my special song, and realized who I was when I became aware of osprey.

the part that is devotion

Nature entices you to follow the path unwinding from your brain; and sometimes, I'm guessing by personal experience, the path appears as a dragon on one side of your skull. If you meet someone along that path my question will be, "What dragon are you following?" after hellos and the courtesies of course. I suppose not everyone is led by a dragon. It is often said that there is nothing new under the sun. Tell that to a blade of grass, or a crocus for that matter, that has come up through the cold, damp soil of winter and popped its head into the air and been kissed by the wind and the sun for the first time. We have not troubled our thoughts with the whole world of shade and shadow, the colonies of lichen, moss and the immense connections of the dendritic trails of mushrooms and the like. Terence McKenna believed that the mycelium spoke to us but the only way to enter the conversation was through hallucinogenic mushrooms. On the way to the river, on a March day like today, my heart starts to sing and my body relaxes; my eyes catch small movements of ripples in the water; and the weeds. Maybe, just maybe, Terence, there are other ways to enter the conversation.

    Some believe that those in power tell the story and guard the narrator in a tower at an undisclosed location. The wisdom quoted here is from those that live near and know the scattered regions and forests, near the small ponds, and beachheads that aren't well known. These few remaining places are off the map. They're the hidden spots where those who know, keep track of the rare and beautiful. Perhaps you have a place you protect and are reluctant to share. These places are for those who walk the wrack line, or touch their canvasses and paints with and without their brushes; it's for those who love words, even the letters of words, as symbols and sounds as much as sense and sentences.

    Being of this world, no sooner do you realize something important enough to wake your brain with the 'aha' moment, than you forget the revelation as quickly as it came. People forget messages from the gods. We forget our ahas, and we forget our inspirations. I admit that I have forgotten the path that brought chills down my back, and through both my lobes. The realizations that our body recognizes before our mind can express them. I forgot and then remembered, that osprey were water dragons. There is the above, really, when you think of it, it is the great above. There is the below, and now we know to think of it as the great below. As in Inanna, the great Sumerian goddess, who went from the great above to the great below to rescue her love. Somebody, somewhere is always diving into the deep, the dark, the unknown. They may be propelled by hunger or love. They may be searching for their daughter like Demeter searched for Persephone across the entire world, many times over. Or they may be the daughter searching for her mother through time and memories. Water dragon may be unaware it is osprey and osprey may be unaware that it is water dragon. I have learned that if you can write these important messages down somewhere, even if you forget where you put them, one day, because we are creatures of habit, you will come across them again. Many things develop from a daily devotion. That is how I remembered this time that osprey are water dragons. And that is how I know to go to the bulwarks as often as possible to wait for the return of osprey. That's the part that is devotion.

    Daylight decreases when osprey leave. Daylight increases when they return. Not only did we inherit this world from Rhea, also known as Gaia, but we inherited the migration of the osprey. We inherited Demeter, daughter of Earth seeking her daughter Persephone. I do not know how long I have had a dragon in my head. It might have been there from the beginning. It might be you have a vestigial toe, that birds have "fingers" in the wings, and dolphins who went on land, then went back to the sea kept the remnants of fingers in their fins; as we kept the ancient, and unlikely dragon in our heads. A dragon may one day say to you, 'Pay attention.' If you have waited under a tree until dawn to be human, or osprey, or dragon or loved, pay attention. Somebody, somewhere, something in the world around you has left something, however faint a reminder, that may lead you where you need to go.

    If that pull from the unknown is faint, or if someone or something has made so much noise that you cannot hear it, paths are not taken. Two years ago, the cell phone company raised their tower even higher. They changed everything. It seemed an inhospitable place so high up, so many odd mechanics in place and little room, it seemed from so far away, for an osprey nest. I have grown impatient with waiting five months to see my osprey. But I wait. I worry for their return. And now a tower so high.

~ ~ ~

Something always happens if you wait long enough. This is always true and as Carolyn Casey quotes someone else, some things are true and sometimes they are even truer. Lynn and I drove down Great Bay Boulevard. The Rutgers Environmental station is off to the right at the end of the road. It is a large building but looks even larger than it might because it is surrounded by wetlands and the only thing trying to rise above the sea level, which is where you are when on this great road, are the phragmites. Or, if you wait long enough and look with, as the shaman's say, soft eyes, you will see a male marsh hawk, grey like clamshells dried on the beach, lifting from the marsh and rising only to drop down and disappear again. They are also known as the northern harrier. I wondered if I waited long enough, would I find a way in this world that delivers me to grace and creativity as easily as Great Bay Road does. Part of its allure is that you are often below sea level on this road. Two years ago, I stood with Lynn and my good friend Virg and looked into the shallow waters off a quiet dock. We watched the sky in the water and clouds, like a meandering river, moved beneath our gaze.

As above, so below. From above, the water dragon will open the water with a burst, grabbing its fish to take it back to its nest or favorite branch to eat. When I was a kid we'd cannonball into the pool, knees to chest, hoping for the biggest splash. Olympic divers slip into the water hoping for the smallest disturbance. Only the osprey comes up with a fish.

At my home, there is a being who I call Spirit of the Land. When I asked her name, she quickly replied. But I forgot it faster than an eel can slip through a bed of eel grass. I once saw Demeter in a journey. As you often do in the journey-lands, I knew her name without asking. Yet she seemed so young I thought she was her daughter. I would have been more comfortable meeting her daughter. I felt 'not enough' to be in the presence of the goddess of all that grows. Both the Spirit of the Land and Demeter have come to me with quick realities attached to them. Both have human, expressive faces and long tails like a comet.

A picture of the meandering Escalante River in Utah looks like a blue dragon. The curves in a river will change the life and body of a fish. We do not know the life of rivers and yet make decisions about their meandering every day and try to right their curves to our purposes. Only a few years ago, the Whanganui River, which winds through the North Island of New Zealand, became the world's first natural resource to be granted "legal personhood." Will this river now be allowed to coddiewomple, and travel in a purposeful manner towards a vague destination as rivers do? It is their way.

As I came up to the bulwarks, the water near was moving fast out to sea, so there was a sense of streaming; and members of the herds of gulls were wading or walking in the streams. I could hear the little dimples of sounds being lifted and pushed by their legs and pads. No splashing, just the tender music of webbed feet. I wonder if the cold played a part in the sounds. The disparity between where I was and the invasive thoughts of the nasties, office people who enjoy the misery of others, had me in tears. The air was cold and also moving. The mud flats will be arriving. Or so it will seem.

Evening was slipping on. The air was grey. My fingers were bone cold but it did not matter, I was there. I was waiting for the mud that the new crabs scurried on, moving around the reed plugs and mud bubbles. Just a little while ago the river was enough for kingfishers to dive into; or herons, the stalking grey blue derelicts of the river's banks, to squawk at. Now, the tiny, staccato movement of plovers would leave their marks as light as faded labels on herbal tinctures on the mud. The river is a river even when it is just mud. The river is a person.

When the tide slowly slides back you will be able to see the sky in the river and your reflection on the thin film of water. If you're gazing down as you stand next to your friends, you'll get to see each other with the meandering clouds passing by. Now, you're a part of the river too.

wounds and feathers ~ 4

When I arrived, the sixth child, my people no longer knew their relationship to the land. But my mother always knew summer in a way that has me associate her and my whole family with this season. We did not know of birds or even nature. The very first time I saw a heron flying, I was certain that I had discovered a living fossil, a real, live pterodactyl. I would say I was beside myself, but Lynn was next to me in the passenger seat. She was thinking the same as me as we headed south on the Jersey Parkway, '*We found a dinosaur!*' Fortunately, it was long before cell phones, because surely, we would have called everyone, including the media and then, well then, they would have had to have gotten the nets out and lock us up for our own good.

Only just a few minutes ago, I saw some herons flying from the mud to the trees, where they wait for the river to return their fish. They think they own the back end of the river where I go to watch. It's not just holding onto a memory; I still see the pterodactyl in the heron.

~ ~ ~

I am aware of this deep sense of joy when someone sees me. When you know that the part of you that you might call your soul or spirit, is recognized and heard. The feeling could be like salamanders when they trade gills for lungs. Air! It's like finding a shard of old pottery and being connected to the working, living realities of those that came before. It's a connection that frees you. Maybe it is not forever. Maybe you're only free to breathe this air for a brief time, like a phase in an amphibians' life. It is a joyful experience. It feels wide awake. When I arrive at the bulwarks, the river, the mud, the air itself, is imbued with songs and calls, rattles and gurgling. All the river's clan, the flora and fauna, even the flow itself, is part of all this talking. It runs through my veins. Don't ask me how. Jeannette Armstrong writes about her family's language. "The Okanagan word for "our place on the land" and "our language" is the same. We are what we see, touch and feel beneath our feet. Those places that draw us back again and again, are part of the connection we have to that which cannot be divided, or taken from us, because it is in the fabric of our being, just like language and land and fins and feathers. We are that. I am part river mud. I can be mucky, of course muddy, and pucker and plop and dig deep enough and part of me is in the roots, moving into the plants as salt running up its bio-elevator and growing into the plant tops bobbing from the weight of redwings.

My mother wouldn't have known the word 'clan.' Nor would she get it, that I felt like the river was my kin. She wouldn't make fun of me, but I know it would be odd for her. Like many others, I am a bridge between worlds. She is in the spirit world, but we talk. The other day I told her that "I am my mudder's daughter." She laughed. She knows now about the river and me. She knows I miss my card game with Virg. That is the way with those that pass. They know from friends and from rivers.

Governed by my intuition, I am moving past my hesitation but wearing it like a cloak. I am sharing this with those that are here on the land; with those that know and feel what I'm writing about but maybe never shared this without self-consciousness. Times are such that I just have to tell you all, everyone reading this, that we have river mud running in our veins. And there's more news coming.

You can know something but that doesn't compare to feeling it. I hold a knowing, it's an embrace of my wetlands where my osprey nest high on a cell tower. Like I said, I have a sense of urgency about my osprey. Will the osprey build? Not a sprig or a twig on the tower. Last year, they seemed hesitant to land on the new tower and were late to getting around to building a nest. I'm anxious to see them again. My love for them is joined by the love of those that are drawn to the wetlands and waters, often not knowing why. And many that know why and ride this bond like a thermal so that their love can circle around and soar with the birds. I hope when I leave for the spirit world someone will hold a place for me in the thermals. I'll be playing cards with my mom, and Virg, but I'll listen for news of my river and osprey.

Tikkun olam is a Hebrew phrase that means "repairing the world." For the sake of the world, for the sake of harmony within a group, a group that includes the osprey of course. I'd like to take up and be a part of the Tikkun olam crew. For the osprey's sake, which means for the river's sake. You know, for all that connects us, let us stop and repair the relationships, clean the air between us and bring harmony to our lives. If you follow the migration of the fish like the osprey do, you will know that it's for their benefit as well. It is the idea of kaizen, continuous improvement. Repairs are ongoing and respond to understanding the relationships that create harmony.

Harmony is also known as wa. As I slip through time, I've noticed that meanings have blurred over the years. Wa means gliding through the day, a sense of wellness, of joy for no apparent reason; and joining, not one life but life connected to all that feeds our hearts and bellies.

Riding along all my thoughts like a shadow are the words of writers like Aldo Leopold. He was worried about ecology, how the connections between plants and animals that should be working together were being damaged. He wrote *Sand County Almanac* just over fifty years ago. Well, things are so much more in need of repair now. It can be painful reading his concerns or Rachel Carson's siren words because things weren't nearly as bad then and I would hate to see the pained look on their faces if they saw what was going on now. They are the Papa and Mama of the environmental movement. They reminded us of the relationships, and tried to convey the meaning to our families who had travelled so far from their language that they did not recognize their own land.

Many times, also riding along my presence at the river, or whenever I get to see osprey, I hear the singers and songs that I still find full of passion. The other day I heard Laura Nyro sing *"We met on a Sunday...."*. I imagine the feeling as the osprey sits on her eggs. The song played through my head until the male returned to the nest, soaring near and moving around the wind, with his catch. *"And I missed him on Monday"* But he wasn't gone that long. *"Well I found him on Tuesday."* And then she dated him, and kissed him, which all seemed really quick, and then *"he didn't come on Friday"*, but *"he showed up Saturday"*, and the female osprey sang, *"Bye bye baby... (dis ronde ronde ronde ronde boppa doo, oo oo oo)."* And then she flew away with the fish.

~ ~ ~

What if our wounds were replaced by songs? Or what if every hurt and harm we experienced eventually caused a feather to grow? How do you change these wounds to wings? There are people who help you transform the pain so that you can soar. They may be well known or they may simply be the stranger you meet by the water's edge. Or someone like the older woman I met in the New Hope, PA drugstore. The pharmacist thought I was her granddaughter because I walked up to where she was standing and started kidding her about the items she had gathered in front of her on the counter. She told him we weren't related, "We're simply two people that recognize each other as soul mates." This exchange launched me. I had never heard anyone so easily say these words out loud and I knew instantly how true they were. Has someone seen you in that way and given you the push you need so that you can leave the shore where you were hurting and move on?

      I have grown more feathers. They're around my middle and they're close to my body so my tee shirts hide them – and if their tracings come through the cotton, I imagine it looks like the crepe skin we old ladies get. I wonder if they will grow on my arms and legs. As my bones get lighter, I wonder if I will be able to fly or if I'll be like a penguin or an emu. Of course, I have always wanted to fly.

    Every wound can leave a hole in your life. As Townes Van Zandt wrote, "we all got holes to fill." The metamorphosis helpers, aides de metamorph, may find ways, such as helping you grow feathers, to move on. She left my life. I grew a feather. Exxon Valdez, I grew a feather. She did not acknowledge my contribution. I grew a feather. My mother died. I grew a feather. The last river dolphin in the Yangtze went extinct. I grew a feather. It is said, and I have heard this myself, that if you wait long enough in one place, this has to be the right place, you can grow the feathers in pattern. I mean, maybe I grew feathers before this and just didn't notice. Maybe they grew during the night but fell off in the morning. Over the years, I have seen a lot of feathers in my bedroom.

~ ~ ~

Rumi shared some thoughts that might apply. His words about the "breezes at dawn have secrets to tell you" are ripe. You should listen to him if dawn is calling you. Homer's rosy fingered dawn also beckons. There are pre-dawn flights of migrating birds. Hundreds of thousands passing through the night. Rumi says, "You must ask for what you really want. Don't go back to sleep." I want to hear them move through the air before the light gives them full bodies. I want to fly with them. I want to be one among all of their many thousands. I don't care if they're robins or osprey; I just want to fly through rosy fingered dawn with them.

~ ~ ~

I dream of a wild way across the whole continent. Others are also speaking of this dream. Wildlife crossings are good. But I dream of a wild way, a wide, undisturbed, swath of the country for the wild. The Pacific Trail, The Appalachian Trail. Walk them through. But the wild way is not for us. Many unknown hands take care of their piece of the trail along the AT. They might not hike it but they like to be a part of its tradition. All your good deeds, no matter where you are, are part of the trail. Charles Bukowski asks us, "Can you remember who you were, before the world told you who you should be?" I remember my dream because I still have it. I dream of a wild way across the whole continent. And I don't want to go there, I just want it to be.

waiting ~ 5

I got to sit and watch the eagle in the pine tree for a very long time. There are not too many better ways to exist. It eventually flew past the mudflat, over the widening stream of the river. The tide was coming in. It landed on a small, solid sandbar just on the other side of the stream. And then it drank the river. Three times. A few minutes later it took a few steps around. This spot, I swear, the exact same place, not an inch to the left or right, is where it flew to when Lynn finally came to join me and see the eagle in the river the other day.

    There were herons, willets, swans, and a whole group of dark birds, just past the ripps. I am still wondering what they are. Such a good long time with the eagle. When it finally flew off, I turned to leave. My bum was hurting from sitting on the bulwark. I actually think I could leave because my heart was full and I told myself I could have another cup of tea despite the time. Whether I sleep or not tonight doesn't matter. As I turned to leave, robins were enjoying the pools that shrunk down from yesterday's flooded areas into discreet bathing holes. I was laughing by the time it was the redwings turn. The splatter and splashes were little Zen poems. The song of the red wings was in the reeds by the river too.

~ ~ ~

If someone was telling this tale beside me, say my mother or siblings, or the mothers from our rooming house, or Hilda's daughter-in-law or Irving's daughter who met us on the beach, my summer friends, all of us who went to the beach together; all would say I was like this, they'd say, with two fingers held together, with the ocean. It means I'm tight with the ocean. Inseparable. Or, there's a special relationship and it's hard to define but it's a close one. From the depths of my being, yearning that could not be surpassed by anything else in my world, was an ache to be by the ocean or in it. I lived all year long in Newark for the three months of summer in Bradley Beach. Then I found Cousteau. He was hidden in his Silent World in the small Newark library by the hospital where I was born. I knew then, that whatever I was supposed to be, by word alone acknowledging I'd eventually grow up, I would be a part of that brine and watery life that is an oceanographer's. As it turned out, I wasn't. It isn't the first time I let time and tides pull me off my path. The first thing that pulled me off was a constant nausea whenever I was on a boat. Later in life, when my kid-self was eclipsed by time, through sheer dumb luck, I found osprey. The first time I saw my osprey was swooping down for dry river grasses to build its nest, it made the hairs on my arms fly as high as they could. Everything in me reached toward the sky. What is the name of that kind of grass? I knew it the other day. Pickelweed? Lemongrass? Nope. Eel grass. The eels like to lie in this grass which roots at the bottom of a tidal river. And it's good camouflage. For me, the world's worst birder, having bins hanging from my neck while I wait for osprey, the salty and exalted one that has connected me to my kid self, I'm thinking I'm protected by some good camouflage too.

Let's be honest here. Lately, I'm pulled to see the eagles. Either passion is a tricky fickle thing or an inner energy gauge is tracking what pulls my attention and I see with my heart. This is known and accepted in some cultures. Here, we sometimes have to overcome embarrassment to speak of such things.

When I was on Marconi Road just a little while ago, nothing. Nobody in the nest. I thought I missed the eaglets fledge. Well, that wasn't the case. A photographer waiting out the eaglet, told me he'd been there a good long while and saw one wing flip up. Hope wicked my being. Soon enough the eaglet was on the rim of the nest and then moving and preening, opening its wings. Shaking. Feathers ruffled by the gentle winds. Then the parents came. One adult at nest level, the first to return, dropped something in the nest. The other, not ten seconds later, flew to the nest. All three there, right there and then. The sky is richly blue there and I'm looking to the sky through the green leaves and sometimes through the pine needles, a perfect and most loved view.

the disappointing herons is one of the songs of longing

The very dangerous park opening has a deep cut in the dirt from runoff that could easily break your car's axles. Once again, they did not. I parked, brought my convenient folding seat/cooler combo that has a strap allowing you to sling it over your shoulders, my bins, my medicine pouch secured in my lower left leg pocket and my sad keppe to the river. Before I situated myself by the bulwark I saw the eagle over the nest area. It was high up, but I could see it lower its Cossack legs and let them hang as it readied to land. I believe it was the female. She came down quite a 'ways in that relaxed position and sailed slowly through the air to the top of the foliage umbrella over the nest. There she remained. Seeing this eagle so frequently, getting to see her fly or drop its legs for landing; or drinking the river, and chasing the geese, such familiarity with her always feels like a blessing. Probably not so much for the geese.

  I also saw a white heron, right there in the tree on my left – only about six or seven feet up from the river. Work has turned me blue, not the good kind of seeing the sky through pine trees blue. All these regular happenings, the eagle dropping her landing gear, the heron just sitting in the tree, felt like a sign of grace. These were easy moments to be with. Unlike waiting for the osprey during the imbolic; which of course is easier than saying goodbye to them in the fall. Every time they leave it feels as if something is torn off my body. As each osprey fledges, it's a sweet sight. Proud mother feelings goosing up and down my legs. I don't think of them leaving then but this is what I remember when they do leave in October. When they hang on till November, I worry. The trees in the area of the nest become the fledges temporary homes. I start looking for their familiar shape and white streaks near branches if I'm a distance. Be careful if you think you see one. It could be the disappointing herons who roost there too. They don't lift the heart quite as much as the osprey but they light up the trees when they lay siege to them and it brings a smile.

    Not long ago, my friend struggled with her dream to begin her memoir. She wanted encouragement and it brought me down to humble. I emailed her that, "It's a sweet precious thing to have that quality of time and conversation with your soul." My response to her frustration was, "One thing for sure for me was knowing what I needed to do before I died. And also, btw, I was told to do it. And I'm doing it cause I like to listen to the whatever it is that speaks to me and whoever it is that loves me into my blue streaks." Virg emailed back. The subject line was "writing takes a long time." My response, "an old memory from Newark: it sure does Ginger." Ginger is the name she used for her writing self. She even had a unique email for that self. "Virg, I hope you are glad you did this and happy with the work. It's good. Keep going when you're ready to go again. I once came into a basement room of a church in Newark. Old women were sitting around the largest table in the world working on a quilt together. About twenty old women, each working on a square they would attach to the quilt. Who was that big that they needed such a big blanket? Think about making a memoir. It takes many hands and minds; stories and sinew. Keep going. You need to sew the squares." I think she must have known what she needed to do before she started to dance with the Crow Women. She was wise that way.

~ ~ ~

When I was at the back end of the river by myself, I got to see the osprey flying overhead with a stick in its talons. The stick reminded me of a wooden school ruler. The osprey flew toward the nest but swung a wide arc toward the right and then came on top of the nest. I'm learning about the wind from them. There's always new things to learn about the wind. It's the same winds that carried my mother's voice. I know, I know. I used to call her an old fart. I thought it was hilarious. An old fart. And then I remembered how profound I found it that Caesar's farts are still circulating in the air we breathe. What a bridge to the past. This is how I forgive myself, I say, "Kids!?!" Today, I am down on my knees, because I've been captured by the wind. I check them by looking at their effects and listening. I write down their miles per hour in my journal as if whatever speed the wind is that day, and the direction it came from, is so important. Right now, for me, it is only speed and direction. Hawk migration watchers know the winds. During migration in the fall, cold fronts followed by north west winds bring abbondanza, a feast of many migrating birds through Cape May. The winds are everything. This wind and that wind. Each day I have to check the wind. It's not because of the birds or their migrations. It's because the winds are speaking to me and I'm not sure what they're saying. Each day I hope to hear it again and see if this day I can make it out. It is good to know the winds like a birder does too. I run down to Cape May when I can, but it's far enough away that I cannot get there after a cold front when I'd like. But I'm listening to the winds that touch everything outside and pick up an accent from the contact. Only in Ireland two weeks, I came home with a lilt in my voice. The winds touch the wings of every bird and the leaves on the trees; they touch the Crow Women, and sometimes they spin into thermals because they like to weave the birds. Unless, as some say, it is the birds that are doing the weaving. Well then, some old birds make squares and blankets in basements, and some are creating thermals and kettles for vultures.

~ ~ ~

It's entirely possible I never was a bird before. I could have been a reed. I thought I read that a reed's memory wasn't as good as a bird's. They stay put and grow roots. They convert salt to food and are never hungry. They like company. That's why the red-wings sway on their tips and sing them songs. Even if I could choose, I don't know if I'd rather be a bird or come back each spring as a reed.

"We look at things in their fullness."

Living goes on many levels. Empathy alone can explain multiple levels of consciousness. If complex life, meaning humans of course, and birds too, can be seen as physicists see entanglement, the idea that particles that have a shared origin but find themselves separated "by unfathomable distances," would that explain the sense of connection many have to birds? If we needed an explanation, the physicists have one, that the particles are linked. Brian Nelson writes that if you "were to tickle only one of them and alter its spin, the other's spin would also get altered at exactly the same time, even though they might exist light-years apart."

    I have been told by the woman I call Grandmother that, "We look at things in their fullness." She meant from the beginning of a relationship through its course. This is where I understood that I might be hurt and disappointed by a friend or relative now but try to look at the full span of time in every relationship. It is hard to read the pulls of relationships. Sometimes it is hard to swim against their current and we suffer. Sometimes, the sun is out, the wind touches your arms like a silk shawl, and you know that the water dragon is your kin, though you might have been separated by time and tide. All of this movement, the yearning, the pulls, the tides, when they enter your consciousness through unfathomable distances may come through as a perplexing message. Am I entangled with osprey and water dragon or they with me? Are they my family? Is the river and mud? All of it, all of them together, in the span of the movement of my life is hard to read. What comes through now is the message, and mind you, we don't always know what a message means even if we receive the message directly, 'We look at things in their fullness.'

~ ~ ~

Many birds lose the ability to sing during fall and winter because they don't have to establish their territory or attract a mate. An expert postulated that since the part of the brain a bird uses for singing shrinks and lightens the bird's body weight, that perhaps that's a genetic solution which will protect it from predators. But some birds, like the song sparrow, may sing through winter. Late one spring day, here, there and everywhere I looked I'd see one or three swallows at the wetlands. Flying all around the bowl, under and over the small bridge on Riverside Drive. They were a constant in the sky and shadows on the ground. I wondered if they sing in winter. They're flying now and their movement is hard to ignore.

~ ~ ~

Being woman, I am used to dichotomies. Elinor Wylie wrote that being woman she was hard beset. If daydreaming is the same as having half your brain asleep while the other half is flying long distances, count me in. For birds who are unihemispheric this means they might be able to migrate, hunt and eat while flying. Alpine swifts can stay in the air for 200 straight days without landing. Even whales and walruses, and ducks can sleep and swim. In the meantime, in the dreamtime, I might be working on being a bird while gliding through being a human. Being May, the oak tree strings, catkins, started coming out in the last two or three days. They have a transformation path to follow. It could be I'm turning into something I already was but didn't know. Maybe that part of my brain is asleep but also working on transforming. It's like when you're gay and don't know it because you don't see gay people around you; or you're an artist and don't know it because nobody in your family recognizes that you're an artist. They think you're just you. You could be an environmentalist but you don't have the credentials, but you take care of your part of the trail or river. The connection you feel to a person, place, or bird or way of being is valid. It's really real. Sometimes, out of the blue, you may remember your friend, or your sister with a sudden, quick inhale. They may have joined the dance with the Crow Women and are on the other side of the table where the big blanket is being readied, yet somehow they have tickled you. That is real too.

every river

Every river is probably as much a story about birds and other lives as it is about water and tides and the wetlands they touch and transform. Ever river is about the trees running the water into their heights and pulsing the water back down. Some streams take your attention but they all are part of our blue planet's waters. All the branches of the water trees that the tide leaves on the beach leave this message. Everything is tidal, every leaf is part of the tide, both on the beach and high up on the hardwood trees. Each journey we take, following one relationship to the end, is also tidal. Grief comes back and folds in on itself, life continues but sometimes the bittersweet leaves a taste in your mouth. I can see the allure of dark chocolate. But milk chocolate is still my favorite. It lands on your tongue and talks plain to your brain. No cursive, just block letters that tickle your thoughts into oneness. Some friends and some conversations do that. The years have taken some of these voices from me. One night the wind was talking and at eighteen miles an hour, in July, it had a lot to say. It's why I couldn't sleep. It is an amen, a so be it, an affirmation of the known but unknowable. It shapes the waves and tickles the particles that are so far from each other or so it seems. This is why many say their thanks to the winds and lift their prayers to be taken by them. I say amen to the winds, to the great Atlantic, to the tides in every living thing and the conversations with and without words.

~ ~ ~

When I went down to the river I noticed a lot of gulls flying about. I was reminded of the massive die off of moss bunkers, the menhaden, a few years earlier. There was not enough oxygen for them in the shallow river. The whole area stunk with their death. Gulls were constantly flying about and circling the bowl. They are not usually the first thing that captures your attention. The clean-up continued for weeks. I headed out to the river in hopes of seeing the eagles. I hadn't seen them in over a week. At one point all the gulls flew off, almost as if they evaporated. I thought perhaps the eagle had spooked them but it must have been the osprey hunting for fish overhead.

There's been a shift. My dreams are receding like water drying on the slanted edge of the beach as its heading back to the ocean. I am not losing hope but its call sometimes sounds so far away. Everywhere nature is polluted by garbage, and sewage runs into rivers, I am stopped. Worldviews are too big for me to understand. Understanding comes from the anecdote about the local rivers, like the Anacostia where some hard work, some legal remedies and some notice are making a change. Rivers are people. They need friends and community.

yearlong

I look forward to the summer. July has become a favorite month. It is, some days, flat out glorious and what Brian, my brother Jerry's lifelong partner, would call really real. Everything good about summer reminds me of Brian. Myself, Brian and Lynn spent one July afternoon on the beach that languorously smoothed into evening. The moon rose from the horizon's line but because the beach dropped down, it felt like it was just past the water's edge. We watched the kids on the tall, heavy wooden lifeguard stand dangling their legs after they reached the summit and sat down. The sun washed the backs of their legs with a pink hue. The three of us felt connected, merged with each other and every bit of everything that was there, including the moon before us and the sun behind. I wished that those hours which coalesced into a memory could have been a yearlong.

~ ~ ~

Waiting and watching are inextricably connected. Like particles, that have been separated for some unknown reason, they can tickle each other while you're doing one or the other. While I was watching my river, I was just about deciding to go when out of nowhere the eagle was chasing the osprey. They slowly flew right over my head and I got a good look at them when they were in front of me before that. I could see their wings touch and could hear the soft rustling sound they made against each other. Oh, how they would have fanned sage smoke for cleansing. They were that close. Maybe only ten feet over my head. It looked like the eagle was going to kill the osprey but as they passed me and they separated from each other it became clear that the osprey was now chasing and harrying the eagle. They went around the arc of the river to my right and then across the river where the eagle dropped below the tree line. The eagle became visible again by its nest. I could see the osprey rise up and then swoop down a few times to force the eagle to stay in its nest area. Then the eagle disappeared. The osprey seemed to head toward the cell tower but went past it and disappeared toward the North. Later, it appeared again on the tree branch. I never saw the osprey coming.

~ ~ ~

Half the world has lost its sense and the other half is living in a worried compassion. You could be a part of the tribe that recognizes that we live in a parallel time where each joy is countered by a difficulty and both tumble through the days. It's not always the best for spirit to remember life's most chronic yearning. But there you go. You have to shake off these demons that get caught in the poet's net.

~ ~ ~

I follow the lines in the mud or the lines in the water like my brother Jerry read Hebrew. He knew how to pronounce the words but didn't know their meaning. My old boss at work was the same with her Buddhist monks when they chanted. She knew the appropriate way to be within the roof of that small holy house but not the words. She trusted their sounds.

~ ~ ~

There finally might be milkweed growing on our property. It's near the path of bricks that I put in years ago toward the end of the driveway. The bricks, barely visible now, have been accepted by the ground. I don't know what it is with me and paths. I have built a few on the property. One there and another leading to our front door from where Lynn's car door might open. All my paths were meant to be a certain width from start to finish but all narrow down when they approach the place they're to guide you to. I guess I go to the river with the same intention. I want the path to be as wide as it is in my being when I go there. I would prefer if I had no objective. But these eagles, the osprey, the herons in the trees, the hope I'll see a turtle or an otter, all narrow my focus so that I'm frequently looking for them. But then a sweet forgetfulness comes while waiting or a tender memory. And I get to wake up over and over again.

murmurations ~ 6

I came to the river with my usual pleas. The terns kept me company while I waited for the water to join me. I call them the laughing terns because they make me laugh out loud. This world of woes had me down. It was one of those not so rare days when the worry was for nature, all over the world; for the way we treat our most vulnerable and for the birds lost to our avarice. Pablo Neruda wrote that he needed big hands to help him "distill hidden rivers in Antofagasta and restore to the water what its avarice lost in the desert." I'm hoping myself for very big hands to help change the direction of what I love and point it toward honoring, preserving and living with the beautiful blue planet. Our avarice, our greed, is currently thriving while so many go extinct and foul and strained beyond the capacity to be what they are meant to be. Refuge Manager Dan Clark wrote "We are a part of the fate of Wisdom." Wisdom, the albatross, has shaped my mind toward wondering what it's like to be at sea for so long; and to have a life partner for over 60 years and return to the same place each year to give birth. Some would say that Wisdom holds time aloft. I am lost in a cloud wondering what she does day after day flying with the trade winds. Waiting time is an illusion. Talk to the eagle that sits on the nest as ice and snow pile on her head. Is she waiting? Or is she an eagle being an eagle. The osprey sitting on the nest, much later in the season, is not waiting either. She's sitting through long days with the sun touching her head followed by cooler evenings on the nest when night becomes her shade.

Where do you go when you wait? In your body? On your nest? With your brain half asleep traveling long distances while flying through your day; as a deer, waiting under the tree during through the night to be touched by the morning dew so they can become human? What does it mean to think like a woman or an osprey? How long has it been since I allowed myself to turn into anything? Always predicting my own responses. Never interacting with the elements but preparing for them. This is not a nest; this is a defense. This is not the way, but it is what I have known. And this is not about waiting like an eagle, or an osprey, or the misguided deer. I don't know what it's about. Some things are apparent, some remain a mystery.

~ ~ ~

For me, east means the ocean is near. Take me inland twenty miles and spin me around and I'm no good for knowing any direction. Even when I know east, I'm uncertain where the other directions are. Is north to my left or my right? I can smell the ocean sooner than most. A skill I developed from longing to get there when I was a kid. I can smell the ocean when there are only ten particles of it in the air, that's 25 miles out.

It is said, and my experience bears this out, that you could be fooled by a wetlands area, but only if it were tidal. My nose has receptors for mud, brine and murmurs of waves that were once big rollers mid-ocean and breakers that light up the sky when the sun hits them head on. I know my wetlands from all others and can home in on them like my osprey do. The possessive feelings I have are without permission and devoid of generosity. Possibly devoid of accuracy. My wetlands smell includes the elusive aroma that can be called 'just down the block from my house' and the teasing lilt of the moisture from the ripps, sometimes carried by a strong wind, bringing a mist wave of sentient water carrying compass aromas that tell me I'm home. There is no other home like this. The first thing I know in my body, and somewhere back in my mind, is east. It's not a direction, it's a bouquet. That's just me talking. Imagine coming back from the southernmost point of your journey to your nest at the Jersey Shore. There are a few ways my osprey might know it and I might not have any of the faculties they have to hone it, but this one. This nose knows my east.

~ ~ ~

My mentor, once she left ancient Greece and came to this world, was an odd bird by all accounts. It is no wonder that she would one day say, *"Birds are the constant."* There is no authoritative history of all her movements, but it is known that throughout all her moves, she looked for birds. She moved through Long Island via her mother's birth channel; then she moved through marriage and childbirth and art and forays through many local arts communities both teaching, absorbing and collating data from many other sources, including: Zen, hiking, homeopathy, grandchildren, politics, France, Japan, Maine, Massachusetts, California, New Jersey, Colorado, and conversations with chipmunks. She must have had a compass. How else can Mentor of ancient Greece find his way to being a grandmother in Colorado during this time of the pandemic? Even with a compass. She once shared that she was going in many directions since living in Colorado. *"Floating maybe. Good to have the space to find more of the world and more of myself. But sometimes challenging to have left my milieu and habits behind - the familiars. Birds are the constant."* What I have learned from my mentor is yet to be determined. Wisdom may fly many miles over the ocean. But if you do not have a constant, or if east is only known when you're standing in front of the ocean, how can a mentor help your brain wake up?

~ ~ ~

My mentor would meet me for breakfast and sit, leaning forward to tell me important things. First, she'd order a spinach omelet. I am a carnivore. If, like my beloved osprey, I could fly down and scoop up my meals, I'd get eggs with sausage, home fries and toast. One eyelid would shutter down protecting me from the glare of diner windows, and diners waiting to be seated *"Did you know a flock of butterflies is called a kaleidoscope?,"* she'd ask after ordering. "I didn't know that. But one time, the first time I was at the Cape May Hawk Watch...," oh, she seemed to indicate as she sat back that I had told her about that experience already. But, I had to just say it, "Did you know, that for all the world, when the air is filled with monarch butterflies it looks like the whole world was turned into a kaleidoscope?"

  For good reason, a group of cormorants are referred to as a gulp. One October, just two days before Super Storm Sandy devastated our shore area, Lynn and I were heading home from the ocean in Spring Lake. We came up a side street along Lake Como heading to Main. It's Jersey, most people aren't thinking there's an abundance of wildlife. On the way back with our fill of watching big waves heralding the storm; with, mind you, a cyclical optimism that this storm, like most, would have the muscle of charm and not the tragic outcome we all endured. Hundreds of corms on the lake pulled our attention as we drove along Lake Como. Never seen anything like it. That alone was enough. The corms were moving west on the water, and we were riding parallel following close to the curb. Every corm that dove down came up with a four- or five-inch fish, momentarily flapping before we watched them wiggle down into the corms' throats.

       The corms in the west, closest to Main Street, weren't catching any fish. As the east end corms got closer to the Main street end of the lake, they'd lift up only a few feet above the water and head back toward the east end. They hit the water feet first causing a lot of splashing and their bodies landed with a definitive cannonball. We heard all this going on from the car, about 40' away. It reminded me of the music of women doing their wash in the river. Their rhythmic splashing sounds were in unison, as they wrung the clothes and then beat them against the water to clean and rinse. It took a while to register that all the corm splashing was also deliberate. They were herding the fish. The corms waiting on the west side were suddenly catching fish too. The corms of the east were both feasting and herding the fish toward the corms in the west. Close in time to this I had also seen dolphins herding fish right off the Bradley Avenue beach. I could see the fish jumping out of the water trying to escape. I had no idea that cooperative hunting was something birds also did. I only knew my eagle was likely to try to steal the fish from my osprey. Not everyone is a cooperative hunter.

~ ~ ~

Never fear that there is no creative energy left in you and that your time with the palette is done. I feared the void. I stayed away from my writing area as if it were contagious. Endless space, alone, cold, and without meaning, the void has been around. Sometimes, like a predator, it stays just outside the perimeter of my fire. It is loneliness. My marsh buddy, Mrs. Teale, once asked me, 'How is your loneliness doing?" She could have smacked me on the hand with a bamboo stick. Is it odd that my loneliness was a companion? We think we can control time. We track it, set limits for this activity or date memories. It's just not feasible. The sun, the moon rise, the birds sing aubades, the morning songs, and some even the night songs. Night closes down and shadows caused by the sun disappear with the evening songs. Loneliness is like time. I am uncertain if it is the void but it exists. And it is doing just fine.

The remover of obstacles came as a gift. Ganesha, or Ganesh sits next to my desk but I don't always see him. I am sure he works and takes off some time and then works again without many people noticing. The male osprey brings the nesting materials and the female will arrange them. The work is ongoing and the nests are sometimes colossal montages showing that osprey are beachcombers as well as pragmatists. When my cat Molly had a very upsetting test at the vets, she was directed to a specialist to see if there were blockages. I prayed to Ganesha. I must admit to having an affinity for him. I had only noticed Ganesh that day by accident and didn't know he was the remover of obstacles. His presence was synchronous. There are so many gods and all together they are the Swiss Army Knife of creation and destruction. Ganesh, very close to knish, making him even more familiar, took care of Molly, who, in turn, often takes care of my loneliness. Somewhere between here and there might not be a void, just could happen to be the space where good things happen.

and another deep well

My mentor was not one for mystery until she was. What a strange combination she would seem to be at times. Most pragmatic. Tight and concise sentences. If milkweed were her seedpod, she was the pod or seed, not the silk. Yet, she would say *"Before I came there, I was there already."* Another deep well she got me into. Perplexitude. Mutual arising from a mutual love of Alan Watts. I would say, "Look there's this bird that has my heart." *Oh, which one?* "Well, every bird I watch, I'm a flooze." She doesn't know this kidding so she waits for the bird's name. "Osprey. It's the osprey." *If you write about birds, you will also be writing about water.* Of course, of course. It's

Watts. It's the *Watercourse Way*. Mutual arising. Spinach omelet and eggs with sausage. Laurel and Hardy routines often end with Hardy, the har-hardy one, saying, "Another fine mess you got me into." And Stan Laurel, like my mentor, slender and frail, hiding mischief in her little notebooks she kept for decades, asks another question.

"Did you know that the shape of an egg depends on how much time a bird spends in flight?" This does not follow upon kaleidoscopes but circles back to it through the fiber optics of curiosity communing with our spirits like shadows never leaving you when everyone else might just. I thought about Wisdom and her eggs. I thought about nest eggs. My mentor was talking about the pure joy of her grandsons. I don't have that joy. She knows. *You have the water*, she says. That's why writing about birds is writing about the water. She knows the connections. I'm following my nose. But she knows. We are the blue planet, the blue egg in the universe. One meaning of nest egg is to lay an egg as to induce a goose to lay another. Now that my mentor has talked about the shape of eggs, I wonder if there are other eggs in our universe or if our blue planet is a nest egg for other galaxies. How would a goose know these things?

~ ~ ~

Everything real is about form and struggle. Forms may emerge like a newly hatched osprey with a head too heavy to hold up while they're protected by their mother/father, birds higher up and closer to the sky than I can imagine being. The closer to the sky teas are said to be the best. If the osprey fledge and learn to fish on their own, we will soon have more flying fish directed toward a branch or safe place to be eaten. The fish has its own story. I know there is struggle. I'm amazed to find beauty in all of this and most of me and my brain would like to ignore the struggle, the death, the rough patches and sip that incredible tea.

~ ~ ~

Nothing in my brother Lenny's world ever directed his attention to birds, except me. In the heat of a Henderson, Nevada parking lot, I stopped and asked him about this talkative bird on the tall light posts. What is it? *It's a black bird.* Gee, thanks a lot. It has so many sounds. *Yeah, they're here a lot.*

    A great-tailed grackle has many sounds and talks a lot. A real yenta. Len and I don't know what to talk to each other about. But he knows yentas and I let one bird lead to another and told him about my osprey. He said write Jonathan Livingston Osprey. Okay, but what if I turn into one? Yeah, that went over. If I were to write how the heart returns to soaring and stooping, with my gambler brother in mind, I'd have to start with the fact that he moved to a place that is nearly always summer. We are our mother's children no matter what we did through time and no matter what we end up focusing on. A hawk's spearheaded drive toward the flock causes it to create murmurations. Are murmurations about sounds or shapes? How many people have heard the sound of thousands of starling wings rustling like the soft fluttering of baseball cards on the spokes of a bicycle while never touching each other? Feathering. Starlings murmurations are evolving images that shape the sky. Sometimes their shifting patterns are for protection from a stooping hawk. And sometimes they are undulating clouds of birds forming and reforming different shapes for no apparent reason. Even a hawk on the attack could lose focus. Everything real is about form and struggle. Sometimes the dance of starlings will fool a hawk. Sometimes birds singing in parking lots reminds a brother and sister what they have in common even if they never paid it no never mind before. I'm sure we talked about other things but I can't remember much else from that day except that the rest of my time with my brother felt holy and dissolved into wellness.

the chick chirps back

All the myths that have owned me and let me live in their archetypal realms have also come to be the many sides of a human wishing only to love the world into strength and balance so that it may be and be as it may. I wonder, since we're a part of the blue egg, if we have a memory of ourselves as a chick. My mentor asked me had I known that the female Gambel Quail calls to her chicks while they are still inside the eggs. No, never heard that. Good that I hadn't heard that because she enjoyed telling me, *"The chicks chirp back!"*

~ ~ ~

Hope should not be tethered. Look up into the sky, or across a field, or into a pond, or a poor excuse for a river, and see the wrinkles in the sand that the tides and winds create. Talk and share, feast, even feel despair. I don't know what pushes mere change to transformation. But I ended my day listening to the sweet whistle puffs and clucking, and the beautiful okalee call of the redwings.

Friday after work and the gym I came home and gave Molly a rub. The light coming through the windows and skylights was enticing. Everything was illuminated. It was just stunning. An effervescent light seemed to be building all week. It was fully present Friday. Even Barbara's Tom said people couldn't get over the sparkling blue sky. It was arresting. Everyone experienced a sense of wellbeing too. Lynn tried to capture it in photos. The quality of the air and the light as it moved toward evening seemed to lift a gauze from your eyes. It wasn't just the blue. It was the range of sunset yellows; the span of clamshell purples and the medieval weave of the leaves as night came through. We were all enchanted.

~ ~ ~

My mentor opened up paths for me I had known before but lost in the rush and hurry of life. What is it like to migrate from several thousand miles a year? If you're an osprey, there is the wind, the push from within, the menhaden and thee. *"Wander Mountain-Born walked the mountains each day,* my mentor shared. *"Her breath and heart beats mingled with the ragged land writing evanescent poems."* As she goes, so goes my head, filled with the little miracles my mentor shared. This woman whispered poems into the air. A chef says that his whole soul is kimchi. It is what he ate. His culture, his family, the stillness in his blood, is kimchi. "Everything I am comes from kimchi." The truth of this sifted swiftly down into my mind and experience. Everything I am is chicken soup. Which is why I am drawn to fresh bunches of dill in every supermarket. I am drawn to connections I can only faintly trace like the water running past the dry reeds, reflecting the sky, a passing cloud, an osprey's nest in the Sedge Islands, an unrecognized cry in the suburban night. There are many threads to follow. All of them are important. If you stop and take that breath every good guide wants you to acknowledge for its simple beauty, you might, as I have, realize you are leaving your kimchi trail in the world. You are leaving your own dill trail. Traces of everything you have eaten, loved, seen, created or even forgiven, are trailing along like a comet, leaving fallen particles everywhere you go. There is no separateness and there is no denying you are a part of this world.

~ ~ ~

To those among us who have experienced these things, you know that nature will come and recognize the big moments in your life. When my friend was dying, three baby Cooper hawks came to the telephone wires near my house. The night before she passed, an owl paid its call. The reverse is also true, we humans will recognize the big moments in nature's life. We know this time for our Earth is one of them. Almost a year to the day before Virg died, she emailed me and asked how the waves were. I told her they were nonstop and sweet. *Were they as many as the last time we swam?* She said that last Sunday she couldn't even finish a sentence because I was riding so many waves in. I remember coming back from the tow path where my friend often walked, where we buried her ashes. My hopes were big. My heart ached to be freer and yet bound to what I love and want to be a part of in a bigger way as my Oracle predicted.

~ ~ ~

The one I learned to call the Old Woman, the one I have met in the journey-lands, and perhaps in other realities, is sometimes known as Gaia. She is direct. She will tell us simple tales, *"This is what happened"* she would say. Then she tells us how simple actions like following your heart may have ripples and make you vulnerable. In this time, we recognize the ugly use of power to suppress people. The danger many experience doesn't just lurk outside the edges, it comes forward, it is bold, it is out for blood and power. All over the world there are people who have had their lands stolen, their rights squashed, their lives utterly changed. Migrants and immigrants forced to leave because the will of the powerful can move them like pieces in a game. Their deadly games roll over and try to bury whole peoples and their cultures at a time.

I once bought a red Tibetan pendant from a couple at a fair. They told me the necklace offered its wearer protection. I have used it when facing the nasties at work. But it seems it was not enough to protect the couple's people from the Chinese government who confiscated Tibet as if it were a piece of jewelry. My own country has forces of power and groups of people that see people of color as a threat. Great harm is done in their name and their shameful treatment of these people. Many complicit silences are broken during this time. But the road toward equity is long and the pain of generations cuts deep.

    A dangerous old woman, some call her Clarissa Pinkola Estes, would add this key note, *"There is a bigger heart rhythm behind this."* When I go to the river, whether to see my osprey or needing solace or just because I need to and can't come up with a why, I am aware of a bigger rhythm behind the motion in the water, the circles the water left moving out from the mud or the clams or crabs; the puppy ripples, the reflections. All this, with the plentitude of green and grasses always has a rhythm. If you sit there you will feel it. Old birds still ride the waves, move around the tides and such, don't you know. Virg of the warm and humid Mississippi, could tolerate colder water than me. But I wouldn't let her go in and not go in myself. Pride demanded I stand with my friend, my weather lookout, and my Oracle in the freezing June waters. "I must go down to the seas again, for the call of the running tide/Is a wild call and a clear call that may not be denied..." Borrowing the words of a shamanic teacher, "*my true purpose in writing this book*" began as a way to share my love for this place I call home. What I really came here to say now is that those I miss and love are still a part of it and that I fear for the most vulnerable among us, the wildlife, wetlands, streams, rivers, even the mighty oceans and all the marine life in those deep worlds. I fear for the quality of our air and the dendritic web that connects all of our lives to the earth. That's partly why I'm trying to figure out the tides, the ebb and flow, the high and low, the give and take, the waves riding across these like a skimmer on the back river.

A funny thing happened parallel to grief for my friend and family. I fell in love with the green world. Not just the mesomorph muscled love of sports or waves or mountains or anything you can name, but the quiet, contemplative love of the complexities, tenderness, even the necessary violence of life and death in the natural world. I have fallen so deeply in love with life while mourning that I was unaware of this happening even as it snookered me and drew me into my middle age.

~ ~ ~

It's easy to sight the eagle's nest across the river from my spot at the wetlands when the leaves are there or not. There are three trees I check. The middle one is the guide line. Follow the line up to the highest tree, eagle nest. I'll tell you something even truer. I'm determined to tell you what I really came here to tell you. The time is critical. Every location is important. If souls have weight, I'm asking you to gather that weight now and take it to the skies and be with the birds and the love of planet, and water and the little spritzes and tinkles the fish create on the surface when they're scooting by. We are leaving a trail, let's put our heart in it.

I was going to write the book Lenny suggested, Jonathan Living Osprey. Skunk, the little osprey in the book would befriend a woman and teach her about love and migration; as well as the trifecta of an osprey's life, that life on this planet is made up of just three ingredients, a weave of light, water and fish. In this story, which even in my mind, was a thin shave away from my experience, Skunk still needed her nest for many weeks after she learned to fly. This also has the benefit of being true for all osprey fledges.

One way Skunk knew it was time to go was when nobody brought her a fish on the bare limb that had become her safe landing zone, no matter how long she called out from her hunger. *This is where I have begun to project my* human concerns. One jagged flight over the nest showed nobody was there anymore and she didn't see anyone in the trees around her. That was another sign it was time for her to go also. *Still being human,* Skunk didn't know if she'd meet up with her nest family again. But she knew she had to head South. All of this was going to be ahead of the story of how their friendship developed. How did Skunk get to meet the woman? Just let me come out with it now, how did Skunk get to meet moi? Predators never forget a face. When her parents flew away to fish or get a break from the nest, she'd peer over the edge of the nest and she'd see me again. Skunk noticed that I was always there and I always seemed to be either looking up her way or looking across the way where Skunk suspected danger lurked. That is where the eagle's nest was, and her parents would often cruise the air with a show of force. Although everyone knows an eagle's parents are near and they own the area.

I happened to be there the day Skunk got her first catch. Shamelessly, I will admit that I delighted in Skunk's misses. What a splash she made each time but that never deterred Skunk and apparently the fish never left the area so Skunk could make many attempts. Adult osprey often make off with a fish on the first try; rarely do they need more than three. The little one needed ten. I never wrote the story Lenny suggested because I wanted to share this one. It has the added advantage of having my brother Lenny in it as well. Like me, I believe he would have been proud of my little Skunk osprey and laughed with sheer delight for her determination, and felt pride when she finally made her catch. With each plunge I worried if Skunk was exhausting herself. She seemed more like an ungainly pelican than a water dragon, It's true that osprey seem all about business so how did Skunk recognize laughter? Lenny would say, "They do that." Authorities on the topic say that predators recognize a range of tones from "I'm hungry" down to "Danger is near." Recognition of the middle ground includes play and laughter. I know I'm anthropomorphizing like there's no tomorrow here, but I'm sure Skunk recognized that tone in my voice. And it is true. Those that know me know that my heart fills with joy when I see and hear osprey. Older folks remember the days when osprey eggs, eagle eggs too, were too weak to form. Their populations dropped. DDT, the chemical responsible caused what Grandmother Rachel called *The Silent* Spring, the spring we feared when the apex predator birds could not produce young and their voices where silenced.

~ ~ ~

This spring of the human pandemic, it seemed that my osprey weren't retuning at all to the tower. I was frantic. I reached out to people on the Neighborhood list, "*What happened?!*" I'd hear back from some, "*The cell tower people. Those ?!%$&%###. They took the nest down.*" It's true. Last year's nest, a sizable affair, many osprey nests weigh hundreds of pounds, was gone. It's also true, and I felt guilty about this, I had to find another osprey nest because my heart was breaking and the nest would hold its pieces together. I found one in Avon by accident while I was outside a pizza place picking up dinner by their take-out window. I heard an osprey cry overhead and nearly fell cup over kettle, as my old neighbor would say, watching the osprey soar over Pizza, Etc. The woman handing her order to me laughed at my joy. I got in the car and followed the osprey to their nest atop a telephone pole just down from the Avon police station. I happened to be there just in time to watch their courtship. Two males were trying to impress the female. One of them dropped a stick meant to land on the nest. That would have been like roses and chocolate to a woman from the 1950's. I laughed and cried; and smiled so wide I thought my lips could touch my ears. So many osprey cries and clearly someone was going to couple and use that nest. It was so close to my home that I could go there anytime to be near them. Forgive the possessiveness of this, but I adopted those osprey right then and there. And yes, I felt guilt and joy combined. Later, weeks later than I sure expected, my osprey returned to my cell tower area and I had an abundance of joy. Yes, there are many ways to survive a pandemic if you're fortunate. One of them is loving osprey.

~ ~ ~

My understanding of tides was they came and went. I like that about tides. It has come to my attention that tides are tricky. Many have said this but their words didn't catch hold until I witnessed it myself. Now I understand. Oh, watch the tides, not only will storm tides rise slowly, surely, deadly. But, every tide brings a subtle change. They may seem the same if you're a casual observer. It may seem that little has changed since the last time you were at the beach or the river. Yet, the iterations, the repetition of each tide, each low and high and neap, when you can't tell the difference between low and high, and nigh tide, each one, is changing ever so slightly, traces really. Over time, over days and months, decades, years, all the tides you and your family have known, show change. You can't see it standing at the beach, but there has been a profound transformation. The power of repetition is best seen from a distance.

  When your transformation is apparent and creates a sense of urgency, you may have to leave everyone you know. I am a dill person because every Friday night my mother made chicken soup. Dill, is a part of one of the many skeins of Lena. Much of my mother's yarns are knotted together but many are just long strands. It doesn't matter because they are all balled up and, in that way, they are in relationship. That's important because as all things are connected, and I believe this with all profundity and certainty, then all things whether knotted together or not, are connected in ways that make up an entity. In this way, my little patch of the world is in relationship to me all the time. This is where I brought Greg the artist and told him I'm writing a book about here. *"Here?"* he said, totally incredulous, not hiding a sense of the absurd at all. He smiled and said, *"Okay."* This story is also about the wetlands, which as it turns out, feels like the waiting spot and the launching spot, the right spot for everything. I don't know all about the soil or waters or the air or birds but my heart aches when I hear how every one of these is in danger; is threatened; how bird populations could be cut by 50% if this keeps up. "This" that is keeping up is hard and complex to describe. I'd say it was indifference but that would be simplifying everything so much as to be carelessly indifferent to the causes that are harming what I love most. All are dancing on the borders of old frames or storytelling, memoir and iconic moments caught in the au jus of light dancing on water.

~ ~ ~

I wrote my mentor to ask if she ever wondered if she has a relationship to everything in nature. I wrote, 'We know our families. We even remained connected to those that have died through memory and the foods we love and shared. What about the air, the wind, water and the fire in the lives of other beings we don't see as kin right off? Like birds, for instance. I think the stretch between us and crickets is harder to map. Or fungi. Maybe that one is impossible. For a long time now, I've wanted to embrace the whole wide world. Everything. My favorite places. The feeling of the evenings when it's either the quiet or summer that is teasing moisture out of everything in the ground. I inhale deeply. The little patch I know of the world, this place that Greg thinks is so small, is delicious. He once demonstrated how to paint. *Be free, let it* flow, he guided. We all knew there was an edge to the canvas. It was large and laid out on work horses, but there was definitely an edge where freedom could spill onto Peter's dining room floor.

     Many times my mentor may not respond to my emails. Or she will write something and I will work on wondering what she means and how it relates. This time, she shared she has always loved the woods as much as people. There are people she loves, many, but she does not accept human relationships as the top of a hierarchy of kin. She is an artist. There are many colors on her palette. And, further, she is a water colorist, and a sketch artist where lines no thicker than a fine thread tell you 'this is a tree,' 'this is a house,' 'this is the wind playing with my grandson's hair." She is most often a serious sounding person. I have rarely heard her laugh. But she smiles with her understandings and she is jovial with the juxtapositions her mind plays with as she ponders everything she's caught in her seine.

~ ~ ~

Embrace the wide world that your loved ones live and have lived in. Embrace your favorite places. This is how you love the world back to health and keep the moon and stars in place and the ocean where it belongs and the shore safe and the wetlands, some call the earth's lungs, vital, and the fish breaking the surface sparkling in the sun. Embrace all that you love and tell the world, out loud, right now, what's important and why it's important. This is the perfect time to do this.

~ ~ ~

The sun sits upon the nesting osprey's head weighing it down with heat that is only interrupted by a passing cloud and the nights. The little osprey in their skunk phase gain strength every day. It is easy to see the transition from the egg to the skunk osprey to the sea hawk, sometimes called the sea eagle. I am not certain if I can see the transformation to water dragon. Weeks on end for me can be a haze of work and woes, but one of those days I learned it was Dorothy Allison's birthday. She said, "People want biography. People want memoir. They want you to tell them that the story you're telling them is true. The thing I'm telling you is true, but it did not always happen to me."

Everything here is inspired by actual events. The journey continues. It's the nature of such things to always head you to an unknown destination even when you know where you are. There are secrets I'm sharing and telling you even if you don't feel you've received any clandestine information. There is movement within stillness and as everyone knows you can hide an awful lot of something inside your own skull. The idea of a water dragon is pulling on me. I want to follow what feels right and true. Whatever is true for you, remember you can always find home from every direction. It just might not be where you left it.

~ ~ ~

Every tide brings a change that the chart's deceptive predictability doesn't note. My river is tidal. I come there most often when there's mud which means it's low tide. At the back end of the river, I call it mud tide. The streams that stayed by and resisted the call of the tide, remind you there's actually bigger water nearby. They have youth in them. Their lines remind me of puppy bellies. They seem to swim and move with delight. There is hope and play mixed in with tree reflections framing the sky. Semipalmated plovers walk on the wet mud, herons stake out deeper streams. The eagles take advantage of the mud flats and walk around like ladies holding up their layered gowns. I talk to the river as much as it talks to me. Both of us use different voices decorated with threads of sound that weave and winds through the leaves and grasses. Everything we see becomes a subject of our banter, the skies, the clouds, the ripples and slicks, I do recognize that I'm speaking for the river here. But I begged it's pardon for this indulgence. Okalee is a safe haven of renaissance and melodies. I often wonder if my osprey can hear me saying, "Hello beautiful," a delightful greeting I learned from my sobrina, Olga. And hopefully they don't know what a flooze I am for other osprey.

~ ~ ~

As a kid in Newark, I developed the habit of writing my address and extending it out as far as I could to the galaxy. Last stop was the Milky Way. Many kids get a fix on where they are in the universe this way. My home for most of my life now is at the shore. Black-eyed Susan's have walked all over and set up stakes. Small gardens are here and there, and slow growing green, or depending upon how recent the rain, browned moss, provide a carpet under the pine congregation in the front and the oak settlement in the back of my house. Maybe it's through the moss and moss bunker connection that me and my osprey are connected. The beach where I swim is not far off. Osprey catch bunker fish, or an occasional flounder, and then head inland to eat and feed their young. My beach is so much so my beach that when I'm on another beach I lean in its direction. Do my osprey and I share the same way of knowing home? I have swum in my part of the Atlantic even while within my mother's belly. My home seems to be a sure place, established; and yet it feels like I am always returning to it each spring with a profound sense of discovery. My state has a border in a country which has a border on a continent which is outlined by two large oceans and defined by many lands and people and cross-traveled by butterflies, including the migrating monarchs, birds, herds and domesticated animals, some who get loose. There is a frame, there is a small piece of sanctuary and there are many ways to paint the day and see your connection to all around you.

~ ~ ~

Rediscovering the bigger heart rhythm may be about returning to a home where you can acknowledge everything you touched and saw and heard as a part of the fiber of your being. And hopefully, where, like the river reflecting the sky, you are also recognized for all you are and all that makes up your heart-mind. The bigger heart rhythm may be about the tidal nature we all have, humans, plants and animals alike. How many times do I remember something and then forget it and then remember it again? This is not always about the depressing hopelessness of Sisypuss, pushing the rock up the hill only to have it fall down. It is about the cycles of hope and reality and how we move up and down hills in our lives; how at times we're in a valley and although we have achieved some good and some security we haven't moved to a place where we'll always be on top. Plateaus seem like the heights or the dullest place in the world. They are neither. They're just a part of the road. They're not going to go on forever. Neither will your groove and neither will your sea dingles. Trust while the wind is loud, and you cannot hear or feel your heart rhythm, that it will come again. Whatever we know about winds, the solar flares; the moon's influence; everything seems to have a cycle. Instead of this failure to be patient, why not think of these days if they cannot just be days, as sea dingles? The center is always moving but the tau is never far away. Pablo Neruda wrote that "One bee plus one bee does not make two light bees or two dark bees: they make up a cycle of sun, a mansion of topaz, a hazardous touching of hands." The work of many hands creates the meals we love, from the field, to the market, to pot and pan, or root cellar and wine barrel. I told my mentor that water within some plant's leaves follows the lunar cycle. Botanists call it leaftide. Everything has its ups and downs, highs and lows. My mentor seems even tempered, like the unlikely steady flight of the heron, whose chest rides like a keel in the air. But I know the strange conjugations of thoughts she shares comes from the back and forth she's had with her left and her right brain.

~ ~ ~

When summer ends it can feel like life is stopping. I struggle with the blues, with loneliness, and longing. I don't know how to migrate south with the osprey. Yet. The annoying question will arise, '*Are you a human being or doing?*' Who the hell knows? I would like to be more fluent in the sacred. When you find a place that feels like home, why would you leave? Labor Day is rough as you'd expect labor to be but this holiday is not that event. We don't pay attention to its meaning. All my life it has simply meant that summer is ending. Although I told Lynn last year, "It was like the joy couldn't help but break through." We got up late that Labor Day. Even so, when I asked Lynn to go to the beach, she got ready with no hesitation. The waves, the water, the air, the sun infused me with joy. I got long and frequent looks at two groups of dolphins that hung around for over twenty minutes. I chased the blues away just as the menhaden were probably being told by some inner guide it was time for them to leave. And when the menhaden leave, the osprey are not far behind.

~ ~ ~

My mentor knows why leaves change color, but she asked me one day anyway. Is it because the osprey leave? *"No, it's because the autumn palette revels in earth colors."*

Many people don't despair for the wild and nature. Many, every year, go back to their favorite summer places or visit their favorite parks with the family. It is hard for some of us to share what we find so beautiful and threatened when many don't see the underlying fragility. If you can remember your family's story, where they came from, perhaps chased out of their country by a deadly and coercive force, you might be able to see the connection to your kimchi or dill spirit. Sometimes the foods we eat are the only link to our culture. It is no surprise that many immigrants to this county live on a land that belonged to the people native to here, long before Europeans claimed their stakes. Some of us living here for a couple generations reach toward an ancestral connection that is linked by a weave of light, water and fish, and herds of caribou drumming the earth with their migrations. Some of us have felt loneliness merge with soulful summer days linking our hearts to the weather, to the eternal, invincible summer. And some of us flat out need to adopt another line of kin as we move from there to disparate forms of connection. My people's tradition marks the journey of soul through many levels. Those that die are remembered and move through the world of soul when each memory is evoked. What if there is nobody to remember you? Or, what if, and there is solace here, the world is made up of light, water, and love of life? And each part of the world you love, each special place, person, osprey, otter, turtle, each breeze is a part of the weave of the eternal and you are held in an embrace by all that is woven into this moment? We could all then revel in the colors of the earth, the smell of dill and the taste of kimchi, the beauty of each breath, and the particles of light we touch on every path and leave on every trail.

  Balance is precarious. e.e. cummings wrote, "*this is the garden: colours come and go.*" Not everyone has time for complexity. If you appreciate the delicate balance and don't know what weights to put on this side or that, how then can you help make things right? If I can make a difference, I know you can. I have felt the need to share the beauty I see in this world; and hope to show others what many know, it is a part of us, so much so, that it's in the fabric of our skin and our deep memories. Some people are here to help us remember. Some will point out the illuminated blue sky. *It's so rare. Come look.* Not one of us, not one leaftide, teacher, or osprey skunk, should be shunned into silence, corners or limited abilities. If we help the osprey fledge and learn to fish, even just by loving them; especially by providing and protecting their nest platforms, we're helping them live to their potential.

~ ~ ~

"Did I tell you that I saw Virg turn into a crow?" My mentor said I did. After thinking I was becoming the crow in my journey, Virg did. And she flew off. I called after her, "Where are you going? Will you come back?" She called back, and said that it was *'hard to fly with so many questions'* on her.

I was concerned for my little Skunk. The microwaves from the cell tower were a cause for worry but I was concerned about the sediment and level of water for Skunk's trial fishing excursions. This means by proxy that my concerns were also about caring for the tide that comes in and out. Each change it brings, no matter how small or seemingly invisible, shapes the world of my osprey. It is said, *'As the osprey goes, so goes the world.'*

my kind of sacred ~ 8

There are days, you may know these, where you deliberately wander through everything that will lead you to your kind of sacred. These days have no path. But the great luxury of wandering, the coddiewomple, is that you may wander in a purposeful manner towards a vague destination as rivers do. These are the days you have enriched yourself and decided to play with all that feels holy and sacred. I would take a day like this once a month during the last years of my menses. I know that I was dipping into a stream that flowed with many traditions. Is all blood connected in this way? What I yearned for then may have been the same as today. Leaning forward into the present, with so many fibers of my being in what some would call the past, I know that the dream of a sacred place for wildlife is made reality here and there by those that work for their lands and waters, whether in small groups or large. We are too often woken by a reality too harsh to accept. And yet the truth we know in our bones, where change blows through from a wisdom beyond our ken, is that everything begins with the dream.

~ ~ ~

There were times, I would tell my mentor, that I'd hope the new DNA testing would show I was related to people that revered nature. It's possible, somewhere in my line, they did. I would think far back to some old Russian shaman. And then I'd wonder if women were allowed to call out to nature as I do, as my adopted kin do. Osprey are on every continent except Antarctica, so it is possible some blood relative of mine knew their ways, and waited for them, but by a different calendar. Unlike my mentor, the Old Woman, was an impatient teacher, once told me that there are such things in life as *waiting times*. I will arrive at a moment and wonder, now that I am older and don't mind waiting as much, if this is a waiting time.

There are many that have helped save national parks and parcels of land, and bodies of water, from overuse. They are protected areas. To many, that have lived here long before Europeans, they may have been regular haunts for different phases of their lives; especially, if they were a people that migrated. My dream of a wildlife trail across the whole country is that it will follow a path that much of the wildlife have known in their bones. *I often wonder when will I begin my work on the trail. What am I waiting for?* I dream that the migration pathways, treated as sacred, and where there are historical and historical migration stops for a vast number of birds, these lands and waterways will be protected. The drumming of herds is in the music of our heart beats. Seeing videos of herds of elk, vast numbers of them, running across the land, reached into my deep. I have never been able to let go of knowing that the sound of their hooves on the ground vibrated throughout the area and moved into the land which then roamed in its multitude of ways, through grasses and winds, plants and foods, into the bodies of my ancestors. All people are connected to the earth. Many bow to its life and mystery in ceremony and song. I am listening to what pushes me and what Walt Whitman has said is what we should do, "Love the earth and sun and the animals, …dismiss whatever insults your own soul…"

~ ~ ~

When we humans feel things in our bones, we cannot always name the source, but we trust what we feel. My mentor says it is because we are connected to the source. When you're in that knowing, she would add, it is knowing without knowing. *'It is hard for water to know it is water.'* Without making a sound, Skunk, reminds me as I watch her grow each day, that Persephone, and her mother Demeter, who have called to me through all my years, is a story about seasons and waiting times, as well as being reunited and gaining wholeness. Skunk will head south for her first winter and she will not return until one full year of her life has been lived in the south. After that, she will come back when the flowers start to bud. All creatures have the go. We are migrators. And because we will return, we have to protect the path.

~ ~ ~

The fear is realized. One quarter of the world's bird population is gone. In 50 years, half the bird population will disappear. It is time to pitch in to help every part of the ecosystem. This is the time. When nature thrives, we thrive, in wholeness, in wellness. The wilds need us and we need them. It is one system of wellbeing, not one household or one neighborhood. We connect by something more lifegiving than surveyor's lines. You can see it when the tidepools are clean and they fill with so many kinds of life; you can see it when the fields are fallow or growing and the buds are promising fruit. Likewise, the dead empty feeling of knowing something so much bigger is wrong. The fish kill pales against seeing stagnant waters and empty skies. The signs can be daunting.

~ ~ ~

Although I only remembered this recently, my dream has not changed since I'm little. My mentor might note that, *all realizations are timely and synchronous with events, whether they emerge into your consciousness or not.* I'm sure I still have some mysteries floating around my consciousness. My dream was that the world would love the oceans and stop the pollution. I would be a hero like Beowulf and figure this pollution out and stop it. Now I know that dreams touch all shores and includes all life. That is my kind of sacred. Just a tad of a shift. None of this was hurried along by my talks with Skunk. But all of it was as you would surmise, rushed by the crushing pressure of current events. Even the national parks are threatened by development. As a kid, the Boogeyman did not have a set look so I never would have guessed he came in a suit like any other business man, where this country can allow for corporations to be people, but not rivers. Not yet anyway.

    It is not every day you are told you must go to the great hall where many warriors have died before you. But if today is the day you must face the monster's mother, and she is really pissed off, it would be good to have a strategy. We will fight the spiraling down misery of the Grey Men's bottom lines with dreams. My weed and seed idea for growing more Black-eyed Susan's will take on a new dimension in the world. I will join others and where the Grey Men, you know them, want to nip at the edges of the Grand Canyon with drills, we'll dig a hole and plant a sanctuary. Weed and seed. Right there at the border of You Won't Dare Go Near the Canyon, and I Don't Give A Flying Fig About Your Profit Margin. Those we save, rescue us. You see it on bumper stickers from pet adoptions. It's true on every scale. Marine reserves, coral reefs, tidewaters, land trails in public trust are sanctuaries for all, including people, as is my back end of the river.

~ ~ ~

It may seem like it, but love is not tied to one person or one family or group. It's the mycelium, morphological, Gaian web of interconnecting flows of living, vibrant beings - flowers, animals, birds, bugs, fungi, lichens, mosses, oceans, seas, streams and their sweet rivers. That's why you need a high perch to observe where it is and be able to focus on that. Let the wind blow everything else off. That's just dross and I trust the winds to recycle it.

~ ~ ~

One day, I may wait under a tree to be a better human only to find that instead I have turned into an osprey. During the time my osprey is gone I try to hold this place for them, the bowl of the river, the widest sky around other than at the beach. Their nest site in view and their ripps, bend in the river, and eagle neighbors, and herons and kingfishers, the whole Okalee chorus, abides while I wait for their return.

~ ~ ~

Sanctuary can be found in unexpected places. When I first went to the beautiful Sedge Islands in New Jersey's Island Beach State Park my eyes and heart were filled with green grasses, pickleweed, and the sweet knowledge that the ocean was near. One man, said, '*Let me see how I can help the osprey.*' Then he said to the State, "*Why not buy these lands?*' Then when he saw people on their boats polluting, he said, '*Why not write a grant and get them pump boats to use so they don't need to dump their waste?*' Pete McClain was the one man with good questions. The Sedge Islands are New Jersey's first, and currently only, marine sanctuary. People can share it with the osprey and birds, with the pickleweeds too, because as everyone knows, pickleweeds enjoy company. The path can be a watery way, as well as a dry pilgrimage. But it will always begin with questions. People are notorious for wanting answers and often miss those that come without words. If you hug the sedges and glide under an osprey nest, you might feel a little bit of the mercurial, quicksilver eternity that I did. You might feel peace. You might be recognized by Skunk or her kin. You might just be moved by wisdom.

~ ~ ~

I am pulled by desire, the strongest current, toward those who want to clean up polluted bodies of water, restore areas to their natural vibrancy, and protect what is still wild. There is a field of energy that has been steadily growing in this direction. Every steward of the land and water is part of this field. Is it possible that the osprey lives in this field of energy? Like the particle that can be tickled on one side of the universe, the osprey feels the connection to the people that watch it and mark their calendars for their return as much as they do for spring or fall on the other side of the universe. The person and the osprey together create a unified field. This wandering morning, I promised myself I'd go to Okalee. When I was there, I realized that you cannot organize wisdom. Wisdom organizes you. For all we know, wisdom is a current that merges with desire to form the oceans. The Oracle has said that *'loneliness is from a false sense of separateness. Belonging comes from tending the path.'* All streams flow from a mother stream. Who can love you like your mother? But can she understand the yearning to be transformed into a bird? Where family may wish to keep you, close friends accept the need to fly. The acceptance of friends is legendary.

~ ~ ~

Chiaroscuro is about shapes emerging from the background. Here at the river, it is also about sounds emerging. It has a consciousness element as well. In that story, I was going to write that Skunk spoke to the woman but it was only when the woman teased apart the sounds of the river that she realized that some of the osprey talk she heard was directed at her. I think my Skunk did speak to me. And then I had to wonder if it was only now that Skunk returned my conversation or had it been going on since we first became aware of each other? Just like bees are known to do the wiggle waggle to tell the other bees at the hive, turn this way, then go South, then turn and go through one dry field, and you will soon see the flowerheads drooping over from the weight of pollen. Although Lynn and I would take on a stereotypical German accent and do the bee directions with all words starting with 'vee.' So, viggle vaggle left and right to tell your bee buddies, *It's past the dry field, you'll see, keep going.'* Viggle vaggle Skunk, I'm watching which way you go.

~ ~ ~

It is a good day when you see a monarch butterfly returning to the milkweed that its ancestors were born on. That Lynn just asked if I checked those plants for eggs, and I had; then minutes later seeing the monarch laying her lay eggs, that is the Tao speaking madam. That is the Tao. Today, I rise on the wings of monarchs after a long dark spell. All loneliness out the window. Every day I head into work as I take the turn to the highway I look up at the tower hoping for a sight of my osprey. Seeing them helps me get through my day. Returning from the job I look for the tower as I head toward my exit home. I look in the trees on my side of the wetlands as I cross the little bridge to my side of Okalee. Some say that truth is known last by the one that needs it. You come 'round when you come 'round and there's nothing to shorten the journey. Well, the work is done. I'm drawn toward nests in the trees because I search for the gathering places, the hollows and havens of materials that birds have found for their nests. Quietly, a great blue was stalking along toward and near the wreck. Eventually, it flew off and made a god-awful sound, like a heavy smoker clearing his throat. As it did, it flew across the way directly in front of me and quite near a great egret. This heron's long neck seemed very white. Maybe it swallowed a swan. Yesterday, there were nearly 40 white mute swans there. If they're mute nobody would necessarily know the heron ate it.

~ ~ ~

I am glad to have a peak at the turn in the road. I found an old letter when I was 32 to Jean Houston about how my writing teacher didn't like myths and wished I'd stop writing about them. I was re-interpreting them. It was only later in my life that I realized I am reliving them because they sometimes seem to carry the voices of my ancestors. My twenties were the dark ages. I could hold a torch and walk through the cavern of my twenties' self-consciousness now and see my dreams painted on the walls. But I'd also see my hesitancy, my holding back and not holding on to what I loved. It's true that I was finding my voice and that I had raw courage but many could steal the air from my lungs and I would let my passion lay flat on the ground like a deflated balloon.

~ ~ ~

It is said that fate is tied to fate. Have you noticed this? I have but often only after the fact. At first, I thought I was too preoccupied and then I realized, the skies were emptier; and I cannot ignore the fact that I am growing more feathers. If my fate is tied to the fate of the birds, is yours? A Holly Near song filters into my head when the overwhelming crush of the powerful wishes to undermine bird migration laws, or ignore the evidence of the damage that large-scale gas and oil extraction create. The root of all this upheaval is the same. *"And the junta knows, and the junta knows."* What if three billion people went missing instead of birds? How do we recognize loss of life on a human scale but not on the connected web of life? The junta is our ignorance. Exile, extermination, extinction. The opposite of sanctuary. Our fate is tied to all fates. Just as harmony is tied to all harmony.

~ ~ ~

Like my mentor, most teachers are fond of asking questions that uncover the bits of you that you hide from yourself or plain don't know because you are water and you're swimming. It's like going on a treasure hunt for them. Their questions are their crew of workers. The crew does all the digging. *'How about digging over there?',* a teacher might ask. Even if they don't know what they're seeking, they know when a question doesn't do the job. *How about over there then?* The crew digs over there then. My friend Virg once asked, *"What's your favorite bird?"* I answered without hesitation, "The osprey." *"Why?"* *"They come back to the same nest and remind me of the hope of spring and the dream of summer."*

    I shared this memory with my mentor. *'Oh, yes, I know that dream,'* she said and then it prompted a story she remembered. In a subway filled with the moist smells of people, grime, a world class violinist played one of the most difficult pieces in anyone's repertoire. Some stopped to listen, some did not. Some saw the beauty and had to stop. In cities, people are used to beauty coming in unexpected places. Some stop. Some do not. But even those who did not stop, one wonders if they heard the beauty or was it just a sound that did not draw them. Or were they in such a hurry because of necessity that they could not stop? When do we perceive beauty? When do we stop for it? Questions hold promise and can touch parts of us that information may not. Do you know that your Sedge Islands are sacred and sanctuary? There are no signs.

chiaroscuro. ancestors ~ 9

Admittedly, I found nature late in life. Now I know that I am here to honor what was sown in my bones a long time before I went walking. Alan Watts wrote that "...if everything is allowed to go its own way the harmony of the universe will be established, since every process in the world can 'do its own thing' only in relation to all others." I went my own way. Bungled a lot of things up too. Finally, I found a connection between my dreams for a clean ocean, the wetlands and my osprey. Leonardo da Vinci used the technique of chiaroscuro, light and dark, shapes emerging from the darkness of the canvas lending them a sense of dimension. It is funny how time creates the same effect in our lives. On our canvas, we sometimes do not see the effect of events or relationships until something is called from within us and we then look at our reactions to experiences and our history differently. It is then you may notice that an event that seemed minor, repeats. Maybe it appeared through different relationships. This then is pulled to the foreground like shapes on a canvas emerging from the background, and you see themes that had been playing in your life all along. Maybe this is what Mona Lisa's knowing smile is telling us.

    My mother was fond of telling me that she had no idea she was pregnant with me when she went on a vacation in Florida. She had great fun diving off a high diving board. She enjoyed this story because she said maybe that was why I was the way I was, suiting whatever brain faux pas she was teasing me about at the time. Most likely when I tossed her gin card. That's the fastest I ever did see her move, picking up that card. Now I wonder, if I was gaining the perspective of a fledging osprey and my wee beginnings in my mother's diving bell was coding my DNA for a first flight. Or, is it possible, that all these years feeling the yearning of Demeter's search for her daughter Persephone, that somehow, I knew I'd be searching for my mother in return, because I lost her too soon? They say it was Hades that took Persephone to the underworld. I know it was Winter.

Or does my osprey remind me of this story because they bring spring and summer? It is autumn when they leave. And you know that is followed by the inevitable winter, just as there was winter when Persephone was taken by the god of the underworld. It is not only through time that we recognize patterns that emerge from our background. We see ourselves through new friendships, the tap of love, and sometimes in the clouds bleached white by the sun.

My mentor knows how often I'm drawn to Greek myths. She is more fond of metaphors than stories. She will search through a phrase that gets her going so that eventually she is caught like a kid fascinated by the mirror reflecting her image. She will point out that I have done the same with Demeter. It is true. Her story compels me. I have seen her in my journey-lands and was surprised to see that she wasn't distraught with angst about her daughter. Perhaps she knew Persephone was safe and would return in her own time. She was among her peers and feeling the joy of just being in a beautiful sanctuary.

It is in this way too, following what draws my curiosity, that I have felt a kinship with chosen ancestors, with the wetlands and the osprey. As I grew to recognize and appreciate them, they emerged more and more in my awareness. They came to the foreground. I pursued being in their company. And in this way, many times in the course of my days I have the stamp of synchronous approval since I'm placing myself in their realms. They hold pieces of the hologram which, as it turns out, are pieces of my dream. My wetlands and my ancestors speak to me about the continuity that exists in life. This is big web territory. Kind of similar to having kids and grandkids. A larger, more inclusive web that includes the lands that we know and live on.

I was called a change of life baby. That was reference to my mother's age not the labyrinth path I took from that first plunge into the deep dive with my mom. Those initial high and deep dives may have caused more ripples in addition to my mother's kidding.

~ ~ ~

I went to the wetlands with the intention of finding my osprey kid. I could not tell from Skunk's quizzical look if she was nervous or gaming the situation she was in. I was just standing there. That was the situation. If she was trying to figure out the best way to communicate. I only had to find the means and slice the difference between us with understanding. I look at my osprey like I would the clouds or the distant blue, for what they bring, a sense of place and a sense of belonging. When I see my osprey at Okalee everything feels more right. Like many who project their way of being onto wildlife, I have felt my osprey could read my mind. Or at least know me and gather my presence was benign. They say body language is 80% of communication. Our bodies translate our unspoken thoughts. Is my love seen from the bulwarks to the cell tower? My mentor is silent on this topic. Virg has said, "Of course. Love is the most visible of emotions because it shows through your eyes and smile." I do tell them, "I love you." Early loss has taught me to leave nothing unsaid. Our relationship is generative. 'Me and you kid, we're still growing. I know you have courage. You're the lion, the roar, the strong heart. This is the mystery work now. Being present to what we will become. A field has emerged. Mutuals arising. Sweet tunings of understanding.

~ ~ ~

However, I might explain my heritage to Skunk, I ought to pay attention to what I say, because it might just help me understand some things myself. As big as my families, both sides, once were, they shrunk to nothing. Stories about my mother's father were legendary. But my father's parents are the only grandparents I knew. They did not speak English. I remember sitting at their feet and nodding my head when they spoke to me in Yiddish. This always reminds me that my mother was fluent in Yiddish too. One day we were on a bus in Miami when a man in a bus addressed her. She was really upset after what seemed like a very pleasant exchange. I asked her why. "I am forgetting my Yiddish." It was such a new way to see my mother, as someone that was bilingual and lived in at least two worlds. My Yiddish is just the relics of our shared humor, a bridge to her other world, I am not fluent.

Skunk's got everyone she knows as family right there in the nest with her. I told Skunk that 'I'd trip all over myself if I had to walk around with a nest under my feet.' I explained who my blood relatives were rather quickly because I related more to my chosen ancestors. I am sure that the road to all my blood and chosen ancestors meets up many on roads. Yet, while one family seems to have shrunk, I have found that I have a growing sense of kinship with the other. As my mother would say, go figure. *'And Skunk, somehow one of my many grandmothers is sometimes called Gaia.'* "Who's that?" *'She's actually Demeter's mom, Persephone's grandmother. And, I have a suspicion that she might be the Old Woman who once shook her finger at me and told me I had better write. She admonished me. I have never forgotten her but I only knew her as this crabby old thing.'* My mentor tells me she's a wise old lady. *'This I know, when they align, Gaia, Demeter and Persephone, the triad, is a formidable force in the world. Each one of them sometimes shows as a bird. Humans and birds have a long history together. Like us.'*

~ ~ ~

I don't know when I started to call the older woman I go to in my journey-lands, my Grandmother. But it is a term of respect that feels right. I seek her out whenever I go there. The times she is not there, I'm disappointed and feel a little uneasy. She is old. I cannot tell how old but she feels old enough to know *way back when.* I have to tell you that I'm not old in the journey-lands. This was not a conscious choice on my part. I can tell I'm younger. Not by how I look because I don't see myself but by how I feel. And I I recognize being seen as a younger person by those I encounter there.

I adopted the idea of calling her Grandmother from many sources of indigenous writings because it became apparent that she holds that place of respect elders should have; and the relationship I felt with her, I mean, the physical part of being near her, reminded me of sitting at my grandparents feet. She is my teacher. I go to her with my questions and concerns. She holds a place of honor and respect among all the other beings I know of and meet in the journey-lands too.

When she appears as an older woman, which is how she most frequently appears to me, I'll often find her sitting on a bench next to a soft path that borders the marsh. Her bench faces the marsh. I can see open water beyond that whether the marsh is wet or dry. When I approach her, I always address her formally and tell her I have a question. She indicates in some fashion for me to speak. And then I tell her my question. She will often indicate for me to sit next to her. Sometimes, that is all I need to feel a sense of deep, loving contact and my questions dissolve. For years, I couldn't look her in the eyes. I do now, but just briefly.

She rarely speaks directly to me. Mostly, she shows me places and takes me on brief trips to demonstrate or provide information I have to puzzle out in answer to my question. Sometimes she'll take me by the hand and we'll walk down the path; sometimes joining others. She'll gesture across the marsh and whatever I look at is part of my response to any spoken or unspoken question I might have.

    She will sometimes appear to me as an eagle and before I would know how, I'd be on her wing or back and flying. As an eagle, Grandmother has taken me up to the tops of trees and flown me all over the journey-lands. All this talk of mothers and grandmothers is foreign to Skunk as it would be to my own mother. Skunk only knows that her flight feathers are still not ready to lift her into the air. Many of us have also found ourselves in the same circumstance. Wanting to fly, to lift ourselves up and not having the flight feathers to do it yet.

    As unlikely as it might seem, the journey-lands are very much like my wetlands. Parts of them most often remind me of the Audubon center in Wellfleet, Massachusetts. I used to travel there and felt a strong connection to that place from my very first time; and that bond has always remained with me. From the first time I went there, I wanted to live there and would dream scheme ways of doing that. In fact, that is where I was headed when the flat tire occurred on 95 and I became aware that there was a dragon in my head. Go figure.

~ ~ ~

Look how birds move through the air. A neighborhood Cooper's hawk takes long slices on an angle then weaves like a heavyweight boxer through the branches. Crowds of starlings, some call them constellations, are like animated clouds descending on the other side of the river. Individually, the geometric shape of a starling is close to Neruda's 'constellations, like dice cut into squares by the cold.' Except that they take a triangular exception to the air space and crisp up the blue sky into sharp angles when you see one at a time. My osprey holds the sky in an "M" shape. They don't have the huge wing paddles of the eagles. When osprey hunt, you can see every movement of their head and know just after they get the news that there's fish or no fish there. If they see a fish, they lift in the sky readying to plunge. I'm held in place watching that vertical lift. Sometimes there's a swing and a miss, it's actually an unsuccessful dunk, and they sail off.

  I am in love with birds. I love knowing that they cut through the light of day and the night during migrations. Some organizations track this on radar. Sometimes a bird song will hold us securely in the moment we hear it, sometimes the background cries of gulls tell us summer is here. I don't know when they hijacked my heart, especially the osprey, but I'm grateful.

~ ~ ~

Before I left the house, I was sitting at my desk but pulled by the awareness of all we are losing in nature. I turned to look outside and an osprey flew over. Never saw one through my study window before. Why is it that every sighting feels like a blessing? I'm trying to figure out how to speak about my relationship to non-humans and also how to describe the land and waterways. Our language doesn't easily show inclusion when it comes to describing our world. It is possible that holograms do. Two intersecting beams of light capture an image and allow you to see dimension. I can imagine being in the space of the image. The only accurate way to share what I feel when I'm at the wetlands is to have you imagine being in a hologram with me. Not a snow globe. An eco-holo. Eco means home, and holo means whole. There's another word that describes our whole home in use today, biome. This refers to the community of plants and animals in an area. But none of these terms describe how my wetlands connect me to my ancestors. For me, I need something that describes the whole enchilada, the gestalt, and the world of my river and mud. If a hologram were to break, each piece, because of the way it is made, would still hold the whole image. It is like your family. You are a part of it and everyone you know as family makes up the whole. When you're off in the world or apart from your family, you are still a part of them. People will say 'You have your mother's eyes,' or your father's walk. They will see you and also see you as a part of a larger group. My family, my ancestors are more than I ever knew and extends well beyond my people kin. Because we are failing our world and so much is endangered, we can no longer deny that pieces of our world show how interconnected we are.

    When something fails, whatever it is connected to is in danger of also failing. I have to wonder how much of our lives then are also failing; and what would be the measurement for that? Would it be how we treat each other? Or how we honor the land, water and air? Or how we act as if we live on a carpet detached from the "natural" world?

    We may not at first recognize that the osprey needs the menhaden to migrate or they will not have food. There is a relationship between these fish, other wildlife and humans, as well. "Menhaden may be the most important fish you've never heard about. They're not only prey for iconic wildlife—from humpback whales and dolphins to striped bass and ospreys—but they also are the East and Gulf coasts' most-caught fish—and the second-highest catch in the U.S. behind Alaskan pollock." Responsible, sustainable ways of living should take into account the vast net of both large and small connections which make this world go round. We learn this early on as 'the knee bone is connected to the thigh bone.' Make no mistake about it, all the bones are connected and the road they lead to is called life. The sphinx moth pollinates the ghost orchid in Florida's Everglades, the crane fly pollinates the orchids in Jersey Pine Barrens. As kids we all heard that some seeds wait many seasons for the heat of a forest fire to be released. Everywhere we look there is a connection, some rare and special, some common as clay. This world, as big as that might sound, is our home. Every part of it is connected. Broken holograms will show the whole image in each broken piece. That is true. But each broken part of our home, our biome, is a lifeline and we have to protect the connections. We are nowhere without our families, whether we know our forebears or not. It is obvious that we would not be here without them. Many may scoff at the connections some see and some study. Just past ridicule is the vast and wildly trafficked web of life.

~ ~ ~

    I once spent a delightful afternoon of daydreaming time in the water with my friend Virg. Between the waves I rode in, there were many that day, we talked about how dreams for a common good float above the clouds of thoughts and group together like a flock of birds. When the gathering place gains a certain density, that's when an idea emerges into the general consciousness. It becomes something like a stream in the river. Suddenly, it's easy to see against the backdrop of a busy world. I told Virg that I had spent all these years longing for an end to pollution and never understood that my dream needs to be wider and more inclusive. Speaking as the Oracle then, because Virg was the source of the Oracle, she pronounced "We need many people to hold this dream." A vision has come down like rain on a desert. Now this dream has touched the seed waiting for the time that was right as rain; and the seed that is the dream of many, can flower.

define the land, water, and air

Somewhere in our people's history, we are all connected to an eternal life line. If you need a reference point, when you stand still, let's say you're in the present. To one side is the past to the other the future. When you move, time moves with you. Who am I to ignore Einstein and more importantly, the cultures of many lands across all of history? I never felt a connection to my ancestors, blood, adopted or spiritual, until late in life. Now I do and it's connected to my concerns about the birds and wetlands. All of it really. Every time I walk the land, the cushy give of moss under the shade of the pines, or the beach or walk to the bulwarks, dry or muddy if it just rained, I am journeying with my ancestors. If you go to the way back when, they have been this way before. I want to feel this connection. It is not always present, but when it is, there's a certain sense of right. Everything feels aligned.

It us uncommon for most people in my neighborhood, and most of the country as well I'd gather, to speak of the land, water, and air. It's where you live, no matter how many stories above ground. It's where you shop and get your hair cut; or buy your groceries. We may be fooled by the purpose of our communal space and forget that they exist on land, and near water, and we may not pay any attention to the air around all these common places. If you remember that there's a few ingredients to your world - land, water and air, you can appreciate why we must protect the path. We'll walk it again and our relations will too.

Along the path, there are the connections, the lifelines, that little by little, if we also take note and take care, will make the work of protecting the path more sure. There are many ways to do this. It's as simple as knowing what the quality of the water is coming out of your faucet; or what goes into the food you just had for breakfast at Lucille's Country Cooking in Barnegat; or how healthy the osprey kids are when they break loose from their egg.

ancestors, family, continuity

At my mentor's suggestion, I journeyed to an ancestor who lives across the river. I walked on the mud then when the water was deep enough I swam like a deer just holding my head up and moving toward the Marconi side. I must have looked like a strange water bird. A few months back I saw two deer swimming across the river to the other side. Bad birder that I am, I kept trying to figure out what kind of ducks they were until I finally saw them reach the opposite shore and walk on the deer path. A young guy once told me about the path but I could never see it. That is, until the strange ducks turned into deer and walked on it.

My ancestor and I met almost immediately when I journeyed to the other side. We looked at each other for a while then we climbed onto the osprey platform I knew from my side of the river. It was worn grey from time in the salty winds. I had never met her before but I felt a comfort you feel being with an old friend. Was she another reason why I'm so drawn to looking at the eagles from across the way from Marconi? She made a sweeping gesture with her hands and I took it to be a demonstration of our connection through time. There was no need to ask questions now even though they were piling up in my thoughts. I saved them for later. I just needed to be with her. And so I was for the time we shared. Some encounters take time to absorb and appreciate. One day I will write more about this meeting.

~ ~ ~

Molly has what looks like a second set of eyes above her eyebrow. I believe this feature is designed to scare you, and, at the very least, make it seem, even when her actual eyes are closed, that she is watching you. Stoner, my first cat, daughter/mother, had exquisite eye make-up. There exists a détente between most cats and their humans. It is a recognition of our mutual need for each other. And so feline beauty allows you to pause and take in something that is immeasurable but arresting. It could be an age-related experience but I'm noticing the skies more and I see the same beauty there that feels just as familiar and just as intimate as Molly's stretched out paw kneading the air. That is it, the familiarity. A deep secret, this has been rising in my bone marrow and informing everything in my body and soul, I am kin to the world. You may think this is projection since every important blood relation has passed. Loneliness has been my companion since my siblings left our home and moved out into the world. I remember feeling sick the day my sister Claire was getting married and I learned she would no longer sleep at home. Loneliness has travelled up and down my bones. It is not my siblings' passing that has deepened my sorrow. It is the daily death and extinctions, the mindless polluting and parceling of the natural world because I feel and know that my kin are in everything. My family did not celebrate the world that I'm describing. But I do now. What I long for, is that you find the sky as beautiful as anyone that captures your heart and pulls on your imagination. The uninterrupted early mornings' face is light and ephemeral. It doesn't last. Until, that is, remembering beauty brings your head and heart closer to the sky, into the realm of the birds and winds, and the dream of a world where wild and human are all able to thrive. My mentor would sometimes grieve about nature. She would tell me that until humans take responsibility for and mitigate our impact, we will continue to lose the world. That is how she said, 'lose the world.' When some people see the rough times in the wild and difficult realities they welcome the comfort of their homes. And then, I fear, they forget that it is a borrowed comfort, a comfort that transformed so much to be what it is. But it came from the wild. It is sometimes hard to believe that even a refrigerator has undergone a deep transformation from it's original source materials. It is said that all wisdom of the ways is first steeped in respect because that is where understanding begins.

~ ~ ~

On a rare Okalee day, Virg and I got to see the buffalo roam. It was a rare day there because Virg was with me. At one point two swans were flying in. It's nothing new to see swans but to see them fly in for a landing is always a treat. Virg wasn't familiar with the small buffleheads. She could only get buffalo heads out of the word I used so we stuck with that. She enjoyed their dunking and when she saw the black and white, she seemed to take the same joy in them that I do. We saw black ducks, widgeons, listened to the red wings calling back and forth behind us and to our left from their phragmites perches. We saw red knots. Virg said they were the teachers and the other sanderling type birds we saw, about 15 to 18, much smaller in size but with really long bills, were the school kids. There were five red knots. Described in Peterson's as a "dumpy wader with a washed-out gray look." Virg said that sounded like her; and I said I'm right there with you.

~ ~ ~

Just at magic hour, finally, an osprey on its tower nest. Don't know where they've been. You know, many of them are from Brazil and they like to party. I went down to the river after eating dinner, which was after a long day at work of feeling alienated, unliked, and out of orbit. The lead that builds up in my system from a day of meaningless chatter and positioning at the job was buoyed by whatever it was that could not be denied because it was summer. The colors were sharp but smooth, like the setting sun through the back of a red caladium in the terracotta box on the porch rail. You may fall in love with the world at this time of day. There's a storm coming on and it's supposed to be a big one. High winds, heavy rains. The wind was speaking and taking over the landscape. First, I saw seven Canadian geese thirty, forty feet out at most, bobbing and floating on a gentle current as they headed toward the opening to the river's bowl. Then I saw the eagle. Few things are as reassuring as the command of an eagle soaring. Dusk settled in bringing moist air and choppy water. The eagle continued to soar. Just the sky moved. Its wings never did. It soared in front of and then past its nest. I could not look at anything else, yet by watching the eagle I felt like I was seeing everything. I had to go down to the river, the sweet river and sky, where the terns dive and kingfisher rattles and the eagle flies over high. I had my Grandmother pouch with me. This small brown felt pouch holds my special stones and shells. When I was younger, I collected rocks and minerals. I still love them. Over the years I have realized that I feel a deep connection to them that is very much like my initial fascination. Their beauty has me marvel at all that is hidden but common if you know where to look. They hold my attention. I feel affection for them. I know the story of how each stone came into my life. As I spoke to spirit, earnest and not complaining for a change, I felt as if a cloak were placed on my shoulders. It was a sweet sense of connection to all that was around me, seen and unseen. I saw the first sun dog after another eagle flew back into the area I call the bowl.

    I shook my pouch and breathed into it. I'd never done this before. When I left the wetlands, I was singing words and then just sounds that drifted into chants. Sometimes words would creep in, but I felt this was just some overworked compulsion to tidy up my experience. I remember the sounds that came from my belly to my mouth and filled the car. Some were playful. I experimented with tones and phrases. That was after I saw the second sun dog. The eagles can see seven times better than people. They must have seen me smile. I had seen one soaring a few weeks back but this was right in front of me and I could see both clearly without binoculars. Seeing them always feels like a blessing. When thoughts of snidely people at work come, or the work itself which does not feel good, I tell my sadness to "Stay with the blessings." There were many from this time and I was able to return to them. The sky was open and sweet like the moment. That's when I saw the second sun dog.

    Taken by the current, the swans were gently floating sideways. The seeds from phragmites edging the bulwarks were blowing sideways like snow in a blizzard. The sun coming through the clouds would have challenged everyone for more names to identify the shades of blue. The sky is everything. I journeyed. Was told again, patience. The word 'agency' came to me direct from the Grandmother pouch. Then my heart filled thinking of my mother. For me, all roads lead to summer which is how I know I am surely Lena's daughter. Summer finally delivered me to my wetlands and my osprey. The eagles came in low from around the bend. Every time I see them, I drop logic in wonder and it melts my perception. I found a small insect just to the right of where I stand at the bulwarks. It looked like crisscrossed pieces of dried grass. It had a natural camouflage but for the shame that I found it.

turtle crossings and crow women (sanctuaries) ~ 10

They say your journey-lands will change as you put more energy into them. I sometimes forget to do this because I'm so preoccupied with questions for my Grandmother. Questions can crowd your head and leave little room for looking around. No wonder some song birds lose the ability to sing in winter. They need enough brain power to find their food. I was seeking Grandmother because I had lost my way and felt despair. Even so, before heading to the bench where I often see her sitting, I turned left and walked to the small pond that was just a bit down on the trail, past some bumpy tree roots and hidden by brush. Since the first time I saw tiny bubbles near a wet log in the pond I look for the bubbles as soon as the pond is in sight. The bubbles turned out to be an indication of the black turtle's nostrils. The small terrapin bubbles can slow you down enough so that you don't hurry past the good. The good is just being there with the turtles and wonder filling the vacuum from the absence of thoughts.

  When I was about ten, I'd search out the giant sea turtles that crawled on the pilings just past Hogan's, the ice cream and sundries concession on the boardwalk that divided Bradley Beach from Ocean Grove. Hogan's was a white clapboard building. The paint grew thicker through the dozens of summer seasons I knew it. There was a large gap underneath the boardwalk where Hogan's sat. There was just enough ocean to allow the sea turtles access for a nice respite on the pilings where the ocean ended and

Fletcher Lake began. I'd rent a row boat for fifty cents from this older, blond haired kid that lived right across from the lake. My mother didn't even know I did this. I'm not sure if his mother knew he rented their row boat. I'd get in the boat, row toward Hogan's and hope to see the turtles. The days they were there were all right. I'd hover at a respectful distance to watch them. They don't move much when they are taking a spell from the ocean. I imagined how good the sun must have felt sinking into their limbs, surely tired from their long swim.

 Sometimes when I went rowing I would have to fight off other kids that tried to knock me out of my boat and dump me into the lake. It's funny how that never seemed unusual or frightening. It just was what it was. Besides, I was strong and they couldn't best me. I also knew not to head toward the turtles if those kids were around. If they had fun trying to knock me off, a turtle would be that much of a better target. And my sea turtles needed their sanctuary.

 Fletcher Lake is the first body of water I ever heard was polluted. It was the first time I ever heard the word pollution too. That never meant much to me as a kid until the day my nephew Ange, about three years old, watched me throw balled up bread into the lake to see the sunnies come to the surface and grab it. He wanted to try. I rolled some white bread between my fingers and loaded his little fists with the doughy pellets. With his first toss, both he and the bread went into the lake. All I could do was bend over the low bulwark and stare at his submerged face under a glaze of scum in the polluted water. *How the heck did he manage that?* 'My sister-in-law is going to kill me,' rushed into my head before I picked him up out of there. Then, I gauged the sun and how hot it was hoping he would dry between there and our summer rooming house. That didn't happen. First words out of her mouth was a squeal which kind of sounded like, "What happened?" And kind of felt like I was in big trouble. I mean, several decades later, my nephew is fine. There's a moral to that story. Polluted lakes and people can clean up. And you can't trust three-year-old's not to get you in trouble.

~ ~ ~

The few places I go to regularly aren't all that exciting. They're just sweet. Some, like my journey-lands, are indirectly accessed, but most are easy to get to once you know where to go. I think Virg would have loved Lucille's in the Pine Barrens if we could have made it there together. The big sign above the kitchen reads, "Life isn't about waiting for the storm to pass; it's about learning to dance in the rain." Well, that's a lesson. Lynn and I were fortunate enough to meet Lucille. To many she was the Pine Barrens. We all have the land in us. The water and the sky too. We're dancing in the rain folks. There was something about Lucille that felt like she could be your long lost grandmother. This is not to take away her youth or to dis her blood kin. For a woman to represent an entire ecological area, succinct and unique as the Pine Barrens, she must be a formidable person. That was Lucille. And her joint, a local food establishment, feels like home as soon as you walk in. Sanctuaries can be breakfast places, or a piling leaning from the constant pull of the tides, splintered and drained of color from the sun. With Lucille's it was all that and its proximity to the rare blue Pine Barrens' gentian which make it even more so, a place to honor and respect. Lynn wasn't sure if the bog nearby or Lucille's pie was the draw for me. I'll say this much, the promise of a meal after an outing is always welcome.

~ ~ ~

The worry demons chased me. That's why I was hoping to see Grandmother. How many pilings remain in the world for the ocean-going turtles to rest on? There's also a world or two of difference between pond turtles and the ocean-going giants I got to see. The Atlantic moved into Fletcher Lake. Amazing transition from a mighty ocean to a small lake, which was only, really, a narrow water lane between two shore towns. The gap between Fletcher Lake and the ocean has since closed. So much in the world seems to be narrowing. While worry filled my head, my chest and middle grew more feathers. Normally, I might doubt there was a correlation. These days, anything seems possible. One day, I'm thinking I might just fly. But after the thrill of it, where would I set down to rest? That got me wondering about sanctuaries and places that were safe for all of wildlife. How do you save a space for a sea turtle? Or a pond for the nostrils and the rest of the little black terrapins? Marine sanctuaries.

When Virg flew off, I mean, she actually did fly off, she told me it was hard to fly with so many questions. If you know anyone like her that's gone off to be with the Crow Women, I guess we can give them that, throw the questions overboard so they can fly. But Crow Women, in my experience, are a might tight with a word about feathers and sharing information. It seems to me their dancing has something to do with keeping things going in the world. They dance in a trance with joy and have little time to share details.

There are those among us, who are water dragons, those who are wood dragons and so on, who are destined to visit the Crow Women but move in different circles most of the time. What distinguishes each kind of dragon from the other are the transformations that help them evolve. Each one depends on the lands and oceans, the waterways, and winds that they need to thrive and transform, in order to fulfill their dragon destiny, and to enjoy their winding dance.

As I was leaving my journey-lands I saw my mentor. She had been hovering. I think. She says, no she does not hover. It seemed like she was waiting for me. It was, after all, unusual to see her outside a diner. We walked along a trail that lead us to my wetlands. My journey-lands connect to the wetlands where I watch the osprey. I had known this but never had I moved from one land to the other with another person alongside me. Everything looked different. My questions about turtles and territory evaporated, as it turned out, in my journey. Besides, Grandmother was not there to provide guidance. As we walked together, I told my mentor that I see Virg now and then in my journey-lands. There is this narrow path that Grandmother often walks with her peers. I trail behind. There is an elevated area in the middle of the path but off to the right. The raised area at first seems to have a solid structure around it. But it is a circle of wind that you can slip through. I know because I have slipped through. When I did, I was silently acknowledged by a circle of women, all dancing around another vertical column of wind or energy that was in the center of their circle. Each woman wore a costume, or so I assumed it was only a costume, of a bird. I thought that I could see their faces despite the crow hoods that covered them. But I have since wondered if I only projected what I thought and did not accept what I saw. Were they crows as tall as a human? I knew when I danced around with them, that I was accepted as a visitor. I knew also, years later, that when I saw Virg step through the circle of wind and poke her head out, now at least two times in visits to my journey-lands, that she belonged to the community of Crow Women. If she was dancing with the Crow Women, I'm sure she knew about dancing in the rain. I began to wonder if Lucille might be dancing with her as well.

the miso walk ~ 11

One thing I have in common with osprey is that we're both beachcombers. There's a special bond among us who roam the beach. There are those that search for sea glass and have been doing this for as long as glass bottles have been plentiful. Blue glass reminds me of images of roaming rivers that curl like a blue dragon, the bends as soft as the curves of the glass smoothed by the ocean's tumble. Blue beach glass is at the apex of a beachcomber's world. But the apex is actually a plateau that derives its character from the frame of mind you enter the beachcombing. When locked in the house all winter with work and chores, the first day in February that I go to the beach, just to be there, feels like a vacation even when it's cold and damp. I am soon drawn toward the necklace at the water's edge. My mind unfurls and without even trying, my body relaxes. Perhaps red glass is more rare than blue. It does not matter. I wander the beach, finding this smooth shell, broken but beautiful, and without realizing it I am moving like a water dragon. I move up where the tide crested, but where the water recedes, there is a downward curve, and I move down closer to the water. As I follow the wrack line the beachcombing has now become the ocean's labyrinth walk. I match the mindless mindfulness of the labyrinth but hug the boundary of the sea. So, it has been said and so my mentor, who I have decided to simply call Mentor, roams the beaches of Sandy Hook frequently. She will tell you that you cannot artificially cook glass and find it to have the same qualities as glass that's gone from boil to simmer and back to boil again at the water's edge in the salty sea. And you cannot expect your mind to uncurl without letting go of the intention to do so. There are standards and there are practices.

    Mentor told me that these same standards apply to miso. *'Why miso, why now?* I wondered to myself. Although, my mentor's mention of the blue glass had my mind hop to blue dragons, and that had a deep resonance with me. And then I realized it's because it reminded me of the dragon who was curled inside my head. I sometimes wondered if it was the one speaking to me and I only thought my little Skunk osprey friend was talking. I also wondered why the dragon curled inside my head had not paid me a visit since that first time. But the infrequent opportunity to walk with my mentor brought me back to her words. Time is precious and she is like blue sea glass.

    I am sorry to say that I missed the start of her thoughts on this topic because my mind drifted again thinking about the Crow Women and Virg. Was there something Virg was trying to tell me when she poked her head through the wind column? When I resumed listening, Mentor was saying, "Because all of life is about tastes and smells, seeing beauty, the discoveries, the sense of fullness that wonder brings, the making it what it is or helping it along to be what it can be. We sometimes get set in the direction and more oftentimes are bumped off course."

    Again, my keppe was open to wandering thoughts. *'Maybe this is why rivers and bees do the viggle vaggle? Or is there a greater purpose in all the turns and curves?* I could not stop my mind from taking a few turns. Maybe my mentor was hypnotizing me? Some have said that the sex of a fish depends upon how many twists and turns its mother took back to the spawning area. For one creature, a turn or bend in the road just provides a different view, for another it can be as profound as changing the course of its life's story. Even changing the course of another creature, because all stories in nature are related.

    "A traditional miso craftsman will tell you that their microorganisms work harder when someone is watching. They talk to them." And then with a fake stern look at me, for she caught me drifting, "Microorganisms can listen and you cannot!"

    I thought, '*The work of microorganisms is not often in the news.*' My mentor gave me another sideways glance. I could not stop to hold my focus. I will lay blame to the rarity of walking with her by my wetlands so far from our usual meetings. She said there's a lesson to be had from one that works with miso for everyone talking to flowers and trees, birds and everything else not human in this world. I agree. What is humbling, my mentor shared, is that the master craftsman said, "I don't make the miso. I just create an environment where the microorganisms make it."

    Ah, now I could understand that she was not just talking about miso. Which is wonderful and delicious, and adds umami to all foods it touches. Umami is that uncanny flavor that takes you on a journey. You're off before you even realize it. What happened? Deliciousness. That's what happened. This is the fifth flavor that brings deep satisfaction and translates to deliciousness. I knew sweet and salty. My mother had sour in her repertoire which I firmly rejected as a kid. Holidays is when bitter might came round.

    We know more about everything now. I would guess my mentor recognized the miso master as kin. They had so much in common. She enjoyed telling about the oak barrel that he used to make traditional miso. The wooden barrels, grown and made from oak in the United States traveled all the way to Japan for this purpose. The barrels have air pockets which provide the perfect environment for the microorganisms to grow. As my mentor would point out, so many worlds within worlds.

    We approached the broken part of the bulwarks where I like to sit and watch. There are a few worlds here as well, both seen and unseen. I was lost in thought about perfect and imperfect environments. Sanctuaries and turtle crossings. Protected marine areas and wildlife bridges so that animals are not hurt by automobiles. Nature reserves and open spaces, some with butterfly gardens. Road crossings to protect migration paths. These thoughts like Li Po's "wind from the pine trees trickles on my bare head."

~ ~ ~

Basho said to write out of the heart/mind. There is no separation from the heart and the mind, there is a crossing, just as people are now understanding the need for animal crossings so that they can be spared the danger of traffic and move under or over the road while following routes that have been taken by their predecessors for ages. The heart/mind has been followed by some for ages but there are known splits and these are telling apertures in our history with nature. Where some see through to new possibilities; and some see only the economy of resources.

    I have to wonder about the dragon that appeared to me. It has been a few years now since that time. And I have been feeling, like many, that not only have I lost my way but that I had better tie myself to a purpose now. So much is at stake. Experts are talking about mass extinctions. The world that was once so big has become that much smaller and therefore more vulnerable to our impact.

    It is said that only mature dragons write. I think it must be because it takes a long time to merge your heart/mind in this world. Many face the darkness before they rise with the sun. Most who create positive change step away from who they were and everything that they think they know drops off of them like spangles and beads whose threads have worn thin with time. If what many say is true, there is a reason to change this wardrobe which no longer serves. First, it is good to know who you are even if finding your way means crawling through a dark night.

    Then, it is true that meaning arises from presence. I know this because my mentor told me it is true. This is why the sideways glances when I am not paying attention. She's always ready with a lesson but it is uncanny really that they never seem to be lessons. I only get the 'ahas' after we have met. However, this unexpected visit and this attention to my attention.... hmmm, something tells me the metaphor of our relating is being extended to my concerns.

It is funny how recently I have felt my mother's presence. Leaping Lena. She leapt because she was known to not wear underwear and her friends thought it was funny to lift her schmatas up to see if that were true at that moment. Leaping Lena, just like the herds of caribou, leaping and running so fast with the power of their great numbers. Maybe this is how that leaping translated into my mother's genes. Something in her, something prehistoric said to her innermost being, 'Don't wear underwear and we will make you leap.' There is no leaping in isolation, only in the herd, that's why her friends were part of the makeup of this recreation of her genetic code. There is no miso in isolation. The microorganisms love company, crave attention and their master's presence.

A wise person wrote that isolation is devoid of meaning. Meaning must have connection. No audience, no miso. I have known connection through love and listening. Ecosystems and the beings they contain know connection through levels of moisture rising and falling within trees and plants; or levels of salt or places to lay eggs with food sources nearby to feed the nesting mothers and the coming chicks. Ecosystems and biomes are big ways of saying everything is like an egg, seemingly self-contained with all the nutrients one needs before pipping through the shell with its egg tooth, creating the small aperture which eventually turns into the entranceway to whatever destiny the egg is carrying.

Imagine the living mechanisms of ponds and fields whose edges around the world touch bays, estuaries, mangroves, and rivers. All living systems are edged by active connections with lives most will never know. But the egg cannot survive in isolation. Meaning, and life arrives from connection to sources, trails, waterways, and winds.

Now, the dragon may not understand winds until it has reached its 100th year, but it will feel them and thrive because of them. They say that Mercury is the messenger of the gods. But many would say that it's the winds. Most will agree the winds are important. But we also look for water when we look for life.

The water the water the water. The essence, sand and dust of our loved ones, the pull of the moon and unseen forces, all belonging and all connected. Tides come and go. Some call it a cycle. Some see the sets of waves and know that iterations have their changes in the mighty growth of increments. That's what I was thinking. But my mentor was walking along the edge of the bulwarks watching the cell tower. She didn't even turn back to see if I was listening. But I heard her say, "Osprey have been known throughout time to recognize water dragons."

Those steeped in their work know intimacies of interactions that cannot be seen by the casual observer or even the connoisseur. This knowing takes living with what you want to know. Listening is important. Ask any miso master or ask any cow bird that's been raised in another bird's nest. It knows it is a cowbird only when it hears its mother's song. I envy those in the daily repetition of work that brings them to the edge of the wetlands and waterways. But when I remember my mother or listen to my mentor, there are clues that I think will lead me where I need to go.

the Old Woman and morning songs ~12

Summer days should not be taken for granted. Some start like spring and then slide into summer. Beginning in August, some carry a wisp of change, some nostalgia. The light will feel different. It is less direct. Even though you might wish to deny it, you know that the days are sliding into fall. Mentor and I were walking toward late afternoon and no matter how far into the season, the high noon sun was still proclaiming summer. It was a glorious day that started out with a twinge of melancholy because it was down to the autumnal 60's. But it warmed toward the hope of summer at 79 by midday.

    The clouds by the river looked like taffeta and chiffon lifted and tossed by a skilled hand that could capture the air and then allow them to be moved by the wind to add another billow. The river was full of water. I watched Skunk dive and come up with the smallest fish. From where I stood it looked to be no more than four inches long but like many osprey, Skunk still did her flight around and cried out notifying that she had a meal. We both looked up to the bare limb where Skunk was attempting to shake the fish off her claw.

~ ~ ~

Why do old people wake so early? I am getting there myself. Or should I admit that I am there already? Is it like the osprey's urge to migrate, but parceled out on a daily basis? And many feeling that there is so little time to do all that we dream of doing. My mentor's perspective on aging seems to be different than mine. She thinks in terms of energy and the comingling of spirits. Cosmic soup and the dance. I believe that I have forgotten a lot of important things. Like some say about children, so able to see and converse with spirits but losing that connection as they enter the school system. I wonder if I was that way as a kid and also forgot the many connections I now welcome. It is clear as I've gotten older that I have a sense of urgency about the wetlands and birds, and all of nature. And, this urgency is woven into my belief that all who I love and have loved are a part of the ecos. At stake is my connections to my ancestors, the world I love and want to know will continue.

There is something about the beauty of the land and water that is impossible to put into words. It is a feeling. I believe that it is also something like photosynthesis takes place when we are captured by the beauty. There's a dynamic exchange we're experiencing and that is why myself and others just want to remain in the presence of the trees we love, or the water that draws us near, or the mountains.

~ ~ ~

I remember playing with dirt, playing doctor using a cardboard shoe box as my medicine bag, and running up and down the block playing ringalario. This was city block-long hide and seek that went past dinnertime and into the evening. I do not remember any imaginary friends, other than those I spoke to on the porch when I would pretend to have a gathering. Through all my playing on my block as a kid, I remember a close connection to the ground, the air always felt like a layer of skin, probably because I was always sweaty. Love nature wasn't something self-directed or self-conscious of self anything. It just was. I never wanted to be inside.

~ ~ ~

The business of the world might make it seem we are indifferent to the movements of energy and spirit. My experience in my journey-lands tells me that Grandmother and her peeps are not spending any time worrying about what I, or the people that move in the world with me, have forgotten. They always seem connected to an ongoing endeavor. Although, it is also true, except for some hurried lessons where I might be flown to different locations, they seem to be relaxed and enjoying the sun on their face or the company of their community. They appreciate the everyday cycles of come and go. I remember sitting at the edge of the small marsh in my journey-lands with Grandmother and watching the insouciant movement of the marsh hawk as it lifted or descended into the marsh's tall blond grasses. Part owl, part bird, the marsh hawk, or Northern Harrier, has all ways a bird can hunt covered. They not only see with the telescopic vision of a hawk but they hear with the precision of an owl. It is not a good thing to be a mouse in a marsh with a Harrier around.

I have only seen a marsh hawk here once but hawks, as bold and daring as they are, can be stealth. I suspect they have traced their spirits through the trees and over the river many times. My osprey must know.

I mentioned the marsh hawk to my mentor hoping she was as fond of them as I was. She listened and then said something that had the effect of waking me up, although I was sure that I was already alert. It seemed unrelated but she began talking about the Old Woman. I remembered her. She was the same one that admonished me in a vision so many years ago. The Old Woman. I didn't know how much in common my mentor and I had to those in other realms. Mentor said the Old Woman was known to be snappy but wise. And yes, Mentor, said, "She was known as the Old Woman."

"I have a story about her." And she related how one day she listened in on the Old Woman giving a lesson. The Old Woman seemed to be speaking to the tops of trees. My mentor said she did not see anyone there, yet the Old Woman talked and paused as if someone was listening. She told the trees that dragons might exist so that they can walk the dragon's elemental world and whatever world the being they inhabit represents. For instance, she taught, that could be half water dragon and half human. It could be an otter. Although half otter half dragons were quite a lot to handle in the otter community. And it could be a rock or mineral. Half galena, half dragon. "Galena", the Old Woman sang, "lead smooth sea." My mentor only knew some of this dragon information and said it was a rare privilege to hear the Old Woman speak. Clearly, she had great familiarity with the topic. My mentor wondered aloud if she herself was half woman, half dragon.

My mentor suspected that even though her hiding place seemed to have perfect camouflage, that the Old Woman knew she was there. She had not intended to hide from her. Mentor was walking down the path in the journey-lands, where, and this I know as well, Grandmother would often walk, when she heard a noise off to the right. Some bushes were disturbed and not knowing what to expect, my mentor said she took cover behind a hedge of sweet pepper bushes. She thought, whatever or whoever it was, even her smell would be hidden by the flowers' sweetness that curled into the warm air. The Old Woman continued her lecture, "All beings, even mountains or small boulders that roll down the mountains can have dragons in them." She seemed to scold when she said, "Even turtles can be half dragons." My mentor wondered about this. This was new information for her at that time. I wanted to interrupt but she was in the reverie of her story. Even I, so quick to ask questions, needing to know all the permutations of the five W's at once, recognized this as a time to listen. But my mentor included me in her reverie. She asked me, "Why would a dragon take residence in another being?"

    Ah, but she wasn't really asking me because she was quick to answer her own question. "Some things are unknown and I live with their mysteries. But I believe it's so that they can walk or be in the world as the turtle or human so that they can understand. They can only do this if they know how that being is in the world."

    Was I to take this to mean that dragons not only walked between many worlds but were weavers and perceived the world in the embrace of the warp and weft of their combined spirits? They took it to heart about walking in another's shoes, or pads, or webbed feet.

My mentor found this to be the most pertinent point. I know this because I had been following her from one end of the bulwarks to another but she rarely turned to see if I was near when she spoke. Thankfully, the walk from end to end was not that long. Along the way, the skies were a distraction, as were the reeds and the ripples. She turned when I was captivated by another favorite marsh movement and told me, "Those that become dragons may never know it is their destiny to be one until the change happens. There might be clues. But there might be misleading indicators as well."

When my mentor left, she made a delicate bow toward the bulwarks and then toward me. I bowed back as if I were touching my toes. Of course, I was kidding but she was not. I think. I can never tell with her. Before I turned to leave I wanted to give my thanks to the river for the rare time I spent with my mentor there. But I did not bow. I took a deep breath and felt I was pulling in all I saw through my eyes into my body. My wetlands are my home. To actually leave there often feels wrong. I am attached to the everythingness of it.

~ ~ ~

Eagles have a commanding presence and carry a sense of making the possible present. I feel as if eagles know when dreams are moving toward ripeness and ready to pluck into reality. I fold that meaning into my being. Like many birds, they are also messengers. And like many messages, not easily understood. When I see them my heart feels fuller; my dreams vibrate and resonate. Even the sky seems bigger with an eagle flying in it.

These eagles know me no matter how I dress for the weather. I'm the riverside lady. 'She watches for the osprey, and takes great pleasure in the river whether there is water or only a thin silver stream tracing through the mud.' My attention is always eagle until mid-March. Then, my first look is to the cell tower to see if my osprey have returned. Followed by looking to the eagles nesting area. I would be dishonest if I didn't share my guilt, for the eagles are residents and they are here all year long. The osprey remind me of what it was like when my brother Jerry would visit. My mother made such a fuss. 'Oh, Jerry's coming. I have to cook this. He loves this." Oy, oy, oy. My mother. I loved the way she loved that Jerry was coming to visit. Do you think the eagles are seeing my fuss over the osprey and making fun?

~ ~ ~

The wavy lines in our brains tell me that water and waves, wind and more, have been the architect of our heart/mind. No computer experts really know what is going on behind the screen. Something is making connections and there's a density of direction that makes it all work. Since many teachers take on the form of birds, I have to wonder if their calls and songs are for their joy and communications but also something we know without knowing. Perhaps our teachers riding the thermals in the skies is a parallel and model calling out to the waves in our brains. Are their morning songs also a lesson or songs once familiar that we no longer know? Is it possible that our relationship with their songs is like when I sat at my grandparents feet nodding my head because somehow, even though I am not fluent in Yiddish now, I once understood them? Could it be we were all fluent in bird songs? The threat to our planet and all we need to survive is many layered. One layer is our noise and being so wrapped up in the world of humans to the exclusion of all others' use of sound. I sometimes wonder if rising early is how older people reconnect with the world of birds and through them to the many rhythms that feed us which had been blocked out by the hubbub of our lives. Hubbub, a confused noise, makes it hard to hear the songs.

~ ~ ~

The songs of early dawn and the morning flights of migrating birds speak to me. Their songs are hello and goodbye braided to call and charm, beckon and simply listen to. I will stand with you in the morning song of hello and goodbye. There are times the thoughtlessness of friends or family's neglect can leave a hole. There are days when we are too much with the world of people and need the peace of nature. The morning songs come like balm and they come, where I live, every morning. They fly into the air with their songs . Each day sung into possibility. All emptiness is gone. When I listen, I feel a sense of fullness. Many uncomfortable memories are dissolved in the dawn.

There are many reason these times of dawn and dusk are so crucial in our lives and in the lore some have passed down. They are openings to the worlds we may not fully know when awake, but the connection through the songs of birds brings us into a sweet chorus of being, even though we know as we listen, they are fleeting.

Some say aubades are the morning songs of parting lovers. What do most of us know about our connection to birds? By me, not far from the wetlands, the robins are the first birds to sing in the morning and the last at night. That is, until the Carolina wren bounces up and down with its song. Once they encourage each other, if they've managed to lift one of your eyelids, you're sunk. There is no more sleep. I get called into the day and I imagine, called into a blended being of song and activity. If first thoughts and last thoughts could feel as I do now life would be a dream.

~ ~ ~

It was confirmed for me, when I heard the red-wings Okalee call there, that Lynn and I found another home for our spirits at Island Beach State Park. I am not a cartographer, but the places in nature that touch our spirits seem to be connected in ways not always known. Everything begins with a feeling. It is kinship. After being in the womb of our world, perhaps even those of us not "into" nature, respond just as the cowbird does to its mothers song, or the quail, or the humpback calf that whispers back to its mother. Even in the ocean, the sound of connection streams to the source. Our sense of kinship with nature might be broken but it is quickly repaired. Listen. Just shhhhh for a moment. Listen.

~ ~ ~

I have seen myself and others influenced by friends and artists or people well known in their respective fields. And I notice that the good influences are like the gentle movement of water around bends that will also seep onto the dry areas. By opening to another influence we sometimes become more of who we are. I remember going to the wetlands to talk to spirit about Lenny. This is when I saw the eagle come out of the white-blue sky as if it slipped into view from another world. Grief and oak barrels leave openings, small nooks and crannies for light and new life to bubble and emerge. That is why we protect the entire biome. That is why protected areas, not just protected species. We are what we are because of the areas we travel and roam, because of the air that moves across our spaces, or the currents and storms, and the people that touch us like gentle winds.

    Now I remembered, my feathers started growing when Lenny slipped into the white-blue sky and disappeared.

half dragon, half mishugana ~ 13

There was something about the sun that reminded me of a day last January.

It is snowing since 8 am. It was supposed to start at 7 am so it was late. I have a card game with Virg, T and Rena manana at Virg's place. I have cooked all morning and made old and new dishes. Can I really be a water dragon? This is what the astrologer had said and it wouldn't have taken purchase had it not been for that dragon curled up inside my skull. She was all metaphorical. But a feeling has moved into my shoulders. I think I feel the start of wings. The metaphor has switched tracks and moved into reality. I was also thinking how often the story of Demeter and Persephone has come to me. At least for part of the year, winter, Persephone is hidden from her mother Demeter. Secretly, I had thought I might be turning into an osprey. I hadn't mentioned the feathers to Virg yet, but I was certain the Oracle knew. But I was working my way to tell Virg. Why not? If I become an osprey, the eagle will watch me even more closely. And, being bold with a deserved reputation as a thief, she will also look for any signs of fish falling out of the sky. I would be the osprey dropping the fish.

Just like the mystery of Virg's connection to the Oracle is my connection to her and the Crow Women. Missing Virg, I thought how all of us get through the bare bone hours of grief. There is no transformation there, just that passage through iron days. And then when it's time, and everyone's time is different, something may speak to us and we begin to repurpose loss. Use it like a tool that's not working for its normal purpose but can find new life when it's used another way.

I headed to the wetlands and remembered another day in January when I was feeling tossed by the nasties at work. I found my park frozen. Where there were footsteps, there was ice. It was easier to forge a new path rather than trying to walk in another's frozen footsteps. Yeah, so that's what I did. I told Mrs. Teale about it. She agreed that January can certainly bring some difficult times. "I know," I told her, "this is why I think all seasons should be in reference to, certainly in deference to, summer."

~ ~ ~

A crow was on top of one of the trees cawing. It looked young. Its head seemed fluffy and velvet new. I remember when velvet was so popular. Now it seems so old fashioned in clothing but so right for a young crow's crown.

Strikes me how birds don't have wishes but many who love them do. Whether fish or fowl, animal or insect, in a tribe or phylum or not of one, there's not a whole lot of wishing going on. Except us humans. How I wish for something or someone to show me how to be the most useful for my wetlands. If we think of the whole world as our body, the wetlands are our lungs. How can I help our wetlands? We're working with two outs and two strikes. But there is hope. We have a player on third. I'm wishing for at least a single. The wishing, like betting in Vegas, is heavy. My hope is twinned with fret. Any good player can hit a single.

~ ~ ~

The Oracle had to know about my feather situation, but Mrs. Teale, did not. I should tell Mrs. Teale. After all, she is my marsh buddy. She loves the wetlands as I do. And, Mrs. Teale also welcomes all distractions.

Usually, Virg was my access to the Oracle. She, being with the Crow Women and dancing the dance, wasn't available. I didn't even know what the questions were. Just the wishes. I would focus on that for now so that the miserable, light stealing pain of the nasties didn't push me too much. The longing being so long, from 'wonder what it would be like to have the days as I wish. The jobs have never touched what I dreamed of supporting.' To my dream of making a difference. So, I had hoped to ask the Oracle the standard questions I come to her with but there were other things taking precedence now.

~ ~ ~

The sweet gentle ripples looked like illuminated baby snakes wriggling sideways toward the bridge. I can't tell now if I was seeing the ripples in the water or the sand below. A good buddy will tell you not to dip all your energy in the bitter oils. They are there, the bitter oils. Mrs. Teale will acknowledge their reality so as not to create "a cognitive dissonance of positive inflation by attempting to magnetize particles of sunbeams." 'Come on', Mrs. Teale would say, 'just last night, when you were dipping in the bitter oils, I was writing you an email about the beauty of the summer winds.' We did a role reversal. She didn't try to change my course, but being in touch stopped me from unwinding that spool of frozen steps where everything turns to drek; where you're not loved, you feel all alone in the world, and a sense of belonging seems too far past the horizon to see.

~ ~ ~

Saturday, I looked through the rain and opaque sky for the eagles but did not see them. There were mallards and black ducks. The clouds nearly touched the air I was breathing. I wish that I could capitalize on these blessings more regularly. Blessings should be like salt. Sprinkle easily and dance for a while until they settle. Once it does, everything tastes and feels better. Stoner, and now Molly, would lick the tears off my cheeks. It feels like love, I'm sure it tastes like salt.

~ ~ ~

Adventures can take the place of salt. I remember a spring trip with Lynn. We went to Cranberry in search of the Paw Paw tree's berries. It was too early. So, we moved on to Princeton to say hello to the Red Dawn Sequoia we had met. Just past our friend with the squared off pine cones, we found the most beautiful, large pine cone scales. We collected them like they were sapphires and rubies. They can sit flat and look like a throne or a headdress for a royal. Their tree is called an Atlas pine. Now you can understand why the scales were so large. It would take an Atlas to hold this tree on his shoulders. One of its limbs was sheered to either make room for other trees or to clear the path beneath. It was not easy to tell why. But this is how we met this tree. There were little pop sounds that a bb gun might make. The pachysandra carpet would register a mild disturbance. After a number of these pops I followed the projected course of the movement and saw the scales shooting out of the cones. They explode and that's how they spread their seeds.

Mrs. Teale, writing about her favorite color, said, "For a planet dressed in blue, she's created a rainbow of colors once you dive past the clouds and come full on under the canopy. I often wonder if we have to go through a senseless period of development and distancing ourselves from what is remarkably beautiful before we can make sense out of our desires." Yeah. I'm reading her email and thought, 'That may be the disparity that consciousness divided against itself creates. We know we rely upon the air, the soil and water yet it's always a battle to try take care of them. My answer these days is to create a path for all of wildlife across the continent. If we do that, it both eases the tension of humans and animals and it recognizes the need to get along. When we support the world we live in and on, we support ourselves. Then we can cheer on the most advantageous uses of our senses.'

    Spring by the Atlas tree felt sweet and open, even under the canopy that it and the other trees created. For a brief time I was spared the intrusive dread of the weekend's ending. I have too often felt this about returning to the job. The people who I call the nasties create such a toxic environment. Maybe this is all they know how to do. I would go to the river without that push from them but they often send me there to talk to the mud and Grandmother. I would also have to thank my knees. I have them to thank for slowing me down. This also helped me find this home for my heart and soul.

In the March spring I yearn for the joy of the ospreys' return. It feels close and that's a comfort. And looking forward to that pulls me through the winter. Everyone gets wonder shook off of them. We got to look around, pick it up and put it in our pockets. Maybe that's why I go beachcombing. A purposeful time with no purpose.

My friend Mrs. Teale, like many good friends, was always along on the adventure even when she wasn't. But she had been in the dumps. She longed for the love she once felt from her family. She said it was like her skin was warmed by the afternoon sun. Like many of us, she translated the love she lost into somehow being her failure. It is a difficult thing to see your friends in pain. Mrs. Teale appreciates all the world so sweetly. She is open like a welcoming arbor that gives you entrée to a garden. When she was stuck in the mud, something I always feared would happen to the kingfishers, I told her, "Your opera shaman diva heart, I don't think you get how rare it is. You listen. You relate. You cry to the gods. You work at what you need to. You got good stuff going on. What you got, there ain't a lot. You better hang in there or I'll call you a yellow-bellied sapsucker." Her friendship saves me time and again. When I told her about the Atlas pine, she quoted Herman Hesse, "Trees are sanctuaries. Whoever knows how to speak to them, whoever knows how to listen to them, can learn the truth. They do not preach learning and precepts, they preach, undeterred by particulars, the ancient law of life."

I wondered what she would say when I told her about the feathers.

I told Mrs. Teale about the feathers. But I didn't say anything about wings or osprey. Her immediate response was that I should love them into my being. She said to listen to what speaks to me. And then she talked about the Sedge Island waters, how they have called to me for so long. "The beauty of all the blues, the greens of the sedge grasses that form the islands soothes everything that comes into your being. Moving over the shallow waters around the sedge grass, pickleweed and salt hay, I remember you telling me how you lay back in the kayak, glide beneath the wooden osprey towers that decorate your view of the sky. The stillness of the waters dipped and stirred by paddles." She listens.

And she said, "Why wouldn't you grow feathers in response to that perfect sense of symbiosis?"

Symbiosis, together and living. My mentor had told me once about crown shyness. "There are many ways trees communicate to each other, of course. But watch what they do. They will form a canopy but not touch each other. Some think it's a way that trees protect each other from infestations. Some believe it is a way they share the sun and shadows.

Mrs. Teale enjoyed research. She liked best finding facts and moving them as support for her husband's writing about nature. I mentioned the dragons' relationship to beings they might inhabit. I was surprised to learn she knew something about this. She shared that it is, among other things, a symbiotic relationship. 'The lore has it that dragons might be awake when their host is asleep.' She wasn't dismissive of this possibility because she called it lore. She just hadn't met a dragon yet. I shared what I had thought widely known, that dragons can't write until they're 100. And she did not say a word about dragons writing or not. I continued to wonder with her. Ideas came and went that I nixed and didn't share. 'If, like the ocean-going birds, who flew nonstop, some virtually for a year before touching land...' "If we move through the world as part dragon, does the other part know we are moving...' Mrs. Teale might have run down some thoughts herself. I don't know. She said, "Ah, but not everyone has the Sedge Islands as a highway between realities." That's Mrs. Teale, she could pick herself up out of her mud funk with the least bit of intrigue.

half mishugana

It is said that big events will shift your life. Big events may break through to the surface when the small changes have done all the work. What tills the soils better than earthworms, for instance? People might not even notice the change in you until something breaks through. My brother Lenny passed. The full length of his illness, like for many we love, is about saying goodbye while remembering to welcome all the hellos while they are there to greet. My mentor, who I haven't been able to reach lately, told me that his passing lit the match to my fuse. Then she said, "Watch for dragons." And then she had to leave, providing no further explanation. Her exits always felt abrupt. If she were a cartoon character, she would leave a visible trail of mystery like a boat leaves a wake. It is the first time she has talked to me directly of such things. When someone confirms what you feel before you can bring it to the fully awake world, it changes everything. I knew something was shifting in me. Well, feathers for one, but there were other feelings I could not describe or validate.

    I once read about an island-people who had long vision. They could see their fishermen come back one or two days out before anyone else might physically be able to see them. Their sightings went way past the horizon. What comes to the surface may have been known only as whispers or even secrets which can have no entrée to our consciousness until whatever their form they take on emerges. Most people don't see butterflies emerge from their chrysalis. Most people don't even check the horizon.

    Mentor is telling me to watch for dragons. And yes, that alone is sufficiently unusual in my world as to bring a sense of alertness to everything I look at. Is Lenny bringing a dragon into my life for the second time? Did the loss of one quarter of the world's bird population expedite a change worldwide, as well as in my humble self? All the warnings, all the bad news about wildlife, ocean temperatures warming, loss of habitat, plastic particles in our waters, big business still knocking on the boundaries of national parks revered around the world, ghettos getting incinerators instead of clean air, all of this and more have moved my response to the surface. I watch for dragons. The Oracle's silence is sometimes the answer.

I went to the river and spoke to Mrs. Teale on the cell. The woman who smokes and reads the paper in her car in the wetlands parking lot was there. She didn't even look up when I pulled in. Mrs. Teale knew I wanted to reach out to the Oracle but I had no way to do that. She joked about getting that number for me but we both knew, it is not easy to come by. Virg was my gateway.

I remembered Virg's and the Oracle's sense of humor when I needed to fly to visit Lenny and my family out west. Of all people growing feathers, perhaps it is not surprising, because we live side by side with irony, that I have a terrible fear of flying. Oh that karma really is a wheel, as my Irish friend once said when speaking of an enemy. She didn't have to worry about revenge she said. "The wheel will turn." Indeed.

I remembered a most welcome message Virg shared with me from the Oracle when I was about to head west to my family:

The Oracle has returned sooner than expected.... Or, since all time is now, is right on time.

The Oracle has returned to embodiment and is now coping with remembering how to move joints and stand upright. It's supposed to be like riding a bicycle, but it sure feels heavy.

Anyway, the Oracle has pondered your question and has the following to offer: you are safe. Or, rather, you don't have to worry about the airplane flight (the Oracle is grateful she doesn't have to go through security when traveling). Your self-produced anxiety voice, however, is ever lurking over your shoulder, trying to bring you (not the plane) down. So, while you may be miserable, you will be safe. The Oracle recommends relaxation exercises, thought-stopping, Rescue Remedy, homeopathic remedies, and - possibly - drugs.

Blessings on your trip. The Oracle will be over your other shoulder, should you need her. She has no trips planned.

Love and blessings,
The big O (not Oprah)

And not the O man either, otherwise known as Odysseus, my O man. And not Penelope either, otherwise known as the weaver of time and space.

~ ~ ~

It was September. The deep blue of sapphire, my birthstone, captures the beauty, the bliss of summer nights. We were driving home from a meal together and the air held us in the moist balm of the evening. I told Virg it felt like we were inside an egg. The environment of the egg is our first world. Everything you need is in reach. I can feel lonely in September. Summer is ending. The osprey will be leaving. I forget sometimes to live in the moment. More than sometimes. The reverse is truer. I only remember sometimes to live in the moment. I'm sure this happens to most of us. Maybe it is unenlightened. But the world brings moments and that drive, surrounded by friends and love and the sapphire night stands out. Thank the gods for living in those moments along the shore.

~ ~ ~

Last fall, Lynn and I were at the Manasquan inlet, right across from Red's on the Point Pleasant Beach side. I had been curious about what's on the other side of the inlet and I could see an ice cream store, another pull. Adventure and dessert awaited. As we walked along the guard rail, we saw a three-foot-wide stream crowded thick and deep with fish alongside the cement wall. They were streaming in from the ocean through the inlets' wide opening but they hugged the wall as they moved. I asked any number of the men fishing there what they were and each one of them told me something different. They were sand eels. Thousands upon thousands. Stripers eat them and probably had chased the school into the inlet. Knowledgeable fishers will tell you, if you see them in the fall, the stripers are soon to follow. They know because they have caught stripers with bellies full to bursting with them.

~ ~ ~

I live near water on a very watery planet. Water is everything. It orders the coming and going of osprey signaled by the migration of menhaden. Sand eels signal a run of striped bass. Negative ions impart a quality to the air as the channel winds, always present, though sometimes softly so, signal a feeling of well beingness. Lao Tzu has said, "Nothing is softer than water, yet nothing can resist it." The same is sometimes true for changes that will transform your world. They begin softly, like feathers sometimes, and like water, changes everything. I cannot resist water. I must go down to the river and I must go down to the sea.

~ ~ ~

Joe, the old man I meet at the wetlands now and again, showed up. The light rain makes for a spongy walk leading to the bulwarks. When I asked after him, he told me that old age humbled him. He said he didn't mind because the root of humble is humus, the ground, the soil. I enjoyed how he traced words to their origins. I like to do that too. You always discover something closer to what you were searching for. He said he loved walking on the moist, mushy park land to reach the bulwarks for the best view. His hands shook and he couldn't hold binoculars steady. So, I narrated what I saw on the osprey's tower nest for him. He nodded his head when I told him what I saw. He felt all of it through the soles of his shoes.

  When we feel connection to a place or being we take a different stance than when we feel anything else, even ownership. None of these relationships are in silos either. We can feel ownership and connection or any number of feelings around a place. It is the quality of love and the necessity of the vitality for home that moves us earthlings in love with we is called the natural world, the environment, to voice our concerns. No matter if it is a body of water, a wetlands area, an endangered species or an iconic place like Yellowstone that we want to protect, because it's a home for wildlife and our spirit, we choose to speak up and voice our concerns. Yet, I am at a loss to know where to begin to protect what I love. I confessed this to Mrs. Teale. She said, "Just begin someplace and see what happens." She said, "Sometimes you begin with what pulls you and you don't have words but you can share your presence." 'Like Joe', I thought. I told her what Thomas D. Mangelsen, an artist and an activist who works to protect Yellowstone's grizzlies said about his determination to protect his home. He said Jane Goodall "...taught me to never hold back in trying to protect the things you love, that if you act with a clear conscience, you shouldn't worry about the people you'll offend, because if you're giving voice to creatures that can't advocate for themselves, your priority should be defending them and not trying to please those who just don't get it."

    It is fortunate that I follow upon the heels of many who have worked to protect the osprey and the bird populations. Some birds are thriving but as a whole, all bird populations have become more vulnerable over the decades and not less so. I told Mrs. Teale that her work in the world might help since I can see the way it can move people toward action. Love a place and the journey there. Listen to it, feel its presence. Get past the awkward stage of 'just being with it' and let it seep into you. From there, who knows what changes softness will bring. Take someone to your favorite places. Mrs. Teale and her husband have done this. I have. I need to do more of it. You cannot understand how important places in nature are or why they matter unless you go to them. You have to walk on spongy soil or walk the cement walk along the rail while a three-foot stream of sand eels moves down the channel. 'These experiences strike me as beautiful,' I told Mrs. Teale. She said, "Beauty emerges from context and place. And sometimes when you follow your curiosity to see what's on the other side of the inlet."

She once lived along the Long Island shore, so Mrs. Teale knows how easy it is to love whole towns and the shoreline. In summer, it feels as if it is loving you back. Many know the reciprocity of love for this area in every season. Mr. Teale wrote, that for some people, "Summer is "the way it should be." It is as though our minds subconsciously returned to some tropical beginning, some summer-filled Garden of Eden." Summer doesn't always come by the calendar these days. But when it does, I am ready for my favorite season. I remember this past June, a week past the start of summer, the air was warm and moist. There was a breeze. I took a ride along the whole shoreline from Sea Girt to Asbury Park and fell through time. I wish I could love every day as much as I do these. I say it all the time. I love it here.

Rachel Carson, who I fondly call Grandmother Rachel, sacrificed much to bring her work into the world. Fifty years since her book *The Silent Spring* alerted the world about the dangers of DDT – saving our hawks, eagles and osprey in the meantime, she is still vilified by the producers of chemicals. She saw it as "A privilege and a duty to speak out on something so important." She showed how DDT made the eggs of our iconic eagle and all the large predator birds, fragile, and too often prone to failure. The world of the egg has everything it needs if it can remain intact and protect the life within.

'And then Mrs. Teale, here's what Robin Wall Kimmerer wrote, "Knowing that you love the earth changes you, activates you to defend and protect and celebrate. But when you feel that the earth loves you in return, that feeling transforms the relationship from a one-way street into a sacred bond." This is what I'm feeling.'

My mentor knows this because I have finally moved past what was for decades something too shy in me or felt too unsafe to say with this tone but it is my truth. It is time to speak my heart out loud. It might not be for the same reasons, but what Arundhati Roy shares is a monster truth for me. I mean the kind that takes down warriors in the great hall. "As a writer, a fiction writer, I have often wondered whether the attempt to always be precise, to try and get it all factually right, somehow reduces the epic scale of what is really going on. Does it eventually mask a larger truth? I worry that I am allowing myself to be railroaded into offering prosaic, factual precision when maybe what we need is a feral howl, or the transformative power and real precision of poetry." I go to the river sometimes and before I know it, I am howling. I scream. I cry. I implore.

Two lessons we are taught early on in many ways: there are no stupid questions. Listening is important. I've done a good job of ignoring these for a long time. I know I need to ask questions and I need to listen to the answers. What is the relationship between the world we live on top of, like a carpet for most of us, and the wellbeing of all of us, birds, animals, and people? Do you think if we protect one all are protected? I have brought these questions to the river. I must go down to the river, sometimes because I want to love it and I think it has answers for me. I broke through to listening. I'm not sure the difference between this and quiet.

~ ~ ~

Mentor last met at the wetlands. Admittedly I was distracted. The river likes to keep things interesting and my mind likes to wander. I'm starting to recall what I heard as background. Mentor was explaining that it is very possible that half of my brain doesn't realize that it walks through the world as a human, and the other half might be living a life of its own. I thought she was sharing knowledge but not specifics. Back and forth along the bulwarks can be a tricky place to learn about unihemispheric creatures. 'Did mentor say, "my brain"?' I know she has schooled me on bridges. She once told me, I think in preparation because it was when Len was very ill and it was weighing on me, "Sometimes facing a fear creates a bridge, or losing someone who knew your world leaves you no choice but to interpret the world you come from to others. Context is not a given. Sometimes trauma will create a bridge to the other half of whoever it is that's a part of you." How would you know who it is or what? Or when it's active? Does the bridge mean there's also communication between the halves? I asked that one. Mentor, ever ready to throw down paradox and mystery, said, 'What does love and synergy do?"

~ ~ ~

There were no words when my mother died. I had a twenty-five pound Webster's Second Edition and no words. My mother's friend Sarah said about the only thing that made sense, "We must all lose our mothers." My friend's mom Ruth had such a strong personality. Every gesture and look in her eyes said volumes of Ruth. After she died, my friend sent me a beautiful abstract pastel Ruth created, as a remembrance. Ruth always had a look and a tone in her words of a wizened, wised up person. No matter what she said you could hear a second line shadowing everything, "Can you believe this?" It wasn't astonishment. It was more like a sense of this is all inevitable. For some reason, even though she never showed fear, she always felt she was dying. Of course she wasn't, until she was. And I never knew her artwork, which conveyed a fuller palette, soft colors and movement, direct expression without shadows, of a world that was beautiful, in the process of becoming, and loving.

for Ruth, and for all our mothers - when am I not dying

When our cat shakes with purr and pops her head out of her curl and her pads look like a hyacinth breaking ground.

When we fall in love with another heirloom bean.

Whenever we use the intimacy of a nickname.

When skeins of rivulets join the larger stream.

When we smell the ocean in the river and our mind is tickled by the notion of how the salmon makes its journey.

When we listen.

When we light up when you walk into the room.

When the day begins to feel like a journey and you exhale into a deeper world.

When we are listened to.

When we are seen.

When we move under the hush of the tree's canopy.

When a squirrel eats the bones of the bread turning it like a wheel.

When you shake the snow off the forsythia and it bounces up yellow with spring.

When answers feel right.

When we see a wren try to sing with a worm in its mouth.

When we feel the silver we're wearing.

When we have the release of the out loud.

When we let the sun melt into our skin.

When we stop, because there is something about the light.

When we know like Ryokan, that we must go there today – tomorrow the plum blossoms will scatter.

~ ~ ~

I had two streams of worry and one of them was an unspoken sense of urgency that called me to the river. The other was wondering where my mentor was. I was without the Oracle and I had feathers layering themselves on my midsection. Fall was calling summer to its cooler nights. And I had no idea what a dragon would do under these circumstances. Half dragon, huh? Half dragon, half mishugana.

mise en place ~ 14

I could not tell how long my mentor was gone. Some people become your compass but she must have also been my way of telling time and without her I lost track. My mentor told me that people who seem to lead the way usually are finding their own path little by little themselves. There are no certain steps if you're on a quest or if you are pulled by something that has never been fully outlined for you. If she was telling me without being direct, because why would she ever be direct, I am guessing she has been pulled by a current beyond her control. I do know that control was one of the things she tried to release. She said it was like fly paper because once it touches you it is hard to shake off. It is likewise hard to let go of some people and even harder, when they are gone, to find your own way. As it turns out, no matter how old you are or how many experiences you have. the loss of some people leaves holes and we all got holes to fill.

    I also could not tell you how long I wondered where dragons came from. I write from my imagination which has been fed by small remnants of information. I have no direct knowledge. If my feelings were to tell you this story, they'd say that dragons, at least water dragons, come from inside the deep sapphire blue of an egg. Then, I'd argue with myself and say, it might be a deep purple. That is true. Dragons may come from the deep purple like the sea purple of clam shells. Do you know the area on the broken clam shells perfect for a thumb? Where the clam connected to its shell? The deep purples are smoothed by sea water and time. The best magicians are cooks, even if the sea is their kitchen. Time is always the ingredient that good cooks conjure. And those who know salted water should taste like the ocean, know how well the pot loves the pairing of water and salt. And I think, so does the soul.

    I digress. Dragons are not easy to write about even when you're making everything up from the shards of information colored by deep purple, or the azure blue of the midnight sky. If you are called by these colors, you will find them a portal you can dive in. You might feel as if you were breathing in the color or breathing with everything and everyone who breathes. It is peaceful. It is quiet but it is also vibrant. You are inside sapphire. It may feel like the joy of potential, like having a full set of paints ready, or a pile of colored papers or every comfort and love ready for you to involve yourself with them. This sense of presence and imminent potential is what smooths the deep sapphire and purple inside the dragon's egg. If this egg came down the river in a basket like Moses and you caught it with a branch that was just right by the bank of the river and hauled it in, you would see a perfect egg, smooth and rounded on both ends; as big as a mallards' egg, larger than the eggs you know from the market in grey cartons. That egg holds time and allows you to feel what it is like to dive into the deep purple, midnight blue, sapphire night of creation. In these moments of opening and possibility before forms we recognize, before sounds we're familiar with, dwell the dragons. I could not tell you before how it felt to have a dragon inside my head. It appeared when I was in danger and everything in my being was roughed up and on edge. It had me sink into a calm unlike anything I had known. There was a sense of oddness but also belonging. Had it traveled down that river as I traveled on the blacktop highway and converged where our parallel living found a bridge through circumstance? They say that feelings are not facts but there is a parallel to most things in the world. Many people share creation stories with common themes. What is formed in one world may only be hinted in another. What is warm and breathing in one world may only be seen or felt at special times in another. Dragons, like people, are born into different worlds. But I now believe they intersect through bridges created by special events in our lives.

    Some people imagine learning how to become more human from watching deer standing through the cool night and the dawn's moist hours. I wonder what dragons imagine.

~ ~ ~

Rivers can have many sources. Rivers themselves can feed into many wetlands at the back ends of small rivers like mine. Water can be traced like the filaments of mycelium threading their way across a remarkable, vast expanse. Somewhere, there may be a map of all these tracings. Maybe it exists as a layer in all of us when our brains are full and song plays through our heads until winter brings its own demands to focus on surviving. And when water's trails find their endings because of the cold. But when the spring comes and the warm releases the water to travel where it may, so may, in this world or another, the sapphire egg move on the blue dragon river, that runs quiet and smooth, like the Gulf Stream in the ocean. The Gulf Stream could have been doing this for thousands of years before anyone knew its true course. It's only just the past 500 years we know of this river within the ocean. Streams always seem young. Yet, the Gulf Stream, is a busy highway for moving so much and so many through the Atlantic; changing our weather and changing the course of many who would travel near it.

~ ~ ~

Just imagine being inside a deep sapphire egg with the light shining through. No wonder birds are ready to fly and dragons ready to soar. When their mothers or fathers temporarily leave the nest, the sun checks in on her grandchildren. That light, shone through the shell, brings the deep calm of blue, and begins the knowing that those in the shell will soon be familiar with in the skies and the waters. It is said that the dragon represents chaos and untamed nature. What if the dragon, in any of us half dragons, represented our wild nature? Wild as in cousin to the winds, abandoning self-consciousness, and gliding through the slip stream of potential. What if, it just came to me, Virg was half crow the whole time I knew her. Well then, there might be a lot of halflings around. While they are aloft and traveling in another realm some part of their being is informed by our world. Their living may be different from our own and yet share a deep part of ours where bridges have been sown.

~ ~ ~

Like streams in the ocean, our hearts also seem young. You will hear about old souls but very few people have spoken of old hearts. We cannot understand tears sometimes, but the heart remembers many things, including tears. A sweet friend, who I sometimes call a gift from Virg, shared that she didn't understand her mother's tears for her own mother's loss, the grandmother she never got to meet until the feelings were brought fresh like a papercut to her through a poem about the heart never forgetting. When my mother was dying, my niece Michelle came to the hospital to fix her hair. As she brushed my mother's hair, my mother shared how she had done the same thing for her mother when she was dying. We were in the barren hospital room but cocooned in a space of intimacy. We may be aware of the importance of moments, as I was then, but the gratitude to have lived these moments in that quiet space of compassionate beauty will always bring a sense of destiny and depth. I breathed that memory in down to my toes and I walk the earth with these feet and stories.

    When I was most open to telling my mother about loving another woman, she told me that there was a relative who lived downstairs in her apartment building who was like that too. That's what she said, "like that too". But what her tone told me was how she cared for this woman. I think she was a cousin. If she shared her name with me, I am sad to say I don't know it now. But what I do know is that my mother's heart never forgot her and through her my mother could extend her love and understanding for who I loved.

And through her I also have a link to someone that shared something with me and was accepted into the family a generation before my time. Many have been banished and lost their families because of who they came to love. Left to dangle without familial connections, they were estranged from all the context of relationship. Like, I sometimes think, most of us have been estranged from nature. Maybe someone in our families knew someone like that, connected to nature, like a love that was not common among families or at least, not openly shared. The heart will remember the relative who lived in the basement apartment, who was accepted. And our hearts are young enough to remember what it is like to feel the earth is our family and welcome all of it home.

~ ~ ~

When Virg poked through the column of wind to say something to me, I wonder if I heard this or if I'm just making this up. Did she say something about Gaia? That Gaia was one of the Crow Women she was dancing the dance with in the eternal circle of wind? She was pointing like you do when the person you're pointing out is very close. And she was mouthing it with the hiss of whispers, because the person she was whisp-er-ing about was within earshot. Apart from her intention to tell me something she demonstrated that everyone should take 'how to whisper' lessons. I think she was trying to tell me, "Gaia, she's here, right there!"
All good cooks know mise en place. Have all your ingredients ready so that you are free to cook with imagination, free to listen to the food cooking,

know when the sizzle is right, and use all your senses to create the meal. If Gaia is near, everything seems to be coming into place.

~ ~ ~

My at-one-ness times, riding the waves. I often dream about waves rolling and breaking into the small marsh area in my journey-lands. Something shifts when I'm in water. I'm a dolphin. I have finally merged with my dream of the shore from when I was a kid in Newark. While I was a kid it was utterly impossible to live in the moment. Even for a kid that's some feat. All I wanted was to be near the ocean. I realize now, that I also wanted summer. Eternal summer. Or endless summer, like the iconic surfing film that still touches everything in me that loves to be touched by the summer sun.

    Summer comes our way in a boat. The people with long vision might be able to see it returning before I do. But if yearning in spring could pull it in faster, it would be here. I think it should always be here; but I know when it's not that it's just down a ways in the ocean, probably traveling on the Gulf Stream. When you mix me in the pot with ocean and salt I become one with the tides. I might become what we all do when we're in water, the being who remembers her mother's heartbeat. The first heartbeat we ever knew was when we were under water. I dive under as much as I swim on the surface. The water feels smoother than the terns' slide and scoop down to the water after the silver fish. The osprey hover right where people swim. The gulls appear and disappear in the waves just past the jetties. What I become in water is something I've always been even though I'm always changing. I'm always my mothers' daughter. The heart remembers our deep mother and the stream in the ocean she once travelled. When I'm in the ocean, everything feels congruent. I don't know if I've ever known this, but it feels like I'm inside a sapphire egg.

    When I went swimming the other day, it suddenly came to me that it's possible dragons have both feathers and scales, are as much fish as bird. Yet we probably don't have a name for their feathers and scales or something that is as much fish or bird. The wind took these thoughts away like the spray from the breaking waves. But they were soon replaced with this notion, that Virg was always half human, half crow. Maybe she knew this all along. When she joined the Crow Women she slipped into their circle readily and found her home in the journey-lands. So much to take in. Thankfully, there was another wave to catch. There always is when Virg has something to tell me.

~ ~ ~

A warm current came by and caressed me. Suddenly, it came to me that I might have something really wrong about wanting a wildlife path across the whole country. It's a solution that seemed good because it was large in scale but migratory paths are often threaded throughout our lands. And they are not so much large in scale as they are intricate and engrained. They also would not be served by one wide swath across the country. My solution didn't account for the many migration paths that different species have. It doesn't account for many of the people and traditions who are indigenous. Or for the needs and migratory paths of all that fly. I learned about the importance of the sage grouse or prairie chicken to people native to the lands they share and realized my dream should be about reconciliation, reclaiming our part and partnerships in nature; not controlling it. Dreams of protecting wildlife have to account for the paths in the prairies and woods. We have put more things out of balance than would have been done on their own. I want to learn how to live with my wild brothers and sisters who are the skies, lands and bodies of water; who are also known by and serve as bridges to other worlds and our halfling selves.

  I may have a dragon within me now. It may live in a parallel universe, but I believe it shares my path. I want to protect my path and my dragon as it once protected me; even as it might be reaching out to me again across a bridge. Or, possibly, it came here out of a mutual need because of something that happened in its world.

  Mrs. Teale had shared an article with me from High Country News about the Tongass, our largest national forest spanning across native lands. The U.S. has tried to manage these lands without giving the eleven native tribes a voice in this governance. What is lost in this use of power is all the intricacies of a lived connection with the land and what is needed to keep its vitality. Marina Anderson, the tribal administrator for the Kasaan, said, "Cultural needs — for generations to come — are not quantifiable. "The

Forest Service asked me, 'How many trees do you guys need left for canoes and totem poles?' " Anderson said. "They understand that we need old growth: tight grain, beautiful logs, straight-grain logs. What they don't understand is that we don't have a number for them."

We have to get down to the weeds, the native and historical, the well-worn and travelled paths of migration. There's a lot of weaving here. Anyone who has a cherished hand knit blanket or article of clothing knows how hard it is to repair should the turbo spin of the washer or some accident pull it apart. And so it goes with our country's traditional paths and ecological interconnections. Mrs. Teale will know sources and resources when I have questions. She would say, "When do you not have questions?"

~ ~ ~

My mentor recently told me about a writer, Bramble Mulberry Thread, and her creative peers, all women from the 8th century I might never have known about were it not for her. Bramble "wrote her poems on raw silk unhemmed banners and hung them along mountain ridges for the wind and rain to edit and rewrite till they dispersed over the land and returned to their elemental origins." I know there are ways to exist and coexist with nature; with the beauty we find here; the families of flora and fauna, and the cycles of abundance and scarcity. Humans like to shore up for a long time. You cannot blame any of us for this instinct. I'm just wondering if we can work with the weavers in our midst, and ask for their help to weave us back into the pattern of existence we lost. Ask them to guide us toward a dynamic relationship with our surroundings; and release us from the power to control while easing us into the finesse and skill of life sustaining relationships for all of us. Humans too. Take for instance, the Hawaiian Crow, extinct in the wild; brought back to its environs. Failed first attempt. So far, so good, second attempt. We can weave. There are those among us who are dedicated to these tasks. There are holes in the fabric but some know how to work out the patterns and get things intertwined again.

~ ~ ~

My mentor has not shared much about the path but I know she respects it. She respects its place and understands it is dynamic. Colors and light, perspective and age, politics and the pragmatic will affect it. She has shared that much before she took off after some whimsical and emoticon messages leaving me to tease out her meaning. I know her palette is always just a drop away from changing one color to the next, one meaning to another because she loves to play. Although I sometimes fervently wish the path were a direct and easy one to follow, it is a wayward one with many discoveries awaiting. Even being in the ocean, catching some waves and sinking into the water with what feels like the delight of a hippopotamus taking a bath, or a bear in a pool rejoicing in the sudden abundance of water in a human's backyard tells me that both joy and troubles change our path. I don't even think the osprey's migration path is direct; but I am so grateful they find their way back to the Jersey shore. Their presence brings a quiet joy. And I easily slip into breakout smiles and laughs when they first return because I hear their high whistling and chirp talk as they're finding their mates and readying their nests; and when they're coming home with fish for dinner. When my osprey leave I count the months and weeks and then days until I can expect to see them again. They are not easy on the heart.

It is late September. If this is what they were meant for, my feathers are not enough to migrate with my osprey. I have no wings. Mentor is still missing. I paced up and down the bulwarks thinking that would help me summon up whatever it is I needed. I watched the mud come and go. Maybe there was some water, hard to tell with such muddy thoughts. I headed home and decided to clean out one of my stockpiles of personal odds and ends I cannot let go of. I went through a few small piles of papers. I decided to call the piles that remained, every single one of them remained, sundries. It made me feel as if I accomplished something. Then I took to the collected wrack line, said odds and ends, of supposed pragmatic objects and memorabilia I keep in a round basket with a fitted lid. I inherited this beautiful "junk drawer" of spiral bands of corn husks from a friend. I went through pocket pouches I had in the basket that were stuffed with concert stubs and bookmarks from feminist bookstores; matchbooks from favorite restaurants; laminated memorial cards; watch batteries; beat up brown leather watch bands missing the small pressure pins that attach each part to the watch, still reminding me of my Annie Oakley days through which the fantasy, and now some of the realities, I have of the West was still an allure that grips my tomboy psyche; cheap airplane headsets. I also came across faded receipts from Virg's vet, mementos I inherited, noting the remains of Baxter; and then another for Moby. Baxter was her debonair terrier who looked like a retired Scottish scientist. He was always happy for a conversation about any topic. He had a relaxed air about him. Moby was her refined Doberman. Moby the Doby. Sweet like Baxter but more of a listener. His legs worked like collapsible sticks. They disappeared when he quietly tucked them under his thin body taking his place on the couch. A perfected magic act. Moby and Baxter got along so well and of course they shared a singular focus, Virg; which reminded me about a wire bound notebook with Virg's early poetry. I found it on the bookshelf in front of my writing desk. I hesitated to open it, thinking all the emotions like the true Pandora's box would pour out of me. The earthbound, gut wrenching missing, wishing to go for a swim again with my friend; the pull of the long canyon of time when people celebrated their connections to nature. The long ago and what felt like far away. But I did open it and paged through, glancing at some poems with titles, some without. I would guess she wrote these in her teens and twenties. Some poems were tentative steps toward expression; some the layering of raw emotion sharing with the spiral bound paper and her soul, her lack of self-esteem and concern about her place in the world, but also bold, defiant statements of her rights pushing against unnamed repression. I recognized a lot of her feelings as many that I swam through, for far longer than I would hope if there is another reincarnation waiting for me. Each page seemed like an emblem of courage and each caused me to stop and sink into the feelings they evoked because I wanted to be involved with my friend's experience, she was often too shy to share in person. Swimming laps might be easier.

I was relieved to see a big gap in the middle of the book which called for investigation.

There was an eighth inch thick fold of newsprint, maybe fourteen sheets, covered on both sides with ten point, or less, hand printed words. They were browned and musty smelling, flaking around the edges, literally, breaking news. The Egyptians are still uncovering painted sarcophagi with fading colors but fresh reminders of a rich history. What I had in my hands, felt equally weighty even before I opened it. There ought to be names for stashes like these. Maybe something like the name for groups of birds or animals. *A sheaf of kindness, a fold of look backs, a rush of memories*, a continuum, or *refuge unfailing*, in honor of Faulkner, a fellow Mississippian Virg would have taken pride in, who wrote "refuge unfailing in which conflict tempered, silence reconciled." For the past found in such parcels speaks again and offers the hope of reconciliation.

Virg had always been my conduit to the Oracle. I carefully opened these pages and found writing in a sure hand; even, like a calm ocean. But words that had unknown depths and created waves of unending emotion in me. Virg had tucked the words of the Oracle, perhaps from a much earlier time in her life?, into this spiral-bound notebook. She saved them with her fresh from the heart lines of poetry. All the time I knew her this was something woven into her being. She always had this knowledge.

The Oracle's writings felt calm and assured, unlike the tentative and raw voice of Virg's poems. "My little crow, you will know dragons. They are drawn to birds. They are amazed at birds' flight and everywhere they travel and dwell. When some look up at a tree they see the leaves. Dragons see the leaves and the sky around and through them because they're looking for the birds. Sometimes when they see birds through the leaves they think birds are flying through stained glass. They think birds are magic. They are their reference point for everything in your world. They are impressed with the waters birds cross and swim in; the way they land on branches, twigs, and sway on the slender stalks of plants; how even large cormorants land on telephone cables; how they fill trees and take to their wing from a perch or the water."

"Dragons first had no reference to what was sky and what was ocean or lake. They delight in the confusion of reflections in still, small bodies of water and how larger bodies reflect skies and trees while seeming to be moving and yet, at the same time, remain still. They see the sky meet the blue of the ocean as if it were a seamless marriage of colors. They drink in the blues. When they look toward the horizon they see a curve indicating a dome of blue where the sky lies on the ocean. Dragons find this to be one of the sweetest sights. They say that they can taste the ocean meeting the sky. They have found the pleasures of looking at evening skies and the ocean on a full moon night at the dunes. They rejoice in the neon white gulls chased out of the darkness slicing through the path of moonlight. They note how they love watching a lone velvet crow pick through the sand at 5 am; and they take deep pleasure in the hurry of sanderlings as they crest the waves and the way they sometimes disperse like candy from a piñata, some flying back over the crests and some landing on the beach only to immediately chase the waves back to the ocean."

~ ~ ~

Some friends, old or new, share a resonance with you that acts like a canvas. Each new conversation adds textures and colors but the background is shared and known by each so that the new details can be properly savored. They may move in and out of your life like the notes of a raga. But you and they so easily pick up a sense of intimacy, a mother rock of understanding and context that allows for the shorthand of sharing to steep in meaning. This is what it felt like to read the Oracle's notes to Virg. The Oracle knows dragons and Virg had to also, if only through the Oracle. I was trying to ration these words so that I didn't eat them up too fast and lose the sweet sense of comfort I was feeling. Something touched me and spoke to a need I could not name at the time. Partly, it felt as if I found my friend again. And she somehow, back then, as young as she was, spoke to me now, as old as I am, through the Oracle's pages, to tell me how many layers of life there are. How alive everything feels might just feel that way because it is teeming with all kinds of life and movements; and ways of knowing that most give no credence. Have you ever been so moved by love that you did and did not want to move past the moment? That is how I felt holding these pieces of soft paper in my hands. I treated these pages, which I assumed my friend Virg produced as the Oracle's scribe, as I would an ancient scroll or sacred text.

I learned that dragons move into our world at will once they have a found a path. They cannot always control where they will land but they are pulled by a sense of belonging that even they cannot understand but follow without question. Water dragons will mimic some birds, particularly osprey because they so admire how they meet the skies and the waters with equal finesse. Some believe that there is no coincidence that one of the many names for osprey is water dragon.

There were so many pages of writing but what little I read was enough to have me pause. Dragon visited me. I suspect dragon is around again. Feelings can be facts. I have been touched by the life of at least two worlds. More, I have the love of birds, sky and ocean, the beach and dunes in common with water dragons. All of this makes me wonder how many worlds all of us have been touched by and may have never realized.

There was more writing on water dragons but I decided to savor what I already had; frankly, I had to steep in it. And it felt like a boon knowing I have more to read. Looking ahead I saw there were notes about all different kinds of dragons just as I had heard tell. And it appeared to be also true that there are many beings who are halflings. I was thinking that it was not for nothing that the Oracle called Virg "my little crow." And I was comforted knowing that my friend who dances with the Crow Women, has found her circle.

Yet what caught my eye, on the back of the second page, caused me take in a big breath. The Oracle was writing about someone known as Mentor.

~ ~ ~

I once watched my osprey drink the river. There was a crow nearby and I thought it was harassing the osprey. I've thought that over and feel differently about it. First, it was unusual to see my osprey on the sandbar to drink; and then to remain there. Very unusual. I wonder if it had watched the eagle do that and thought, 'Why not me?' Well, the crow kept making short hops closer to it. When it finally got close enough the osprey lifted its wings. Except for on their nest, it's a gesture I've never seen them do near another bird. I didn't want to see crows and osprey in opposition. The osprey's wing movement was definitive, but it felt like a request more than a warning, to keep its distance. The osprey moved a short distance away. The crow hopped closer. This sequence happened a few times until the osprey flew off.

When I read the name "Mentor" in the Oracle's pages, I remembered this crow hop encounter with my osprey. It felt like I was always a student with Mentor. Something I deeply valued. I would hop closer to what she was sharing and it often intersected with what I was working on. She seemed to move so that what we discussed took in wider rings of meaning. I would hop closer to the growing spheres of thoughts and ideas. But she or I would move again. She would dive into a subject that held her fascination and I would not hear from her; and I would not reach out because I was diving into an interest of my own, or the job had me in its current. Our paths seemed to cross when each felt we had to share something. But she was always better at talking about the connections. My burgeoning thoughts might open up like popcorn until they were bursting. But I needed her talk to open this to a form I could express.

    I've always hated formal school. Everything about it was soured by the building once I entered. But I have loved some teachers and recognize that they are different from school although that can also be their environment. Now I know teachers come in many forms, some are birds, some may be dragons, some may be the old ones in new forms. But school, as soon as I think of the word, I remember how I hated being closed in. I'll notice the windows first in any building I enter or have to sit in. That doesn't mean that I don't love my desk at home. I do. But I also sit right next to a window where I can watch the birds. My mise en place at my desk begins with looking outside and then looking at my rock from a Niagara Falls trip with my mother, and halved sand dollars showing the inside ridges that look like text or code, the small bits of thisses and thats that I collect like clothespin springs, click pen springs, millefiori beads mixed with my polished stones and Atlas pine cones in three inch dishes from Asian markets, magnets holding bottle caps in their field, half of a heart-shaped tea diffuser hanging from my clip-on lamp along with bracelets and necklaces I enjoy seeing, maybe more than wearing. I can sit at my desk but I need my mise en place; which is, I also just realized, the results a different kind of beachcombing, some of which includes rocks and shells I took home from the beach.

~ ~ ~

My mentor tickles my brain. She has me jumping around inside my head. Sometimes my heart races because she seems to be a catalyst for me to put words to feelings I never thought to do. It feels like gliding. I feel full and satisfied whenever we've had chances to get together but writing to her, emails and texts, seems so much more fluid than talking. They feel like encounters with another universe and when I return to this world, everything feels so much more alive. I do not have a formal relationship with her but I enjoy the sheer dumb luck of connecting and moving into the mode of play she invites.

She's been gone for a while now and I was worried. But reading these words about Mentor eased up my worry and had me shyly curious. As much as I wanted to know everything the Oracle would share about Mentor, I also wanted to sit with this sense of relationship whose dynamic was just altered in the most dramatic way by seeing her name in this *refuge unfailing* scribed by Virg the Crow Woman.

~ ~ ~

The swimming dragon qigong exercise begins by standing with soft knees. The movements are like the Chinese New Year's dragon you see in parades. You move to the left, and then curve to the right as you lower toward the ground. There's a sense of spiraling down toward the earth. And you do this again, and again but each new spiral you're reminded of your natural connection to the energy and you are aware that the movement is how you connect to the deep pleasure of taking in air and life. You relax and you spiral like all of life that loves movement because movement is life. The free-flowing curves of a river where water and river basin dance. The blue river dragon dance of the river is what the qigong exercise mimics and brings to your body, no matter what age, no matter your path seems dry or moist. The element is water. Water is life. It is sacred because it is the earth's blood. The swimming dragon qigong is what has often brought me to the river. And it's the river I think of when I see my Mentor's name. This is odd because as much as I know she loves to be out in the woods I've never heard her say she loves to swim and be in the water. She once told me though, "Writing about birds is writing about water." And now I see that being with my mentor is also about being with dragons, and Virg, and the Oracle, and no doubt a whole lot more than I can fathom at this moment.

~ ~ ~

Mentor is older than the Gulf Stream and we don't know how old that is. She is old enough to know the language of color and line; and images with haiku captions. All light, like her memo book watercolors and line drawings, are simple suggestions, leaving everything for whoever is looking to complete; or better yet, to drift with the faint, pale colors toward whatever destination you're inclined to travel.

    Mentor last said to me that she's getting very fond of emojis and was thinking that all writing should be in images. She had a recent fascination with cell biology and morphogenetic fields. She once told me that if she were a bird, she'd want to cross the oceans because she wanted to glide between the sky and water for as long as she could. She was impressed that frigatebirds would intentionally fly into the updraft of a cumulus cloud rising miles high into the cold atmosphere so that it could glide more than 35 miles without flapping its wings.

    But of all the seagoing birds frigate birds cannot get their wings wet. If my mentor was a bird I would think she'd be like Wisdom, the oldest known bird. The Oracle did not mention what kind of bird she might be but the writings stated that curiosity pushes transformation and that some beings, Mentor, might be one, could be more than halflings. She could be half human, half dragon, and half osprey. Osprey and more halves than most would hold. I could see Mentor breaking through the limitations of dichotomies and adding half-lives whenever her curiosity pulled her. But curiosity without respect for the ecology of places and beings must find a healthy dynamic. I am sure she had more mission that transition in her movements. Just knowing what I read so far, a confirmation of dragons and a revelation about Mentor, had me singing. I took my self, filled with the song of possibility, to the wetlands. Unfortunately, I disturbed another heron and it went off with a long squawk of annoyance. It always makes me feel guilty. I'm a bull in a China shop, and at the wetlands so far as herons are concerned, totally annoying. And this visit was not balanced by the welcoming eye of my osprey or the eagles.

~ ~ ~

It was chilly at the river. A slight wind can make a big difference in how you feel the cold. Olfactory memories are supposedly the strongest but for me memories are often evoked by the wind. Wind holds memories as well. If the wind releases a memory, it is known as a message wind. I was suddenly dropped into the memory of approaching my mother's hospital room. How I readied myself with invisible armor, a poor job of trying to protect her as much as myself, as if that could stop the fear and grief. We'd greet each other with our eyes first each time I walked into her room. I wish I could report otherwise, but there was always a lot of goodbye in my hello. I could not hide it. We both knew this. One day when things seemed really bad, someone spelled me so that I could get away for a few minutes. They pretty much forced me to leave thinking it would be good for me. 'Fine, I thought, I'm going to curse the gods.' And I did. Oh, how I gave it to them. I was exhausted by the time I got to the beachfront in Fort Lauderdale. Wiped out but trying to stay away for as long as I could, I forced myself into an antique store. For a moment, it was really quick, I left that iron pain and found myself in front of a glass display case; and then a person behind it asking if I wanted to see anything, I surprised myself and said, 'Yes, those beads." "The millefiori beads? They're beautiful, aren't they?" They were. Like many beautiful objects, they had a presence. She told me they're made from a thousand flowers, hence the name. 'No, it couldn't be.' She assured me. I had only a few dollars so I bought four small beads. I still have them. They are beautiful. At the time, their colors and design felt sweet and their cool temperature was noticeable. It still is. It was windy at the beachfront, a little cool. I had to hold the door so that the wind wouldn't take it when I left. Was that the memory wind? When I came back to the hospital I started to dress in the same despair I wore on the way out. I guess it was how I braced myself.

  I walked into the room expecting I don't know what, but some kind of pain for sure. My mother was sitting up. She had a book in her hands. Reading is hopeful. Her eyes were bright. I forget who was there. She was talking to them. She was engaged. She was alive.

  I will ride hope for as long as it takes me.

  That was the memory the wind brought me, and I know the lesson. It was about Virg also. I had been shown that Virg was with the Crow Women. I had to stop mourning her loss. Here she was giving me access to the Oracle again. When I see her again, I have to take the goodbye out of my hellos. At least that. And ride hope, for as long as it takes me.

  Birds were at my feeders and many birds here at the river. Along with them, all of these realities flying about at the same time.

the Old Woman and the fields ~ 16

"Consistent observation is a way of loving." I am not staring at the river mud or the shore across the way. I'm remembering. The thousands, maybe ten thousand or more, starlings that lift and light on the opposite shore remind me that it is fall. I am here because I have no place else that provides me solace like this place. This is my spirit home, this side of my river. There are other sides, including across the way, and those in my journey-lands. But I'm more frequently here then there. Everything reminds me of tides, the coming and going. Here, mud seen and unseen, reminds me that the river needs a good dredge. Upland runoff and the artificial manipulation of the waters have added too much sediment right where I enjoy seeing my young osprey learn to fish. It doesn't surprise me any that I'm waiting along the river's shoreline, or that I found a place in the bulwark that's got a worn piece of wood perfect for my butt. Like all driftwood bathed in salt and briny waters, it's as soft as wood can be.

Many of us are drawn to the shorelines. I wonder about the energy fields that birds are drawn to. Birds may connect to the knowing in them. Just as Wisdom holds time aloft, my guess is that these fields hold all the information birds need. I think birds tap into a memory stream in the air and rely upon it for migration paths and all the knowing that we always find remarkable in birds. Air seems like a natural information source for birds. Easy to connect with even for the ocean-going birds or the birds that live in cliffs where trees can't take root. The sky holds information about patterns of travel and pathways. And no doubt, so much more that birds tap into than I can fathom.

    I am drawn to water. How much do we rely upon memory in water? With most of our bodies being liquid, it isn't surprising that many of us are drawn to places of tides. Lately, after hearing Mentor talk about the Old Woman, I came to wonder if the Old Woman may personify a field herself; and that all things being connected, we can trace our lineage to her, the one who has scolded me to pay attention. Our focus is everything. Remember how delicious it feels to have someone pay positive attention to you. When the air sparkles with synchronicities too poetic to be coincidences, as I was feeling now, I'm told that you are in the Tao. And I was feeling it now because all these thoughts were creating murmurations in my head and the hawk that chased them was my wish to see my mentor and the osprey.

    Birds may connect with a field around them that informs their patterns of migration and all aspects of their movement in flocks or small groups; or even as solitary migrants. I don't know if this is still considered a mystery in my world. I think of the dolphin, whale, and shark migrations. Everyone one of these creatures are being electronically tracked in one way or another. But we don't know the joy and we cannot feel or even taste or describe what might be the inner necessity of their movement, of what compels them, what that feels like. We are only gathering knowledge about their itinerary. Just as I don't know my mentor's movement but remember her love and fascination with all that moves. "Everything moves," she would say with such a sense of awe. Nothing is still. Not even rocks. I know that now. It is not only the water, though flow is its nature. It is the fields of energy and what we all partake of from them, that moves and moves us.

    Even I relate to a field though it would seem that my feet were bound with the mud. My spirit responds when the river returns. I'm not staring at the cell tower, or the empty trees looking for the osprey. I'm remembering. Memories move as well and I suppose that it's just as likely that they're in the field, perhaps brushing against the feathers of birds heading toward Cape May; maybe swooping over their wings and being carried by a wind; taken like spiders into the atmosphere and dropped by their silken lines into the Tao of the moment when I was just thinking of someone and was lightly touched by a memory of them. Some researchers have said that a spider's web is a part of its mind. Could it be the same for those who consistently observe? Consistent observation of my wetlands brought me home to myself. Returning to our familiar places has to have an effect on them. We're touching and becoming a part of them. I can give you a reason to satisfy you now. But if you love something and consistently observe it, a whole field of Tao can feed you for a lifetime.

    Okay, I have caught myself staring toward the South wistfully, wondering where my osprey have gone or if my mentor has gone with them. When the wind reminds me, I take in a breath, and it may not last very long, but for a while, maybe only as long as a redwing's whistle hangs in the air, the wetlands are a part of my mind.

~ ~ ~

Nobody hits the ball the same way; wooden or metal bat. No lefty swings the same backhand spin but every one of them confounds the righties. Nobody crawls the stroke in the lane the same and nobody stops an Olympic swimmer in the middle of the pool and says, totally amazed at their speed, "Who are you?" Nobody makes sauce as good as your mother. Nobody knows dragons better than the Old Woman. Even Mentor, and the one I call Grandmother out of respect for her, and those that keep to the ways of nature and taught me to call her Grandmother, even the Oracle, knows that the Old Woman knows dragons and water and has more connections to more fields than stars in the Milky Way. Nobody knows water and dragons better than her. I like calling her the Old Woman. The Old Woman knows.

~ ~ ~

Of course water dragons especially love water. The day before she disappeared, my mentor was streaming her recollections of the Old Woman's dragon talk she overheard. She wondered if the lecture was solely for her benefit as I wondered now if the stream of her memories had been for mine. As much as I wanted, I couldn't interrupt with questions which would break the flow of her talk like a branch divides the stream in the river. I have watched even a small branch split the water's flow. I like to see how far the two streams move away from the vee in the branch before they merge where the river widens.

"What swims better than water?" my mentor asked with no expectation of a response. "Fish, even dolphins ride the waves, the streams and currents. What is more congenial than water? It embraces everything it touches. What is more powerful? Nothing can stand in its way. It is resilient, coy enough to go around obstacles; resilient enough to wear them away. Strong enough to bowl them over. And water enough to fill a bowl."

"Water takes on the shape of whatever contains it. I am water. You are water too. Every vessel that holds water shapes it. Some waters, like the ocean, come and go. Of course water dragons love water. They love watching birds drink water. It's as if the birds are singing it into their being. Some birds have watery songs. Maybe because they sang water into their bodies. Who's to say that the shore doesn't call the tides to it and that one shore's song is stronger than the other at different times of the day? The moon is given far too much credit. Water will whistle, steam and blow. It will flow, freeze and make long, cracking sounds when the pressure from beneath the tow path pushes up from a frog's burp and causes the frozen surface to split. The sound carries through the winter air like the crack of a rifle." I knew what she was talking about. Lynn and I walked a towpath with Virg in the bone hard cold of winter hoping to hear the cracking sound Virg loved and wanted to share with us as a special treat.

"Sometimes you'll see water dragons running across the top of waves." I have seen something that seems to be riding on top of the sideways waves. It always has me do a double take. It's crazy how the water ripples as if something was riding the aberrant wave parallel to the beach. Miniature currents and ripples will do that. Virg thought the phenomena was peculiar to our trips to the beach. You could convince yourself that small waves, even at low tide, have the call of the wild in them. Whether there is a storm heading our way or not, they sometimes look like something is riding them. But, if I'm to believe my mentor, who overheard the Old Woman, do you know what you're really seeing? You're really seeing water dragons riding the waves. Mentor shared that water dragons, like their namesake element, also can take on the shape of whatever contains their joy. Sometimes, all you need for joy is to see the sky, the water, and the waves, with the gulls' call singing through the moist air.

~ ~ ~

"Wood dragons love the woods. Air dragons love the air. Fire dragons, fire. Of the elemental elements, humans sometimes only recognize five. But there are more and there's no accounting for how many more are created every moment. All the elements create a field of energy. Like is sometimes drawn to like and sometimes the pull of opposites creates differences never before noticed." So, what my mentor was relaying was that the fields of energy can have a push and pull like the tides. Who's to say it is not song that calls one species to another? Rumi said there are fields and I will take you there. Dragons love fields. They love morphogenetic fields, where knowing is matched to those that seek it. They love the energy fields that albatrosses and sea-going birds access because they take to the air and rarely land. People have praised the early explorers, the first to cross a narrow land path to a new continent. They have praised the well-known, boundary breaking human treks to the poles regarded as heroic. None of which compare to the flights Wisdom has taken through long days and sometimes hundreds of dark nights through time. There is a field and I will take you there. Is it a land that's calling you or a body of water? Dragons take on the shape of the joy that calls them. Imagine what happens to them when they are intoxicated by the colorful, neon and pattern transformations of a cuttlefish. Or the knowing touch and puzzle solving moves of an octopus. Or the songs of whales.

"There are dragons that love shamans and the shimmering effect of sage to transform entire atmospheres and groups of people just by touching and conveying information through smoke. Of course, there are smoke dragons."

"There are dragons that love plants and all the ways they move with the wind, that flower and fade into the season. There are dragons, not just water dragons, that follow all the ways that water transforms, channels, carries, moves and provides for fish and water plants to thrive. There are ocean dragons and river dragons and even dragons that love frozen creeks and frogs that freeze through the winters and defrost with the spring."

"There are cactus dragons and a whole host of dragons that thrive on dry land and weeds that talk to desert winds." There are a lot of dragons and my mentor's words about them race on the top of my thoughts just as they might ride waves parallel to the beach. As do the words of Ursula K. Le Guin, that "People who deny the existence of dragons are often eaten by dragons. From within."

~ ~ ~

I come to my wetlands because it speaks a language I know. The winds, the ripples, all the sounds make up a language. My mother feared she lost her Yiddish. I fear that I cannot communicate this language as well as I would like to. But there are others that do and I take heart that I am part of a movement of people that know these sounds and know the words and poetry, the testimonials, and solemn odes, the doggerels and shanties, the rhyming couplets, and the lines of melodies that make up the language of the wetlands, the lands that bring water and an abundance of life with them.

~ ~ ~

The kingfisher was flying around the inside edge of the river's bowl. It made a number of passes, so I got a few good looks at it; heard it rattle and felt the nearness of its energy. All of the wetlands beauty and sounds seemed to pool around me. I was steeping in it, feeling it reach deeper into me, to where there are no questions but a place that feels like a grotto, it's an open place that I wish I had a readier access to. My wetlands are often my portal to this feeling.

When you know beauty is all around but it feels as if you can't steep in it, have hope. You will. The kingfisher flew an arc around the river, before it came home to roost. I was thinking of heading home to Lynn and Molly. Best part of every day. But I wanted to carry this with me, this being everything in this moment. The weather will change, demands on my time will change. But I wanted to keep what I had here. It's not that these feelings are so impermanent or more slippery than a fish. I have watched the osprey enough that I know how to hold onto slippery things. But there's something.

Brigantine is a way I can extend summer and counter what feels like the pull down of autumn. Going there helps me hold onto summer, for a while. Before I left my wetlands I decided to speak to the eagles. I was trying to plant seeds of hope. I told them that when the leaves fell I'd see them more. They know I was snookered by the osprey. But they're a forgiving bird, they're magnanimous. If you think you see a plane, it might be the mighty eagle. Eagles are awesome. Nothing is as captivating as an eagle. Not even half dragons, half eagles. I said all that and more. But eagles knew I was bs'ing them now. You can't sweet talk an eagle. Everyone knows that. I had to be honest. Eagles can see a lie a mile away. I love them. They know that too. I should leave before I sink quicker into the sand. I wasn't trying to curry favor, I just had to tell them that my Grandmother often appeared to me as an eagle.

Rays were coming through the clouds. Blues were starting to turn to that color which is as sweet as love and as sad as some goodbyes but too beautiful to ignore. Bees were at the goldenrod that rose up over the bulwarks. I thought I saw an osprey take wing toward the back bridge. There were many swans all bunched up together just this side of the ripps. A speedy snowy egret was running along the edge of the opposite shore. I'm sure each time I saw it run it was a fish that ventured near enough to cause pursuit. Glad to get these last looks. Hope stirred that an osprey might still be around. I like it when hope stirs.

~ ~ ~

I would like to know the old woman better. But it seems she rarely reaches out to people directly. It's always through intermediaries or in my mentor's case, talking so she could be overheard without a direct exchange. But she did come to me in a journey and scolded me with a familiarity, shaking her index finger as a shorthand, I easily accepted. A certain familial baseline was in the threads in her voice. And I did easily accept those terms in my journey. She came to me out of nowhere, was direct and as real as you can be. If particles have a shared origin, imagine the possibilities that we are all connected from way back before we were even a twinkle in the sky. I'm going to imagine I'm connected to this Old Woman. One particle tickled on one side of the universe, will respond by tickling its linked particle on the other side of the universe. She didn't tickle me. She delivered a harangue. But you know, some particles, especially Old Woman particles, are probably very busy and have little time for the civilities. There's work to be done.

Two particles walked into a bar. The one particle says to the other particle, "I know you, we are inseparable" And the other said, "Bartender, get this particle a drink. She's delirious." The other particle was deliriously happy because she was recognized. She had travelled a long way to drink in this relationship.

no wrinkles no entry ~ 17

Old women are beautiful. I respect them. I listen to them. Many live with the awareness of their connections to the earth. They have always been the sexiest people on the planet. Everyone hasn't recognized this. With our wrinkles, even our crinkles, we hold the loss of loved ones in our bones. Our hearts are tidal. Sometimes they are full, sometimes they feel empty. When we cease second guessing ourselves we have knowledge that bears witness to many worlds. We choose each stone on our way across the river. On each one we can proclaim whatever we need, or we can listen to the stones themselves and see what they are saying because we hear them too. The Farmer's Almanac in 1931 proclaimed March the "Tomboy of the year." Athletic women are accepted now. Maybe we don't have to be just tomboys. I'm jumping on another river stone. This stone proclaims, like March's tomboy, that we are beautiful as we are. Stones speak slowly. Their words bring ease to all the bumps and bruises we took along the way. It is time to praise and honor all of us old women. Consider how many amazing women there are and have been. Those you know or just met briefly. Those you heard or read about, all treasures waiting to be found. Our voices are finally being recognized in a blossoming renaissance. But our voices will be meaningless unless you also listen to the natural world where our sounds come from, where our words are dressed with meaning, where we connect to our life's energies.

~ ~ ~

What if we had fantasy old women councils instead of fantasy football? Who would be on your team? To get started I'm calling on Wangari Maathai, Rachel Carson, Marjory Stoneman Douglas, and just for shits and grins, the woman who introduced the rapid runs in the Colorado to the rest of the world, Georgia White Clark. I'm calling on my mentor. I'm calling in the Old Woman too. How about every woman from the past and present who recognized the need for balance and respect for the land and waters that give us all our lives? How about them? How about your ancestors, who, maybe not recently, but way back, may have been shamans? Imagine making a meal together. The stories that emerge from preparing the meal will feed your soul. Too many of us have been left aside, dismissed for our age or because we're thought to be irrelevant. No more. The beauty of our youth goes deep so that you can harvest it when it is ready to blossom. Every story you hear starts with an old woman but she may never be mentioned. Yet, there is no tale, not even a wiggly tail, that has started without her. No wrinkles no entry.

~ ~ ~

Waiting around the bulwarks always involves me with the wetlands. Whatever is on my mind, this time a longing to know the Old Woman better dissipates when I stay just past the point of 'nothing is happening here' to just being there. The world opens most gently there. I'm in a realm that time has forgotten but not my soul. The air reminded me of a November day. I was driving over the back end bridge and looking east for the osprey. There was a car behind me, so I had to keep driving but wanted to stop. Winds were strong. It was in the high 40s but felt colder because of the wind. Blue, blue skies. Conditions were just right to see the eagle without binoculars because the air had a clarity that fall will often provide. The most amazing thing, I saw my osprey. In November! He was flying low, swirling into his spiral that precedes the dive. A sweet view. I watched it set up by rising and moving its body like a conductor just prior to the first command to the orchestra. Then head down, its body folded like a Gothic M, it dove. Then the splash. I laughed with joy when it surfaced. He shook off the water but I couldn't tell if he caught a fish. The sky was smoky blue where he rose. Just an amazing amount of glorious beautifulness. A signal to one that thinks summer is the only season. November has its charms.

~ ~ ~

Remember Mercury, messenger of the gods? What if dragons are the messages? All day I have wondered about the Old Woman. She's so knowledgeable about them. What if she is the field and dragons are the sun and rain for that field? I know it's a simple wish, but I wish everyone had love and respect for nature and sought to get in the dance with it. With our cleverness and use of tools we have transformed almost all the natural elements of life on this planet. It's some mighty changes we have wrought. And now we know a lot about the damage we have caused. Big business still goes after mining in ecologically delicate areas and damn the consequences. People like me wonder how do we live without creating more harm just by taking advantage of the resources we've grown accustomed to in our daily lives. We're at a point where the world has got to come together and find ways past our differences to steward this planet, and each other. We've gotten to this time in our story where people are talking about the whole planet being in peril. The whole planet. Earth is in trouble.

    I'd like to know how we weave and foster, generate and fold back the good stuff into the very soils and waters we have used. There are many working toward these goals and I hope to join them. Right now, I seem to grow questions as much as feathers that don't fly.

    Wise women have told me that when you love a place that the love is received and returned. And that love does good. Love can mend. I wish this to be true because I have love for my muddy wetlands. I love the bandit skimmers, and every bird who goes there; the resident kingfishers that sound more than show their presence. I got a whole lot of love. I have worried if it is enough and if it will help my wetlands thrive, because I don't know what else to do. Will loving this place add to securing the ecosystem and all that lives there? Including myself. I mean, nobody can tell you what love is so how can you measure it? It's not a barter item. You don't always know if it is returned. There's no math or equivalences involved. It just is, like the wind that came by and chilled my face as I reluctantly turned toward home.

    Everything about my world is based in feeling at home where the waters are at or below sea level; where the ocean is so close you can smell it and the birds that come to the back end of the river, are following routes that they have followed for generations. When I'm there I am stepping on living ancestral paths and standing in vibrant ancestral energy fields; as are all of us migrating and resident beings at the back end of a river. It's good that I'm here. It is enough because the wind will wick my love into the air and it will mix with everything, even the limbs where the osprey often finds a perch.

~ ~ ~

Old women in spring. Old women in summer. Old women in autumn. Old women in winter. Every turn through time connected to the seasons. Every movement a grace played through our lives.

~ ~ ~

Mrs. Teale once told me, "The big birds have my heart. They take it and fly away." She knows where to find her heart and follows it across the country, through the seasons, on the journeys she and Mr. Teale take. She knows my struggles with summer ending. I'm trying to adapt and move from being a one season woman to at least two. Even I know merging spring with summer is a cheat. I recognized a truth difficult to see until recently. The fall colors are a swoon for the soul. I'm connected to the river and it has a beautiful skirt of toasty fall colors around its bowl. It's my place to pray, to talk to the dead, place my hopes; laugh at the terns, and wait for the kingfisher to rise with a sparkling fish in its beak. I look for the osprey and eagle. I wait for the osprey and summer. But while waiting, fall comes along. The ice easily forms on the thin waters in winter. The phragmites dip in it and then offer a frozen flag of seeds to the winter winds. That is my country and that is my flag.

~ ~ ~

The sky is overcast and its cold. The leaves on the last hold out in front of our house carpet our front yard. They seem to keep the stone-cold emptiness of winter away. The river is high and reflects the whole sky. When the eagle drinks from the sandbar, it's drinking the sky's reflection. If I see the eagle, I am also seeing one of the ways Grandmother appears to me.

When I see the osprey, I am wondering if my mentor has migrated with them; while I am here, thinking I was going to migrate but I'm only left with feathers that keep me a little warmer while puzzling my mind. When I see all of this, I'm reminded of the Old Woman who yelled at me and by doing so confirmed my way in the world. The respect my mentor paid her along with her ready and easy knowledge of dragons is always present for me. I wonder about the connection between her and the dragons. I also wonder if many of us have known dragons, or other beings not familiar in our day-to-day world, and just not mentioned it to others. Dragons are in love with birds and bird populations are under such severe danger of disappearing. Some teachers are best known for sharing through love. After years of reading and listening to many, I've come round to believing that is the bridge to healing our environmental woes and stopping what some call an extinction event. A naked, chilling thought that threatens to claim its reality. It's almost impossible to protect something if you can't see or experience it. It might take dragons and beings from other worlds to remind us of the beauty we have lost the ability to see.

the old lady's ragu

First you get on the back of a great blue heron. Then you stalk the shoreline. Later, fly into the rook in the trees. Stretched out, a heron can cover a city block. Their necks are longer than anyone can say, plus or minus two percent. They're like the coastline of barrier islands, like New Jersey's Long Beach Island or Norway's fjords; impossible to measure. You'd need a new math. Herons roost in trees with osprey. I've seen it many times. Nothing like that ever gets old. The light changes everything every second. There is always beauty here. There are deep shadows. But there is often sun. There are lazy, quiet rainy days when the water runs down the tree trunks, slides unnoticed off the eagle's aged yellow beak, drops onto the river and fools the fish near the surface thinking its gobbed-up bread balls.

    Somehow, time passes even though each moment feels like nothing else is possible.

    The water's surface is a perfect skating rink for some bugs. I've watched them and can glide with the best of them. I've covered the surface at the back end of the river ten times. Can't get the hang of the skimmers though, you need a crew for that. Still I glide with the best of them. Until I fly on the phragmites leaping from one dry, crackling stalk to another. Sometimes I just like to bend it just above the surface of the river and watch the fish. Sometimes I go plunk. I have even gone kerplunketty plunk. Or I skip my body across the water as if it were the smoothed inner curve of a clamshell that I often find on the beach. I can toss myself sideways and skip over fifteen times, sliding sweet and low. It is like shine on silver. Still can't make it across all the way but I don't want the eagles thinking someone's coming to visit either, so that's good. They like to keep to themselves. That's why when they soar overhead, and it's around the time you needed a sign, that's plenty good enough.

When dawn comes each day, and dusk each evening, do they realize they never meet each other? One is captured by the morning, whether the sun is out or not; and the other is captured by the evening with and without stars twinkling. The moon is no help and doesn't convey or link their separation from each other. Yet they have so much in common. These times are the bewitching times; and what's more they have a big moment in the calendar where the whole of everything that they touch can cross a bridge to multiple worlds; where dragons and the Old Woman might swim freely from one watery world to another, through a field of energy, like a body of water, blue through green depending on the light. I'm guessing the Old Woman knows my tricks and then some. Bet she can skip across the river in two or maybe three sweet low, long glides.

Old women are not solely in the autumn of their lives. Winter is not the end. Seeing the aging in each other, tender as it is. we also see our strengths. Like the tarot cards, misleading trails seeming to be the end of things are always the beginning. You cannot forget that. Every season in my life contains moments, even days, when other seasons play through with their themes. Just as grief has many stages. Just as joy has an arc like the sun's from dawn to dusk. Just like coming to terms with your abilities and disabilities. How many of us old women are artists but took two, three, maybe five decades to speak those words, "I am a writer."; "I am an artist." This is the time to proclaim your love and yourself, for autumn has summer in it; and spring; and winter is a new beginning. I proclaim, which means to cry out, that I am connected to the earth and this place that I love. These wetlands carry my soul in every movement, every stillness, every living plant and being. When I am here I feel loved into my proper place in the world.

    I have found my true North and it turns out that it is East. And if you head further east, you're at the beach. It's how I line up with what feels like the right direction and from this place I know all other places.

a talk with the Old Woman ~ 18

She used to say to me, "Geh avec!" Go away!, when I was annoying her. I was restless and annoying myself, so I took my mother's advice and I went to my journey-lands. My plan was to find the path my mentor walked when she overheard the Old Woman talk. Time does not exist in the journey-lands, at least not in the same way it exists in the wakeful world. And I figure, if you wait long enough, something will happen. The Old Woman might just be making her rounds. I've been holding tight to the memory of her speaking to me. It was so long ago. Lifetimes. I had to satisfy this longing to speak to her.

My family and my ancestors have not lived in this part of the world for many generations. I'm only the second generation to be born in the United States. My mother was born in Brooklyn. She is the first generation here. Her parents were born in Russia. I did not grow up inheriting a knowledge or an intimacy with any lands, not even my wetlands. But I was fortunate to spend every summer, except for one, and that was miserable, by the ocean, very close to where I live today. I loved the ocean and I loved to play pinball and eat fudgsicles all day long. I lived each remaining nine months waiting for summer and waiting to return to the ocean. Every night I'd lay out all the items I wanted to bring with me to Bradley Beach. It helped close the distance in time. My mother and I moved down the shore when my father died. I was a sophomore in high school.

I wonder all the time what it would be like to have had this connection with these lands through generations of my family's people. My grandparents escaped a difficult world for Jews in Russia. No stories have come down to me about their lives there. I know they, like many Jews, were forced to migrate to Russia also. I have no idea if they ever thought about those who were indigenous either there or here. But I have often felt like something is missing from my words when I talk about loving this place and also loving all the natural beauty in the world. I don't have a continuous lineage like people with long held, long lasting cultures of living in one area for countless generations. My connection to *my* home is profound but my family's connection to place is broken. I wonder if that's why I speak about stones across the river. Without realizing it, I have come to these words because I am seeking to bridge and connect what has been broken in my family line. A difficult parallel to this is knowing that the ecological integrity of every land and body of water any of us are likely to come across in the States is also broken by pollution.

My experiences in the journey-lands are a way to bridge worlds that cannot be found in the mainstream culture. They connect me to an ancestral world; and through this way I have bridged a connection to my wetlands in the wakeful world. Today, it feels as though I have been connected to these lands and waters for as long as long can be, for they are also a portal to my spirit home.

But I want to be sure to recognize and honor all those who walked on these wetlands; those who flew and nested here; and wildlife that have been here for generations. I am not just a visitor but by their standards I may be a newcomer. I am grateful for this beauty, for the bowl of the river, the ripps that always brings me a rush of joy and excitement, and are a good place for the kingfishers to catch a meal. I'm grateful for the eagles that reside here; for the osprey that have migrated here for generations and in recent years taking advantage of the cell tower for a home overlooking this poor excuse of a river.

However you describe it, mainstream culture with its convincing worldviews has not found a way to honor the past or connections that people and their cultures have created for generations. There are obvious benefits and conveniences in our lives that most, including myself, would find unthinkable to live without, like the supermarket with foods from all over with only scant regard to the environmental costs of how it traveled there or its packaging. People and companies are addressing these concerns but it seems only for the more affluent who want to know their environmental footprint isn't harming the earth, when it's brought to their attention; but then they might just hop on a plane and fly wherever they wish, not thinking about that cost to the environment. During this worldwide COVID pandemic, the one thing that stands out is how clean the air is because so few are driving or flying. The cost of our living has often meant that we do not appreciate or respect the land and water. We certainly have not been taught to honor the land as an integral part of our upbringing. It seems to be proven daily, that when we lose our way and do not steward the land, that we pollute, we squander resources, and we harm the integrity and vitality of the land where we have our homes and neighborhoods. I am trying to find my way, as many are, in this mix of cultures and even among the commercial responses that address this, like locally grown foods that pop up now and then in the supermarkets.

    We live in a time when not only wildlife, plants and animals, but languages have become extinct and many more are facing extinction as the last of the people who hold the language die. The irreparable cultural, historical, monumental loss of languages is integrally related to how we see or don't see the land and water. Understanding that this too is important is to understand what has been broken.

    It is true that some of my family have since lived and died on these lands. I never heard my mother describe the land or talk about her connection or her family's connection to it. Or even mention our summers at the shore other than wondering where to rent each season. But I believe that my mother's Yiddish has amended the soil, has seeped into the water table, has left trace elements that climb up the stalks of plants to be wicked by the column at the base of the thermals that the big birds ride. And I believe the sparse Yiddish she shared with me has formed into smooth pebbles at the shoreline. When I'm at the beach and see them, they ease my nushumma.

"Do you think my nushumma is a rozhinke?" My mother would say when I taunted her with a card in gin. No, ma, your soul is not a raisin.

She had Yiddish. She was two souled. At least. I have the wetlands. It is my second soul. And I believe the Old Woman yelled at me to write because she knew that is how I share my soul with the world.

Of all people, Charlemagne said, "To have another language is to possess a second soul." I would say that those who have found a place they love and respect have found a second soul. Whether you are from those with long held traditions, and live on your ancestral lands or are people like me, who have come to love and honor a place, you are walking two souls on the stones across the river.

Thich Naht Hanh said, "If you look deeply into the palm of your hand, you will see your parents and all generations of your ancestors. All of them are alive in this moment. Each is present in your body. You are the continuation of each of these people." I would humbly like to add that when you're standing on the beach looking at the ocean, or when you're near a salt marsh, my wetlands are a salt marsh, you will see the lines and ridges the wind creates on the surface of the water. These lines are, like those on the palm of your hand, the continuation of generations of your ancestors. Our DNA is coded in the winds and the sun breaking on the waves, it's in the ripples and bubbles that the fish and the river's mud create. If you too are drawn to watching the tide slowly fill the river at the bulwarks, or when the birds are joined by all the sounds of a waking world, or to being present when the day moves across the grasses in a meadow and the sun reaches through the treetops, then you are being touched by your ancestors and loved into your place in the world.

~ ~ ~

'Talk is a funny word and not everything said has meaning. Colors and shapes, the feel of your hand rubbing feathers in the same direction that they fly, is not spoken but I understand it. I will talk to you because you also know this. We have common ground and from that all things grow.' I said these words on the path pretending to be the Old Woman talking to the trees. When I thought I actually heard her my instinct was also to hide behind a bush like my mentor. I could not find the sweet pepperbushes my mentor had mentioned but I found the spirea. Spirea always grows in the direction of my heart as it coils its way like the eagles riding the thermal waves toward the clouds.

 Before I could turn around and stand, the Old Woman was behind me. She said, "Maybe the dragon landed in the wrong place because it was tired and taking a rest."

 "What?"

 "The dragon that landed in your head. Maybe it was tired and your skull was a safe place to rest."

 So began my talk with the Old Woman.

 "I took that as a sign. It felt like love. But I wouldn't tell too many people about it because, well, they'd think I was hallucinating."

 "People confuse experience with signs. The dragon is drawn to places for reasons she knows best."

"You really are talking to me."

"Maybe I am, and maybe I'm not"

A dry laugh escaped me as she moved closer. She was no hallucination. I had a tureen full of questions in my head. Nothing that I could actually construct sentences from. No wonder there was space for the dragon to curl up.

She looked at me then turned and walked slowly down the path. Then I saw the tulip trees that my mentor must have seen. They were beautiful. But when I looked up, instead of blue sky through the spaces the leaves framed, I saw birds. The leaves were generously broad and a great canvas for the light and shadows to paint. Then I realized that the edges of the leaves had something on them. My eyes slowly focused until I could see them. There were little dragons on the many of the tips of the tulip leaves. They were everywhere. And the Old Woman spoke to them with her hands and eyes. She began to sway slowly as if from the wind's slight breeze. The tulip leaves gently moved also. The sun shined through the leaves. Each tip had a dragon on it. The light on them had the chatoyant effect of tiger's eye where light seems to move through the bands of yellows and gold. Some were green with a blue sheen that seemed to stretch as it does when the light hits labradorite. It was hard to turn away from them.

Everyone seemed to be moving. Even I felt my body gently swaying as I stood and watched the Old Woman and the dragons move. It felt like I was standing in the middle of a dance floor.

I often wish that I could go back in time and play gin with my mother. That bittersweet yearning sailed past me as I looked up at the dome of leaves and light overhead. When I looked into the scene before my eyes, I saw that the Old Woman was now looking at me as she continued to move. I exhaled and only then had I realized that I was holding my breath; only then did I realize that every thought that came to me felt like a hawk about to strike. But then it would ease up and bring me back to the present. Although I was left with after images, as if these memories had shadows; each like smoke on my mind cleared by the next image. The air had a silky texture. It felt cool and refreshing. I saw four great blues through the tulip leaves. Then swarms of other birds, varying sizes, going here and there. Then a flock split into two different directions just as they were over our heads. As they parted, I could hear their wings make the sound of shaking sheets out in preparation to folding them. Another activity with my mother that I missed, walking toward her with the folded sheets. And then I noticed the dragons leaning over the edge of the leaves and looking up. They were so small. Talking to myself again, 'Of course they're small. They have to be, to travel between worlds.'

    She was talking to them when I came back to that moment. "Be careful around that one," as her arm drifted away from pointing at me and continued to sway. I looked at her questioningly. Some of the dragons looked down for a moment but when birds flew overhead their heads lifted to search through the leaves for them. I just had to ask her if I belonged to the land here. This whole question of belonging surfaced with such a passion; so much questioning just about how to be. "Well," she said in response to my thoughts, "everyone has always migrated. Those that have kept to their lands the longest are threatened every day. They hold on as they can. Those that come to new places do not always love them. They miss their homes. Then they forget what it is to love a place. It is a big mess."

"But do we belong, can we belong?"

"Love migrates. Love has seasons. Love moves with the wind and has its favorite watering holes and migration paths." There was a long pause, as she seemed more interested in looking at the dragons and swaying to whatever moved her for there was no breeze. Like a vapor escaping her lips, she said, "Everyone belongs."

"Did you write yet?" She remembered. I didn't know how to answer. I was thinking, 'Well, I wrote. Yes, but is it writing if nobody reads it.' She laughed without me saying these words out loud. "Silly girl. Silly." Then her arms moved like they were wings and the dragons seemed to take that as a sign for they lifted their heads in unison, then flew off the tulip leaves. I heard a rush of feathers brushing against the tips of the leaves. And they were gone. And so was the Old Woman.

bird dreams ~ 19

The wind carries messages through some dreams. The sun, the rain, breezes, warmth, cold, clouds, all the weather you know, exists in the journey-lands, sometimes also called the dream lands or dream world. In the dream world and the wakeful world, weather seems to hold everything together and is welded with what you're experiencing in the moment. But when it isn't, everything can seem strange and contorted. While I wait for the osprey to return in the wakeful world, nothing is as it seems. The days are segmented like the small green, organic mosaic tiles of the cedar's leaves. They do not make the music of dry, rustling deciduous trees that signal autumn in my east. But they are good for rubbing if you want to worry on something softer than a stone.

    I wonder what birds dream about. I do not recall dreaming about birds, but I have flown a few times in my dreams. My body recalls the exhilaration when I wake and it pulls on me when I watch birds' soar and slide into trees. I do not have the heart to cross the oceans and travel without touching land for most of a year like some of them do. I stand at the shore loving a good dunk, a brief swim, a grateful immersion in the ocean knowing the shore is only a few feet away and the sounds of the gulls and the waves cushion my movements. But I could never enjoy even the thought of a long, ocean journey whether on a boat or gliding over the lonely waves. I wish I could touch the tips of waves like the sandpipers who fly close to shore in a line parallel to the horizon, more than I'd wish to ride through the tunnels of water on the surfer's pipeline in Waimea.

When I dive into the ocean I feel complete. Is that how birds feel when they enter the sky? Winters are difficult because I wait for the osprey to come back and summer to come to my ocean. I dream of sliding through the water and rushing with the broken wave back to the shore. The osprey's return is also a bridge to the ocean I know.

~ ~ ~

Scientists have measured birds' REM cycles. They may be short cycles but most birds have them. So, yes, birds dream. I also know that birds dream from the Oracle's notes. Dragons lay their soft heads next to dreaming birds because the birds' REM cycles start a tickle in the dragon's head that runs through to the tips of their tails. They indulge in this delight and ride bird dreams the way I ride the waves. Some believe this connects them to the blue dragon river in another realm.

Birds that dive for fish and flora may sometimes be seen with dragons holding onto them the way ocean hitchhikers, like the remora and barnacles, hold onto the bodies of sharks and whales.

If you ask a bird whether it dreams or not, you may get different stories. Crows often talk of their dreams when they hold their conferences. They may seem like noisy gatherings from a bystander's point of view, but I have listened to them and I hear dream talk. Not all of it. They get caught up in the business of their days just like humans. 'What tool is best for getting at caterpillars under the bark?' "How many puzzles did you have to unlock before you could access the nut?' 'What if I drop a bread ball in the water?" Etc. Etc.

~ ~ ~

I couldn't stand not knowing any longer. So, I journeyed and waited outside where the Crow Women dance the dance, to see if I could get Virg to repeat what she was trying to tell me. Her visit was brief, but she said they are in the dream when they're dancing. "It's stunning. There are all kinds of colors and skies. We fly through clouds and sometimes hear the tingle of the crystals that hold the rainbows. We dream of other birds, but mostly crows. We feel the cycles of the sun and moon on our velvet wings; we weave into the skies' tapestry of clouds and the places where it touches the tops of trees." All the time she was checking behind her at the elevated crow circle. Then she said, "Oh!" with a deep exhalation, followed by, "Gotta go." It reminded me of the many times we were in the water and a beautiful wave came that I had to catch. But this time, she was gone and I remained on the bench.

~ ~ ~

Some say that dreams are pulled through our minds by dragons. Some believe that the desert winds start all of this up. The winds search for moisture and when they come to a wetlands they hover until the birds begin their morning songs. The winds wait behind the bushes and trees, behind the hills or they lay low in the tidal areas. Some see this as fog instead of waiting winds. Bird songs entice the winds to rise and in turn the moisture is pulled into the air. It attracts the dragons who fell asleep on birds listening to the rhythm of their sleep. Dragons bring back the dreams they captured in the night when they lift into the air.

~ ~ ~

Thoughts of birds and dreams were streaming through my head while I stood there. These got caught in the sein. The others flowed past with the outgoing tide.

~

there is a road to my dreams
I had guides who taught me how to find it
past the tangle of branches and tall grasses

~

a magnetic field pulls
east or south, north or west
while birds hold
clouds
air
mornings
suspended in song

~

I want to fly
dreams chase down dreams
past the nest i never left sight of

~

after my cat woke me
fear pulled me into the day

I wasn't meant for this world
but I landed in my mother's belly
and she took me so far
it's up to me to find the cat food
the shield to ward off the fear
the morning songs the birds offer

~

plankton wander the ocean
a peregrine falcon waits for the one to chase
right where you'd think you left it
the heart has a key

~

the blue dragon
rarest
most often seen by bird nests
listening to the eggs
waiting for joy to open

~

lean against their trunks in winter
the buds are whispering

~

I said goodbye to my old self
knowing I wouldn't last through the day
without forgetting who I thought I was

~ ~ ~

What is the largest living organism in the world? It was previously thought to be a fungus somewhere in the Midwest which covers an area vaster than all the volcanic craters in the world. Even though humans forget, the world is alive. She is sometimes called Gaia and sometimes called Earth. Mostly, even those who forget she's one big alive planet, call her home. Many think they're talking about their one particular place.

    Some know that the birds stitch the sky to the land and the water and then the water to the sky and the leaves to the blue and the moss to the shade. Birds connect the mountains to the clouds and the sun and stars and moon and rain to the trees. And while they're doing that a vast mycelium ghost network passes through soil faster than the old clipper ships through oceans and then pops up as mushrooms in damp forests. Or it touches the roots that multiply to provide rivers of water and nutrients to the plants and trees and flowers.

    All of this life energy transforms into hearty laughter and the songs of birds and summer's cricket chorus. And it connects through the earth or water to find its way to the webbed feet of ducks and the dorsal fins of dolphins. And then filters through the whales' baleen, and the thin coat of ice like Crème Brule on shallow water; where you might also see it shook off the wings of osprey, even swans, and geese. That energy honks through the fog descending with the night; where moisture in the air is suspended like love diadems on the chandeliers of trees lighting the way for birds; birds who can slide past the pointed holly leaves or the cactus needles or the jagged edges of the cliffs or the cold tips of the waves in the middle of a wide ocean. An ocean that slowly moves its bulk pushed by the winds to form waves that roll for miles and days and then blue or gray, aqua or green moves toward the shores and ranges through the rivers toward the edges of the low lying salt marshes and the wetlands. And only sometimes is it stopped by bulwarks and sometimes met by cavities for birds' nests or otter dens and sometimes moves through the briny introduction of salt water to the river's mouth just past the ripps, and then into the bowl of the river that the eagle oversees. This part of the river reflects the sky where the eagle reluctantly welcomes the osprey in the spring who follow the largest school of menhaden coming from the south. All of this pulled together, like the last stitch holding the fabric, then knotted and secured, by the weather or the dragons that ride the dreams of birds because they find them beautiful and know they hold the sky to the land and the sand to the water's edge and the ocean to the dome of the earth that covers our home; and reaches across the wide places that only some have seen with their own eyes and some believe their destiny lies and some wait for the waves to come and tell them stories and bring the regards of many, including the wind, the water touched by the earth and the sky, the call of the birds, their evening songs, the love from the far reaches of their home. Time and winds. Diamonds. The largest living organism is the world. Birds dream the world.

~ ~ ~

I look toward the osprey nest. Joy comes if I see them. Are they dreaming when they look my way?

the blue dragon ~ 20

I became aware of both the days growing shorter and the length of my mentor's absence at the same time. Although we did not see each other frequently there was at least some form of contact between us fairly regularly. Until now. There seemed like there was always something to share in emails or the rare text message which felt more immediate, present. I made the occasional quick phone call on the way home from the office. Some calls, whether on the road or from home, could turn into long delicious talks that felt like they uncoiled every creative knot and all mundane tensions. Mentor has a curious mind and generously shares her research and discoveries. All of these contacts made up a network of connection and the network was down. Until this morning, when I received a special delivery that called for my signature. It was a small document box with no return address. Something told me it had to be from her.

    She would often mail me a book or a collection of articles because she knew I did not read the NYT or any of the magazines she frequently read. She would collect them for me and send the mental pinata when something pushed the critical mass toward the post office. Of course, I couldn't be certain if this was from her. At first it seemed it was when I opened it because I saw a collection of papers. But these were loose newsprint sheets, not the well-known print of the Times or cut out New Yorker cartoons which often signaled my mentor's collection.

Yet these pages felt familiar. Virg had put the Oracle's transcriptions on soft paper. Why is it that I am receiving the most important documents on the flimsiest of papers? I opened the package and found the following notes from a blue dragon. Much below will confirm some information that my mentor has shared and that I have read from the Oracle's notes. Some mysteries are also resolved. And as always, many questions remain for me as they will for all who read this.

~ ~ ~

The blue dragon's writing began: 'Writing tickles the brain. And it reminds me of my first time riding the dreams of a bird. It was an osprey. Oh, how they dream. Their thoughts curl and swirl around just as they do when they're bringing a fish back to the nest. They always circle the nest. At first, I thought it was because the winds made it impossible to go there directly. But you learn by watching osprey that they love to celebrate the catch, to create the anticipation of the meal. The female has been waiting and calling and looking and searching the skies for her mate. And dinner. When he arrives, what a joy! Although, the female's calling doesn't stop until he lands with the fish in the nest. When their little ones are hatched, the calls are joined by the smallest, high-pitched cries from what will one day be the mightiest fishers." I have watched this many times myself and loved every moment. When fish are flying that means osprey are about to eat.

"It is summer, the season for writing. I am a blue dragon. I am one among a few dragons who have decided to write. This is the season that many in this world long for during their grey and cold days that offer little sunlight. Summer's gift begins each warm morning and slowly opens to a long day of sun and a gentle night. Conducive to writing for those called to it and an inducement to dive and lounge with joy for those captured by the charms of summer." This blue dragon knows my heart. So they share the same sentiments. Summer beckons all of us.

"If ever seen by humans, these pages remind them of newsprint. They are easy to write on and accept the ink fully like newsprint. (Perhaps not all the thoughts some may write.) These soft papers are actually the preserved scales of baby dragons that were taken by the wind as the babies began to shed them. They are welcomed by the earth as they settle into the leaves and grasses. Many dragons, who have hopes to write in the coming summer, hastily move about the grounds trying to gather the shed scales. They learned from the squirrels and the birds to store their document materials in trees. But like them, they store so many, with no careful catalog to retrieve them. Many are forgotten and become the nesting materials for the same birds or squirrels they have watched." Baby dragon scales? The words did seem to float on an opaque surface. I went outside and raised a page to the narrow light of the winter sun. The words shimmered and moved. They looked like the ocean's surface at the horizon when the cold winds make the waves look like dark blue whipped egg whites, or like what I imagined were dragon's teeth.

"Many dragons who have wished to write often decide to sing their songs instead. They have learned from birds that the winds carry messages and the trees and even some humans revel in their songs. These dragons wish to be a part of the chorus and to rejoice in the sounds they too have come to love, especially in the spring and summers. Writing seems a bit stodgy and beside the point to these dragons. When would they or anyone read what they wrote after all? And if they lost a summer to writing, how would they follow their birds around or the birds' dreams? They love to do both. Choices have to be made.

~~~

"It is said among all dragons that we love too easily because we were once, in a world that has fallen, not loved enough. When we travelled around the planets in many galaxies, we moved as a group. For a long time, we were a world unto ourselves. We talked little because that was not our way. We did not write at all but carried our histories in our minds and bodies, in our gestures and tones when we communicated. Many gestures or sounds have different import because we couch the movements and sounds to hold layers of meaning. It is no wonder dragons love bird songs for they recognize, and deeply appreciate, the layers of meaning and nuance in them. We understand this is often lost on humans but not on other birds or animals." I have read that some of the best birders can recognize hundreds of birds by their songs. Some have even proven that the same bird, say a robin or a wren, will have a different accent, depending upon which part of the country they live. The blue dragon is right, if we're only recognizing birds by their songs for food or protection and sometimes their regions, we're missing their stories. Stories always fall somewhere between hunger and safe surroundings. I want to know what the eagle thinks with snow piling on its head; or what the female osprey's yearning feels like when the sun is baking her crown and the youngsters are panting from the heat.

"We understand that what happened to us and the world we once knew as home is held in our language. Our language, no matter the form, has the highest regard among all of us, no matter our age, because we know it holds us. We know that to be true to ourselves we must follow what we love. There is always a clear path if you accept your gifts and value the gifts of others. The gifts can be as simple as sharing your life's story or the story of your ancestors. These stories weave time and experience and hold those that gave us life in the fabric of our being. If you could say we had a guiding principle, our teaching is that joy comes from listening. Sometimes sorrow. Both are always in the stories you will hear from dragons. We follow what we love and see the beauty in life. We don't think this is special. As some humans might say, 'it just is.'

~~~

"We lost our home. Since falling through that great hole in space we looked for a home that we could love again. It was a long journey and one that other dragons may wish to tell. I may wish to tell it one day. But what I want to share now is that we found birds here, on Earth. We were immediately charmed. There is no other way to express it in writing. If I were to share it with another dragon, I would curl and glide, and roll, and twist and pop up or appear to be a blue liquid sliding through the sky or a winding river. And then my movements would evoke the land and stones and skies that this river flows through. With sun and breezes suggested through my motion and stillness. That is how dragons most often communicate. But with words only, let me simply write that a world with birds had to be a world with love. And so, we have been here for millions of years because we found birds.

~~~

"Like us, many beings move through different levels of realities within the Earth's sphere of influence. All dragons that once were the world unto ourselves have filtered into these realms. We may travel on our own or on the dreams of birds but we no longer are a nomadic group. Birds are our home and wherever we go on Earth, we are home. We belong because they belong. Our travels, both in riding their dreams and over all terrains, are their travels. Through time we have also found our way through other beings. There are now, since millions of years have passed since we first came to Earth, eons some like to say, half dragons and half other delightful beings. There are even half dragons and half writers. I may fall into that category. Some have even indicated that there are half dragons and half blue dragons. Wit does not escape my kinsmen, the dragons.

"The mysteries of our lives are braided with the histories of many ways of being on Earth and in its many realities. The universe is made up of finely woven threads, and, like the sheen of a mallard's head, sometimes green, sometimes purple, the tapestry is always beautiful. But it is also so common that the beauty is often overlooked." It has many realities. Many realities. The journey-lands. Even states of mind. Joy, sorrow. All of it, they are along for all of it.

~~~

"Until the balance was broken, we lived in a beautiful world. We have found another home here on Earth and have lived here in joy. We also understand the powers that exist and the imbalances that can threaten this world. Dragons remember our first home. All dragons know we once lost our home. We do not teach this history. It is in us.

"We watch and we, of course, listen, even as we continue to love birds and ride their dreams. Many birds that once filled the skies and summer mornings, are gone. We know.

"We also know that some rivers are being legally recognized as persons so that they have protections in the courts. In this world, personhood allows rivers and protections. These and other protections offered to and projected to be offered to larger bodies of water, parts of the vast oceans, and some territories, have the promise that those in power understand that beauty is integral to life and to survival. All of these protections further the opportunity to offer birds and all of wildlife what they need to thrive.

"We found our home here because we fell in love with the joy and beauty of birds. But perhaps it was more than that. Something even dragons do not yet understand. Over eons, some dragons have indicated that we were called from across vast spaces to this place; that something in us and something in birds drew us together. We arrived at a time before humans are as they are today. Even when other large animals died through cataclysmic periods on Earth, birds remained, and dragons along with them. They not only remained, as we dragons, perhaps more than other beings, can recall, they flourished. They evolved and created all the variety and wonders of the known birds that exist today. It is only some birds that are lost forever because of ignorance and outright harm done them. Birds are *the* wonder in our world. Every day, even the birds at feeders and fountains, are miracles. Like the journey through time birds have travelled, so has the joy that this word miracle - to wonder, to astonish, to smile - is built upon. Some people have assumed that miracles are infrequent events brought on by dire need and once in a millennium gathering of unlikely coincidences; that miracles are called upon by unprecedented pain and the horrible emptiness of death's finality. Simply untrue. Every day, birds show that miracles have wings, that miracles are morning and evening songs; that miracles nest to create the next generations of miracles.

~~~

"As long as it might be that dragons have been on Earth, we are still learning about many energies, such as winds and currents, the many forms that water takes, the ways that multiple realities exist and how many beings move into other worlds with ease. Dragons understand that many humans do not see these other realities but we notice how they address them in different forms nonetheless, such as howls, or songs, or prayers and chants. Time is, of course, something that moves through life like a current or stream moves through the ocean. It changes the temperature of the surrounding waters, so to speak, when it is near. It effects all lands and waters and living beings from a distance through the imperceptible movements it makes and creates in its layered realities. Some dragons have suggested that time is also a bird dream that one can ride. I have not had the pleasure of riding that dream. I do not know what shore it may touch or what rivers it may enter. Dragons, in their own understanding of such topics, believe all rivers deserve the rights that people are granted in human courts and that they should be loved and protected because rivers receive the dreams of birds and all life from the oceans and carry them inland to all shores." Time may be a bird dream. Time is a current with layered realties. But the daytime, clock world reality is harming birds. If birds are time and they're being lost, we are losing time. All rivers should have rights. They flow to all shores and are fed by multiples sources. Even time, even bird dreams, even dragons feed the rivers.

<p style="text-align: center;">~~~</p>

"I am a blue dragon. I dance with the rivers. Many of my ancestors liked to celebrate life through dance. I understand the powers that exist and the imbalances that threaten beauty and joy. This is why I chose to write. Words sometimes tickle me when I write them. Some words have me pause and take a deep breath. All dragons that have dabbled in writing know that when words become songs they add to the messages the winds take. And all hope this will help save birds and the lands and waters they, and all of life, need. When many can see the common, daily beauty of birds, and listen to their songs, we hope that like our ancestors who fell in love with birds, that those on Earth who have not yet been captured by their beauty and joy, will be. And that they will, like the rivers, carry that love and joy inland to the many shores and to those who can gain the power and can influence their peers so that they will provide birds and all wildlife protection."

~~~

The last of the blue dragon's words that I received follow. Whoever provided this has lifted my spirits and confirmed what my mentor has shared. I hope I receive more from the blue dragon. I always want more but I also bow to this gift and I'm humbled by the deep connections through time and space that dragons and birds share. My osprey must have more tales to tell. "Dragons believe there is hope for this world. They believe that just as a nest provides a home for the new hatchlings, listening to bird songs and the songs of others who love this world, will protect the beauty and joy that is here. We stayed here because of birds. We may well have come here because something in us and something in birds called to each other. We have also come to love and see the beauty in all life in this world; having watched it evolve for many years. If you are like many we have met, and you feel a stranger to the land; or don't recognize the connections you have because they have not been woven into your skin and stories, have hope. The land and waters know you. The birds know your songs even as you learn your own heart."

a highway between realities ~ 21

Smiley. I got the nickname Smiley in the summer, down the shore. I was a happy kid. I think one or several of my mother's friends, the other mothers at the rooming house, recognized my happiness and christened me Smiley. I had pluck and more so as they braided my hair and pulled my scalp so tight you could bounce coins off of my forehead. I try to remember my Smiley self now and then, but she's melted into the stream of decades. She was the first to see things, to show me how to look at the world. I saw everything through Smiley's eyes and everything she saw was filtered by summer.

I'm told that it's not good to compare. I believe what I've been told. This is mostly meant when I compare myself to someone else where I diminish who I am or what I've created. But I can't help but to compare every day to summer. It's my measure.

But don't listen to me about how to look at your days. Definitely don't compare yourself to how I see things. Trust your instincts because they have been shaped by how you've seen the world from day one. Our instincts are sometimes buried so deeply in our being that they have become a shadow of their former selves. We might even see them as shadows rather than our native, direct route to knowledge. It might just be why I'm so drawn to shadows. Why I remind myself all the time, that shadows are nature too.

As evidence of lack of instinct, I have to admit that I did try to pluck a feather from my midsection.

It hurt. I stopped plucking. But that desire to pluck became a character trait. Little wonder considering I am the heir to Smiley and Smiley had pluck braided into her being. Now, I've got pluck and feathers. Pluck and Feathers. Could be a law firm. The birds are going to file a class action suit against humans who have overpopulated the planet in some areas, and have caused havoc and harm in others. The suit will claim that humans have destroyed habitat, wetlands, wide open ranges and left human bird allies trying to figure out ways to abate the damage.

corridors

There is a new alleyway in town. It's called a corridor and there is now, what Jodie Hilty has named, corridor ecology. You know why we're creating new corridors, or new ways to delineate and protect wildlife paths? Because some people know and respect the historical and ancestral migration paths, be it for large animals and herds, or salamanders and blue gentians. Whether it's for turtles or elk, these wildlife bridges, corridors, are created and financed because corridors prevent driver collisions with large animals. Collisions are costly. The incentive to save money and the need to protect animals is met through the corridor. That is how those who create these passages between the reality of highways and humans and the instinctual migratory paths of animals, have got them funded. Corridors are a way to mitigate the damage we do to wildlife and preserve their paths. Naturalists found a way to help the animals and their winning argument gained support because it was based on saving people money. These alternate paths, connecting two areas intersected by a highway have been successful. There are less collisions, less interruption of migratory paths. It just seems like a diminution of what was once wild and free. But I know the necessity and welcome the solution.

    The ancestral pull to migrate across time honored passages is now crossing, or going under or around highways, allowing the wildlife their realities, and humans' their highways and speed. Take a moment and remember this, time honors these wildlife passages. Time and honor are linked between multiple realities. We may all have paths we go down because they have everything we need to be and to belong to a place. Safe journeys.

you rock

Thanks to the Yurok tribe, the Klamath River now has the legal rights of a person. The largest wildlife crossing, in the busiest urban setting, is set to be built to protect mountain lions and other wildlife in and around Los Angeles. The earth has allies, even in our cities where some are caressing innovative nature areas and a variety of gardens, including community gardens. It seems odd, even foolish, and it is sad, but many of us are not trained from the get-go to love the earth and to consider it our home. We are most often taught to drill down to our own particulars and forget that they rest on the bluest planet we know, our earth. We aren't taught that the inspiration or the beauty of this world is a resource. It's not the cash and carry most understand. We've knocked entire bodies of water and tracts of land off course and upset a dynamic that was able to achieve balance through self-regulation, even through the seasons. Take heart, take care, take a look around and try to imagine what loving a place you're near might do to it and yourself. Somewhere down the line, we all were once as wise as the Yuroks. And now our fate and the fate of all of wildlife is in our hands. When it is in our hearts, hope will surface like an osprey, rising against the weight of the water with the fish it carries, majestically rising to the surface and lifting into the air, and then heading toward home.

different realities make for different folks

Smiley is in me. The life lived between when I was a young Smiley has sometimes just snagged, more recently, embraced, many experiences. I'm discerning differences in realities all the time. Not just the obvious ones from my journey-lands to this wake-a-day world. From road hypnosis to presence. From one mood to another. From speaking to the treetops, or to playing gin with my mother across the card table I now have in my pantry. Maybe my experiences aren't so different from the mind of the albatross, one half of its brain sleeping while the other glides and looks for a fish near the surface.

Different realities make for different folks. From being a person who possibly never saw birds other than the gulls on the beach, or the sparrows on

Newark streets; to someone who waits as though her life depended on the osprey's return. Or from being all heart and running to exhaustion as a kid, to learning to know my older heart. The realities that I love most aren't made of wood or held together with spackle and nails. They have a corridor in them that was and is an ancestral, time honored, path. A path that had no separation from the wild and beautiful. It's a path some call migratory and some know as an instinctual need to travel. I suspect it takes many forms. And that humans also, always getting into the act don't you know, have ancestral paths. It's possible our high speed world and the bombardment we all experience from information overload has created the necessity for our own corridors that connects our ancestral knowing to our minds and hearts.

conjugating joy

The last time we talked on the cell I told Mrs. Teale that it just dawned on me that, 'Although I don't know how to conjugate it, joy is a verb. If I were in French or Spanish class the teacher would have me list all the ways that joy can be expressed grammatically. Here's one example, 'I am going to the wetland to joy.'

She responded with ,"To joy means to love. Love is a liquid that pours into you. Sometimes you see or hear the source and you put your being right under the joy faucet so that you can fill up."

I said, 'Like chocolate fountains. But birds, the wetlands, the waves on the beach. I drink them in all the time. When I was Smiley I probably wasn't aware that I was steeped in joy.'

"And summer."

'I know. I was lucky.' Then we both paused.

'Actually, I was so lucky. So blessed. And now, you've got me, I'm here trying to conjugate joy still woman!. OMG!'

Joy is a corridor too. A long-held, ancestral trail, time honored.

So, I was lousy at grammar. If you're reading this, that truth might be evident. But I have always been fascinated by verbs and grammar folks love to conjugate verbs. I know that sounds racy. With the time I have, and where I am, a long time outside of the nest, if I need to conjugate joy for all my various selves, I can get to the wetlands, and after that, I'm not so sure. I can stay put, like I often do and see joy rise as a heron lifts off the mud, or watch for the surface sprinkles of the bait fish. How do I conjugate the joy I feel? One site on the web notes that we conjugate the verb for each person. We have six different persons in English. Who knew?

If I'm down, or downed, I can get all woozy bluesy or country corn trying to muster something, to whip some energy up from the deep blues I got myself into. I'll tell myself to find my way back to Smiley. So, a few things about that. I know something Smiley didn't. She was in love with the beach and summer; watching the guys play basketball, in that otherwise abandoned playground, in the hot sun, riding her bike around Ocean Grove and up and down the streets gazing at all the summer homes in Bradley Beach.

When she got a little older, she found Jacques Cousteau. She was in love with him. She wanted to be on the Calypso as part of his crew. For Odysseus, who I call the O man, Calypso was his captor. He wanted to go home, and it took the gods intervening to convince Calypso to release him. For Cousteau, the Calypso was his ship. His home was on the water.

I sometimes think that for me, for all of us, who often pay it no never mind, we all have our homes on the water. I mean, this is the watery planet. My smiles come in waves. Sets. Riding joy, riding the waves. I tell myself it's the same good feeling the dragon's get riding the dreams of birds.

Every way that I can conjugate joy, is a good way. Oh, all right. A few guidelines. I know we know these parameters but they bear repeating. Be kind. Don't interfere with any animal migrations. Respect their paths. Respect the elders who deserve respect. Don't do anything by rote. Be easy on the earth. Love all water, it is our life and home. Every drop has a memory of blue whales. Find what you love. Conjugate joy.

between buttonholes

Mrs. Teale was staring at my shirt. It was the last time I saw her before she left to wander through winter with Mr. Teale. We said our goodbyes knowing we'd see each other in October. Mrs. Teale said she'd be back to meet unless she was kidnapped by a sunset, or a starry night, or the gurgling of a tidal water as it plays through the openings in a jetty. Barring any of those circumstances, we would meet at the bulwarks. When she left me I remained at the wetlands, as I often do.

After a while I remembered her staring at my chest area. Then I looked down. Feathers were poking through the spaces between my buttonholes. I'm sure there's a word for that space. Wow. I told her about the feathers but I'm sure it is entirely another thing for her to see them. It certainly was entirely another thing for me to know she saw them. A quick flash of vulnerable went through me like a chill. But, she did not say a word. Everything she had to say about feathers was already said when we last spoke. For her, it was as natural as the moonrise over the Long Island Sound

I remember when Mrs. Teale told me that not everyone has the Sedge Islands has a highway between realities. I bet most people have at least one way between. Most people, like water moving between low tide and high, will move into different forms of consciousness all day long. The Old Woman talking to the tops of trees was looking at the dragons while saying something for my mentor's benefit. She was holding two realities at once. Or was she just looking at the tops of the trees where they meet the sky? Her words were short but her looking was soft and long.

island in the stream

Love exists between realities. It's like a floating island that moves with the currents. Love is found on every continent and in every possible living arrangement. Love is a lot like birds. They're on every continent. They're the most widely distributed species. They fly. They glide. They float. They nest. They dance and they have songs for every occasion, including one for a chick to recognize its mother's call among many others from the same species. I am drawn to birds the way the Old Woman is to the dragons.

I was watching their moves and going to the wetlands every day for a year, no matter the weather or time of day, when I seemed to wake to the beauty of osprey. I couldn't always get there in full daylight. My body holds my heart in place. However it physically stays put, I'm telling you that if my heart could fly it would travel with the osprey, maybe never letting Skunk out of view. My Mentor is now somewhere south. I bet she's watching Skunk grow into the sea eagle she will be, the water dragon fish should fear.

There are corridors linking the hearts in our bodies to our soul's heart, and to the paths in nature that bring us home. My wetlands offered me protection and healing from the nasties at work. Those who used their energy to tear things down and not love each other or anything outside themselves. At least that is the way they presented themselves in a toxic work environment. Thank god I finally left that place. Before I could, fortunately, I had a remedy. My corridor between realities. My wetlands and everyone that lived there, including the mud, all guided me through the different realities of the heart.

I imagine that when the cooling evening comes, teachers who take the form of birds in the journey-lands fly for the sheer joy of it. Some may choose to fly in a flock instead of being a solitary bird. They glide and soar across open areas or cut around branches. Dragons may form murmurations, chased and moved into beautiful forms by their joy. Or they and all who delight in flying move from one host, be it butte or branch, to another, while the sun bounces off of the water onto the trees, illuminating patches of bark, deepening velvet shadows as day melts into night.

    I feel love in the journey-lands that may get pushed aside by the urgencies of others in the wakeful world. All events and movements are without question there, they flow. They happen. That is why it's a journey. There is no need for effort. The results pop up like ruddy ducks in a pond. Or the bufflehead or the merganser that wears its hood with panache.

a world where birds are not in peril

Just this past week, the U.S. Fish & Wildlife Service would not add monarch butterflies to the endangered list because there were too many wildlife priorities already. Audubon is predicting that as much as half of the bird species in North America may go extinct. Half of all our birds. Only those with pluck, and advanced adaptable skills, will survive the next fifty years. This is devastating news and it doesn't get better because each day we learn about more environmental harm. There is hope. There are all kinds of people and groups, even some politicians and geopolitical organizations trying to effect good governance and stewardship of our lands and waters. But I believe our focus, and the work ahead have to have an integrated approach and address all people and all wildlife if we're going to make a difference.

I dream of a world where birds are not in peril. Where they and their migratory paths are protected. Where this dire projection is wrong because all of us woke to a heartbreaking loss of birds, three billion since 1970. This news was so painful it broke something inside me I can't even name. And there are even worse predictions for their future. Rachel Carson wrote about a silent spring. Today she would write about a deafening silence and empty skies. Indigenous caretakers, environmental organizations and their members have been trying to save and repair the degradation of our land and waters. Government programs sometimes help. But this is not enough. It's just not enough. Government help in the U.S. is built, as they say, on a slippery slope, dependent upon who has political power at the time. Members of indigenous groups and organizations just aren't enough. We need a threshold of people to know and care, to insist on right actions, programs, and laws. There are environmental questions of priority that we must acknowledge and discuss. We all need to learn how to reduce harm now and how to generate the proper caring and caretaking that will support all life that is not subject to political whims or short sighted leaders. I think we have to find the right way to live in this world with all the life that is here. We have to seek out each other's voices, concerns, and solutions. We have to listen to those steeped in local and indigenous knowledge. We have to listen to those of us who have learned about our eco areas and biomes and join with all the stakeholders, holding a space for those who cannot speak or for those whose language we do not yet know. We have to broaden our ideas of who and what we listen to. The wind carries words, the plants and wildlife speak to us. How do we convey this to the general public? There is a council of all beings and we should join them. Let's include all children, every age and grade because they are both stakeholders, and the ones that will inherit the world. Show them where conflicts about use of lands and waters arise. Share all the difficulties and the solutions we know of for challenging ecological questions or ask for their ideas. This will increase their skills and knowledge early on. If we educate them about healthy waters, and what makes up the land they live on, they'll learn what cultures previously taught their communities before the great human diaspora, before we were all pushed and pulled by inventions and technological achievements of the last hundred years, and by power over indigenous people and their lands. It will help connect many of us who were separated from their knowledge of their lands and waters.

  Many good developments might have come from this period of human growth, but we lost a fundamental connection to earth and continued to think and act as conquerors. Conquerors don't farm so good; or fish, or pay attention to where things come from so much as they make demands from those they've controlled.

It's not just birds we've lost. We lost our understanding and good sense about how to keep the world healthy. And we never quite learned how to make peace among humans, how to cooperate and join rather than take over and control. It just doesn't make sense to destroy what gives us life. I'm not sure that what we're doing to the environment is any different than suicide. And we have laws against suicide. People are dying too young from air pollution. Up and down the line of our bodies and souls, essential connections to a thriving world are broken. We're endangering so many animals besides our fellow humans. And plants. It's not just dispiriting. It's truly killing us. What is the expression? Death by a thousand paper cuts? Every day, oil leaks in our waters. Every day, more children with asthma, more contaminants in the water, in the fish we eat. We've forgotten about the eagles and osprey who couldn't form healthy eggs because of DDT. We forget the lessons of the past but we all live with anxiety about the present. It's time to listen, to talk and to be good earthlings and take care of our mother.

Main Street

October was too far away for me to wait and ask Mrs. Teale about how to show our love, how to listen, how to place value on harmony between all beings and beauty. I called her and poured a quart of questions into the airwaves. "How do you show Main Street the value of birds? My greater family extends beyond the two-legged variety we know. Birds are my family too. I understand that people like to put a value on things, even what my uncle pelican might be worth. You wouldn't think to put a value on what this sibling or that relative of mine is worth.

"Some sports people like to tear through the woods on their motorbikes and 4-wheelers. They just want to have fun. In the meantime, they're destroying habitat in some places like the Pinelands, regularly. I can hear someone asking me, 'Why should I care about birds or whatever?' It is hard to show them why they should care right there, on the spot. You can't say it's rare habitat you're destroying. It has no meaning to them, no context. Same for saying there's a whole ecosystem here and you're hurting a critical part of it. It's not so easy to show them so that they'd care to change they're idea of having fun."

Mrs. Teale responded to my hairs' on fire call. She said," Well, about birds, you could say that they have shown us how to soar and helped us describe our aspirations. They have pollinated our plants and have, for untold generations, represented our beliefs. Right along with us, they have solved problems and made tools. We can't hide the fact that we know they are intelligent beings."

She was being the calm Mrs. Teale I came to love. I could walk through the Everglades sweaty and hot, attacked by giant mosquitos so much so that I would be smacking myself silly trying to kill them when they were on my body, biting through my shirt and pants, until I got out of there. But Mrs. Teale, Mrs.

Teale would walk back to her car, calm, cool, unwrinkled, no sweat and wonder what the heck was going on with me. She can step back. I try to understand perspective. She just has it built in. I said, "So, tell people the practical, real-world effects of them in our lives? But how then do we talk about how their beauty also has a place? It does. Because I'm afraid if we only take it so far as to show how they benefit us they'll set priorities based upon that. The thing is, we are still learning so much and we don't know what we don't know."

    She agreed. "You're right. We don't know relationships between living organisms and their biome. And because we don't know that they're vulnerable to harm if we hurt one part leaving the other without what it needs."

    "That's right, " I agreed. And while I paused, she continued with her thought.

    "So, we have to preserve and protect environs and all contained therein. Not just for uses and foods or because they might have rare plants or animals. We also have to preserve areas because they hold stories that breathe life into some cultures. Many of us might have known our stories which accounted for the relationships that hold great value, in ecosystems and lives. That's the value we want to listen for and share. And I agree, beauty also has a place."

    And I said, "We sing, we dance, we have even found ways to fly and soar. It's true we took a different path through evolution. But all along the way birds have spoken to us." And then I paused because I was getting emotional and I wanted to talk without crying. I said, "They've spoken to me. I know they grieve, like I do. They love. They know their mother's voice. If they migrate, they return to the same nests each year, and to their same mates. They are faithful."

Mrs. Teale agreed. I think she was trying to help me get past the rawness I was feeling. She said, "Yes, and they help preserve balances in nature by eating pests. They build the wetlands you love through their nesting and hunting. They even clean up carcasses. More values and practical reasons to appreciate birds. But you want to tell people something else, and widen the lens, and open their hearts. I know you do. I'm just not always sure how to do this either. We have to find opportunities."

I was repeating her words inside my head, 'widen the lens, open their hearts.' And then I said, "I would tell people that a world where birds have perished, it would be like a law saying 'You can no longer listen to your music.' It would also be like living in a world where there are hardly any colors. Everything will be muted, sounds, colors, even movement"

"What I know through sight and sounds is uplifting. Their beauty touches our spirits," Mrs. Teale said these words like a teacher might to draw a conclusion to the thoughts and information we shared.

I agreed and said, "Yes, and more, we only know a world with birds. And when the skies seem emptier than they have been, and sometimes I believe I'm seeing that emptiness, it feels like pieces of the world are falling off."

Mrs. Teale took a breath. I could hear her and I felt bad because I knew I was taking her from her journey through spring. But she seemed wanting to share her knowledge. She said, "You are right, we have to show why something in nature has value because we clearly are that far from knowing this without question." She paused and I knew something was taking shape in her thoughts. I was able to wait, because here I was leaning my head hard into the cell phone, overwhelmed with a desire to stop the madness and feeling completely powerless to do so. The sound of her voice gave me hope. "I sometimes think we have to teach each other about our human capabilities first in order for people to care about birds and other wildlife. People mostly relate to people things. For us to have well-being, we need to have the freedom to experience joy, for instance, or to grieve, to experience loss. We have the capability to play, to cry, to laugh, to love. And. there's what Martha Nussbaum calls the essential capabilities, bodily health, body integrity. Affiliations. If we can allow each other these qualities, instead of boxing and packaging each other, I think we would have the ability to recognize how we have to look at all living things through this idea of what makes them well and what capabilities they have. You can't see it in others if you can't see it in yourself. Having the similar experiences breaks barriers. The good we see in ourselves, if we understand the full range and allowed it to be in each other, could be a mirror for how we see wildlife too."

I took that in. I remember reading about capabilities. Then I added that "We could share their relationship with us through time. We have the journey through time in common. And wind and rain too, is a part of who all of us are. We value intelligence, skills, tool-making, song, beauty. We do. But we forget that it's not just us humans who are smart, talented tool makers. We forget that."

And Mrs. Teale concluded that "We would never be who we are without them being who they are."

"Right!" I was elated. And I added, "In all their varieties, on all the continents, in all the skies and trees, and hollows and ledges and telephone poles and as finials on the highway lights winnowing us to the exit toward our home."

"They are our relatives," she emphasized, "but not our aunts or uncles. We share life with them, the same life that runs through our veins also runs through their wings."

"Yes!" I knew she would help me express this. Yes, we share life with them.

And she added more of what many would see, that "We know them as messengers. The carrier pigeons. Once, not too long ago. And, also, many birds are harbingers of weather fronts and seasons changing."

I was feeling more light-hearted. I added, "They are our companions. They are our fine feathered friends. They may not live in our homes or where we dwell but they are just outside. We do not live parallel lives with birds. We live alongside them.

If we're inside, they're just outside, on our, too possessive a word, properties."

Mrs. Teale was helping me so much just by being in the spirit. I called and started this like Homer, in medias res, right in the middle of things. That's why I loved her. She said, "They nest in all our towns and cities. We swim in the same waters your osprey dive in. We share the same skies."

"Right, we share the same shade and sun. We have lived through eons of time with birds. Eons."

"And if we're lucky enough," she added, "and listen to each other and to nature, we may be able to turn the wave we have created. Wind should create the waves, not people. The losses we predict may not be inevitable. We may always share the same lands and skies. And look for their return if they migrate and listen to their songs each day if they stay through the seasons with us."

I just had to say, "And not travel through the seasons as you and Mr. Teale do? You know Mrs. Teale, Main Street is only two miles from my wetlands. There are actually several Main Streets within five miles of my wetlands. I want all of them to know my wetlands and to value birds. This is the Jersey Shore. Everyone loves it here. Go to Main Street and check out all the shops and restaurants. Then come with me to the wetlands. Check out the hooded mergansers. Their hip dos, how they snazz up the reflections in Nollequesset. That's Shark River to you, I'd tell them. But it's been here as Nollequesset for thousands of generations of Lenape. Come on, I'll show you where the eagle nests. That's what I want to say to everyone."

She listened. "I'm someone who wanted to be an oceanographer, a naturalist, a ranger. But this mishugana, half dragon mishugana, between getting seasick on big boats and not able to dissect animals, I quickly found out, an oceanographer? Not going to be me. Somehow being a naturalist or ranger escaped me. My resume does not show my dreams but there's no denying it was a road there too. All my efforts now, in my own unconventional ways sometimes, are, I'm hoping, going to help nature, especially my osprey. But who knows, maybe there are dragons that I will work with to create ways to protect the birds we love together, with the birds input and consent of course."

"Of course," she added good humoredly.

I was reminded that dragons not only represent each element, they touch each element. And from the birds, unwinding like a spool of gold filaments, we will no doubt see how everything is connected to each other.

She sang a version of my favorite Frost line back to me, "You are a guide who only has at heart our getting lost, hopelessly lost and in love with birds."

Well, I was smiling but I also felt tears and barely could get out what I felt. "Birds complete me. I didn't always know how they were a part of my family. But they showed up sooner than the relatives I'm finding through my DNA matches. The osprey was there when I couldn't take it anymore, those horrible people at work and being so far away from my dream. I love them more than I can say."

Mrs. Teale allowed the space to fill with love.

"I want to yell, 'Rise and shine, everyone. This is it. Please, wake up! There's creatures flying in your skies. You breathe the same air they do. And your relatives have breathed the same air as birds for millions of years. They have always been a part of your world. They're beautiful!'"

"You could have been the head scout for the dragons who came here eons ago. And you're right, this is the rise and shine moment," she agreed.

"When I read about birds and other wildlife that have gone extinct, my heart aches. It just flat out hurts. I don't know what to do with that pain"

She knows me. She feels the same pains. Before we ended our talk, I told her how much I was thinking about my generational place on this land. I only know it as a second-generation person, learning as I go. I don't know who walked this river land before me. Or, who sought the osprey out, even just two generations before I did my bumbling wiggle waggle way to the wetlands. But I want to know more and I want to and will do the work so that I can walk in harmony with everyone, past and present, indigenous and immigrant. I say all the wrong things. I'm probably up on the nature's wall for the ten most wanted for anthropomorphizing. But I only know birds through my experience. My family did not put them into context for me. And learning about birds or anything in nature is sometimes taught as if you can pluck what you're studying out of context, memorize it. Know it. Boom, you're done. But I feel that process of isolation leaves out context. We need context. It's the mother. Context is community.

And now, what you said about shared experiences, that it breaks barriers, maybe anthropomorphizing isn't such a bad deal. Fortunately, I found birds, found my osprey and I'm finding my way. It is sometimes coupled with my mother's love of old movies and movie stars. I mean, who can look at a black-crowned Night-heron and not see Edward G. Robinson?" We said our goodbyes. Mrs. Teale had to go and I stayed put absorbing our conversation.

My dream is now in our wake-a-day world. I moved it here, hoping to join all the people working toward protecting and stewarding ecosystems throughout the 197 million square miles of earth. Let's call ecosystems ecos, all right? We have ecos all over the place. We're basically, overrun with them. As my mother would say, 'We're lousy with 'em.' I want to be part of this effort so these dreams have to cross the highway between realities too. And I hope that many others can see its connection to our lives and protect the path, steward bird and wildlife as if all the hope and beauty in the world, and everyone you love and ever loved, and every delight and joy you've ever had and hope to enjoy again, depend upon doing this. Many share this dream. The more we share our dreams, the more they can inform our choices. There is hope. Corridors of hope. And some of them begin on Main Street and lead you to the wetlands if you have a guide who has at heart you're getting lost.

a wind memory

It's now been two summers past the summer since Virg joined the Crow Women. Her absence feels as obvious and present as the warmth I feel from the sun on my bare arms. We were the only two people I knew who went swimming so early in the season. I needed the sun; at least, if the air temperature wasn't very warm. I'd always try on Memorial Day but together, some seasons, we'd even try earlier. Every time I entered the water for the first time in the season thoughts of Virg came through like the searing, sharp pain of a paper cut. It hurt but it was razorlike and quick. Elements of the seasons travel through my emotions like most everyone. This last season, when I went into the ocean for the first time. the automatic words 'I miss her' came to my lips, But these days I try to quickly follow that she is present to me in different ways. Because she told me to. I can enter the journey-lands to be near. I may not be able to see her or communicate with her at will there, but I am in a world that she is also in.

    I remember walking into the ocean for my first swim after Virg passed that July. I just cried. I faced the horizon and sobbed. Grief is a line much like the horizon. It moves. You end up covering more ocean before you get closer and you can see the distance you travelled but you most likely won't know how much more travel you to have to go. The horizon is always beckoning you out further. Virg did not go for a swim with me every time I went for a swim. But this particular time I entered the ocean knowing that

I wouldn't swim with her again. It was difficult. It was tender beautiful too. I searched the sky for hunting osprey. I acknowledged the horizon. We too have become old friends.

what holds us to the world

I stopped at the wetlands this one day, after another soulless day at the job, to refuel. So to speak. I wearily looked downriver to see what I could see. The sun off the ice felt like glare when I first went there. But then it turned to a welcoming light. Wasn't much there, a few mallards hugging the sand bar just inside the bowl of the river. But I had my bins, so I scanned across the way. Checked the trees. I'm familiar with the trees the eagle will perch on down by the old osprey platform. Not there. I scanned from left to right, from the tree line of the osprey platform to just past the eagle's nest. And then I lowered my search and scanned the next level down from right to left. That's when I saw the eagle. Each time, so beautiful. It filled my heart, so I could head home.

I headed back to the car slowly and told the guys in the parking lot that I saw the eagle. One of them heard me first and repeated what I said to the other,

"The eagles are going to think those are something to eat." I pointed at their devices, I think they were small cameras and sound recorders.

'Oh eagles' the one said.

And the other fellow said, 'What did she say?"

And when he heard I said 'eagles and they're really here', he broke out into a big smile and said to me, "Really?"

"Yes, just down that way and they're watching you."

We belong to the world by who and what we love. Whether a person, an animal or a place, this is how we belong to the world. Dragons came to this world and are held by birds. The dragon that came into my head that day on the highway in Connecticut, maybe it made a wrong turn but it introduced me early on to dragons. I'm glad I finally made the connections I now have. I went kicking and screaming the whole way really, considering how many realities it took for me to know about them. I mean, in the journey-lands I was watching dragons watching birds; but in the wake-a-day world I watch birds and look for where they might be otherwise engaged when they're not flying. Until recently, I never thought that dragons are watching them too and even riding their dreams the way I ride the waves.

~ ~ ~

Like a river, all of us have more than one source that feeds us in every reality. We have our mothers and fathers. We have everyone that came before them. The piece that was always missing for me was that we are all a part of earth and we're all connected. Somewhere back in our histories, even when, evolutionarily speaking, we went one way, on land, and birds took to the air, we remained connected. Such divergent paths but the one source, one very large ecos, the earth. With birds on every continent.

Part of what holds me to this world is otherworldly. It's a physical sense of connection with other realms. It's the teachers and guides I've met who have embraced me. I'm also held by other beings who have become a community. I am held to this world by my beliefs grounded by my experiences. I'm held by my hopes and memories. I'm also held because I want to know more about the Old Woman, I want to spend more time with Grandmother, to have more meals with Lynn, to spend more time watching Molly sleep. To have and love time with friends and some family who remain. I'm held to the world when I hear early morning bird calls that thread the air with their sounds as I sip my tea. I do like my comforts. I'm held to the wake-a-day world by what I love here. Sometimes I'm aware that I'm held by the light and shadows, the predictable and the unpredictable joy that will get me laughing out loud, say when Molly seems to be confused by her four paws when she's cleaning, as I always imagined I would be confused with four legs. I often tell her I'm doing inventory as I count her paws. I don't know how she manages.

  As it's true for ecos and biomes it's also true for all our realities, they inform each other. One reality without the others can be barren or dangerous. They won't be a healthy. Of course there are highways between realities. Would you expect anything less? I mean, sometimes I'm overwhelmed with a sense of despair when someone has passed, or when this world has more muscle than memory and doesn't respect wildlife. But there are days when joy moves like the murmuration of starlings and bounces like the light creating the shadows and reflections on the streams within streams at the wetlands. I'm not sure why, but I also want to keep in mind that rivers can have many sources. It seems so important.

Then I wondered if my feathers also had more than one source.

broken and holding ~ 22

I'm sitting at my desk squeezing the coils of my brain for any memories of dragons before one came into my skull. Nothing's coming. I keep whatever is currently a part of my writing life and focus on the bookshelf that hangs over my desk. I have an old wooden box with a hook and eye that separates two groups of books and files on the shelf. I can't remember where I acquired this. It has faint white block letters on it that I can't make out. Inside, I keep the broken pieces of my mother's favorite Johnson Bros. rose chintz (made in England). This china arrived at our home when I was a kid. It made such an impression on me because my mother fussed over it so much. There wasn't much that we had by way of fine and I never knew her to care about such things. The Johnson Bros. rose pattern changed all that. Every piece of it has become a memory hologram bringing my mom back to me. There's an artform in Japan about joining broken pieces of pottery with lacquer embedded with gold dust so that the joints appear to be gold when they are connected. This is gold joinery. Part of this art is about embracing flaws.

    I sit with pieces of my mother's china. My mother, who brought schmatas down a notch through her redesign of the sleeves to sleeveless with her terrible sewing job made worse by her really bad eyesight. Schmatas, literally rags in Yiddish, were the house dresses she wore all the time. It was her signature look. She would tear off the sleeve or even partial sleeve the schmata came with and sew a very large baste stitch around the arm holes. She had to cut out the little bit of sleeve because they made her too hot. She toiled in the kitchen a lot. She schvitzed if the schmata had arms. Cut the arms and sew the sleeve like Dr. Frankenstein's monster, why don't ya, Lena? That was my mom, transforming house dresses back to the rags they once were. Frankenstein's sew job. Not rose chintz. But then there is the evidence that she too loved fine things. I have tried to find ways to join my memories and keep those I miss in my life. These memories are some of the fine things I have now. I love the Johnson china. Like everyone I suppose, I reengage with memories when something wakes them up. They change as I change. It might be true that memory is a river. It should achieve personhood as well. Time is the gold that ties memories together. Sometimes they fit and the bowl or the cup look like they can hold water again. Sometimes, seeing the break and where I glued them, although I have not put gold in the glue, reminds me even more so of my mother. It's her schmatas that I understand more than her china. But both belong to her.

   To join sometimes means to meet up with and go along. If you're a part of the stream, you flow along. Maybe you'll meet up with the ocean. Joining is also a way to bring pieces back together. But I gather that it is not always about repairing what is broken. The same day the Johnson Bros. came into our kitchen in Newark on Fabian Place, so too did we get a new kitchen pull down lamp and a red and white striped pull down shade, both of which snapped up if you yanked down on them. Just the kind of trick memory plays on us. We pull them down and they go in an unexpected direction.

~ ~ ~

I was trying to puzzle out things I had no control over. The way my mind works, I ask questions and move ideas around until they feel as if they're lined up and make sense. My mother's broken china led me to thinking about the Old Woman. I wanted to know more about her. Honestly, that's why I was thinking about golden joinery; about why things that are broken can still function as they were meant to. It's because of the break in contact with my mentor, because of the break with my friend Virg, because of the break in my mother's china, right there in front of me where I spend most of my time pondering, that I thought about the Old Woman. That's why I wanted to know more about her. Because of the breaks.

~ ~ ~

The sheer poetry of the Japanese practice of mending with gold captured my imagination. All of these thoughts brought me to the idea broken is also about wholeness. I mean, it brings me to my mother, to golden sunlight bouncing on water. To the season when the osprey return. My three season bird, arriving just as spring does, hanging through the summer and leaving just before fall is pulled into winter.

Viola's question

My feathers show through the spaces from one buttonhole to the next. There must be a word for these spaces. I cannot join them with gold. Borders, edges, where things join, these places always draw me near. I'm not sure why. Audre Lorde, the great poet and activist, too long gone from this world and only recently acknowledged for her contributions, was an out, gay, black woman. My god, could she wield words and strike the heart. It has been true from my experience that those knowing their power can also show the easiest gentleness. She wrote "...that visibility which makes us most vulnerable is that which also is the source of our greatest strength." It is true about coming out. How vulnerable. Every time we show our love, no matter to who or what, we are vulnerable. Some more so than others depending upon who holds power. Deliberate vulnerability is bold. I feel gentle about my feathers, those that slip through the buttonholes, and those that warm my midsection. I feel not so much that I want to hide them. In some circles it would be weird, or highly unusual, suspect even, to have feathers if you're not a bird. It could also be a tease to the wind. I'm more concerned about the wind's good opinion. But I know that the wind will not take them or me aloft. I have tried. For those feathers that poke through the buttonholes might be like the spirits that can travel between worlds during dusk and dawn. These openings that we have, where we are most vulnerable, might be where we are most free.

Imagine little Edens in all the small pockets between distinct locations we are familiar with. The park, the river, my backyard, the empty lot across the street from you, or the one you pass by on the way to the market. Maybe the spaces between my buttonholes, where the feathers are finding a way through the two sides of my shirts, are providing a glimpse of an Eden. I want to remember my first reaction to new openings. It is unfettered joy. In other words, feathered, not unfeathered. It can move freely. Even fly. Feathers finding a way past an enclosure makes sense to me. The space between the buttonholes, the veil between the worlds, the edge of the marsh next to the road, Eden. How then would we treat each other knowing we're just a step away from something sacred when we move or find ourselves in an unfamiliar place?

    Viola's question tickles me. Viola, dressed like a man, landed on an unknown shore. She asked the first person she saw what land it was. Illyria she was told. "What shall I do in Illyria?" she said. The question tickles me because I have fancied myself a tomboy and such a question of vulnerability is, or was, so unlike me. It is also so unlike me to ask anyone I know this question. Feathers coming through my buttonholes may be one way to ask, 'What shall I do in Illyria?' that feels just about right this time in my life. The question is new again since I found a dragon in my head. Experience is like the surf, it churns the content and questions of our lives. Ways to ask may find us before we find them.

you might not know

You might not know to mourn. You might not know to pause and allow the grief. After all, the birds you see still soar. You might not know to feel the hollow ache of loss for bodies of water or animals and fish that have gone extinct. After all, the eagle still guards the river. You might not know the empty free fall through total darkness, where the wolves of time and industry have poisoned the land and put particles into the air fouling everything, your lungs and the brain cells of our children sullied, literally, polluted by these chemicals and fallout. After all, the otters still sneak past the mystery of the river.

the Great Kibbitzen

I fell asleep at my desk but then when I woke up I knew I needed to head to the journey-lands. And so I did, with the intention of seeing the Old Woman again. Last time I saw the Old Woman she asked me if I wrote yet. "Silly girl, silly," were her last words to me when I replied I did and wasn't sure about the fate of my writing.

    I walked down the same path I often do to enter my journey-lands. Everything was familiar but I was pulled to turn right. I never went in that direction before. Once I turned, there was enough room to navigate my body between the bushes and shrubs, but just barely. I felt drawn toward this direction. I usually let things unfold and don't have that sense of purpose in the journey-lands. In moments, I came upon a large rock. I was about to go around it to the left when I heard voices. One of them, then another, sounded familiar. But none of what I was doing was familiar. So, I decided to ease my way around the rock. It was about four feet high but smooth as a pebble at the surf's edge. My hands made no noise as I used them to guide me and slide me too, around the rock. I had a feeling that if I weren't careful, I could be seen before I wanted to be. I held back before the rock's curve would reveal me. And I listened.

It sounded like the Old Woman, aka the old one, talking in a scratchy voice, as if she were irritated with the words, she said, "The jam, the raga. She can be moved in the right direction. She has to follow this and not the foolish whining nebbish head."

I had to see what was going on. Who would the old one be talking to like that? Jam? Raga? Thinking that my stillness also granted me invisibility, I peered past the rock and saw the Old Woman, Grandmother, and two other women I didn't recognize. I could tell that when Grandmother responded to the old one, she was taking in the irritation and trying to agree, but also turning the current just a tad. She said, as she slowly threaded a needle, "I would tell her, jam, raga, be brave," nodding her head toward the old one, smiling as she added, "don't be a nebbish head," then pausing to emphasize these words, "trust the energy."

They all listened to the silence after that, including the old one but she always returned her gaze up toward the trees. It didn't seem rude, just the natural inclination of her attention.

But then, wait, they were all sewing. It finally entered my consciousness that they were all sewing. Each had a needle with a wooden handle in their hands. I've seen needles like that before for mending canvas sails. I noticed this when one of the ladies I didn't know reached into a pile of white-grey feathers. She lifted the feather in front of her face and eyed the quill part. And then she pushed the needle through and held the feather against a body before nodding her head, agreeing with her placement, and began to sew the feather on.

They were sewing feathers on someone. But they were real feathers and real needles. I could see the points. They were kibbitzen and sewing. Lynn told me how she used to lay on the floor and watch her grandmother and her great aunts sew the sequins and beads onto the piecework dresses they had. This is how many Italian women in the Bronx would earn some money. Piece work. These women in my journey-lands were kibbitzing the way my mother and her friends would when they played cards or Maj Jong. If there was an alternate energy source made from these gatherings it could feed the world, saving people and economies. Or perhaps, that is how women get all that they do done while communing.

"This one would like to think," the Old Women said, actually pointing in my direction, "that dragons especially love tomboys." The two women I didn't know responded like a Greek chorus, "Even now? Still?"

"Yes, now. Yes, still." She still sounded annoyed. But then she smiled. And she looked up. Oh, and she swayed. They may have all moved. It seems they touched shoulders now and then more for affection, but perhaps they all swayed. But the old one, and mind you, none of them were young, she definitely swayed. And she smiled when she looked up. All of this counter to the tone of her voice. Maybe I misread her tone all this time.

  There was talk I couldn't hear. It seemed like they all took turns imitating something they overheard. One lady said, "Dragons melt into the other half that called to them. That's why you can't see them." Then they all laughed, even the old one, as she looked around the group and laughter just bubbled from her lips. Even Grandmother took in a deep breath and bellowed laughter when she could no longer hold it in. Then they were quiet and involved in their sewing. There was a pile of feathers on either side of them. And the other woman I didn't know, started to laugh as she tried to get out these words, each word spit out with laughter, "Their motto is to walk into a world and leave no trace. As if we couldn't see their footprints." They could not stop the sounds of agreement, and the false irritation they tried to evoke with harumphitude. For some reason, that too was funny. And then they quieted and sewed. There was no hurry. This was like a coffee klatch, a ravioli making session. Let not to the marriage of true minds admit feathers. But feathers? They were sewing feathers on someone and I could not be certain, but if you asked me who was lying there, while they kibbitzed and sewed and joked, I'd say it was me. I don't know how that's possible. Or how that could work. But I saw myself lying there. And more than that, I realized one of the old women I didn't know, was a male. I had seen him before too. He was known as Shen. Soul. Shen was sewing with the women. All of them seemed to hold some kind of deference to the old one; not enough to change their behavior except for this one thing I noticed. They all paused if she spoke or if they spoke they looked to her first for a reaction.

    Grandmother said, "This tomboy had a great mother." They were all interested in knowing this. "But who", the two chimed, Shen and the other woman. Grandmother continued, "She was called Lena."

    "Oh", they all said, even the old one. The woman I didn't know said, "We loved Lena." "We did," my Grandmother added. And then the old one added in a sweet voice, almost sing-songy, but no edge, "Why? Because she would often say, "Nu?!" And they all laughed again. They laughed, they swayed, they sewed more feathers.

    And the woman I didn't know but began to see as someone I would like to know, added, when they could catch their breath from laughing, "And we knew, because she could always be surprised with learning something. That Lena." They all nodded their heads as if to say, 'Yes, that Lena.'

    "We love that," the Old Woman said.

    And that was that because something made a sound. Molly? I was pulled out of the journey-lands. I was at my desk. I knew something about my feathers now. They had another source but never one I'd have guessed.

talking to the river ~ 23

I went down to the river to talk to the spirits that be. And I realized that all this time here at the bulwarks, wailing and moaning, praying and talking to everyone I knew and loved, whether alive or not - but never present, talking to Skunk and my mentor, to Virg, everyone and anyone who would listen, the eagles, all this time, the mucky muck, the mud, and the river - heard everything. Everything. I thought at first that the river never spoke to me but how often did I address Shark River, known as Nolletquesset by the Lenape, the indigenous peoples in this area, specifically, directly? I love this river and feel a sense of intimacy with it. I never would have thought a river would be one of my close ones, my karass, but it is, it is one of my deep soul friends.

dear river,
At one point, I remember thinking you might tell this story. This is my story but it feels just as true that every story I might want to tell about the osprey, and dragons, would also be fine if you narrated it. Each day I come to you is linked by the skies and the trees, no matter how they are dressed. Every time I drive by, my eyes are drawn to the area that opens to the bowl of the river. You're the bowl, you're the river. And you're the opening. I might focus on the sky or search for the eagles, but you're always there.

    You know the way people go, "Oh, it's a seagull." As if it were nothing. For me, I go, "There's the osprey." Or "There's the eagle." As if you weren't there too. Seeing might be believing. But sometimes it also seems to be parsing and pulling things out of context.

~ ~ ~

Strikes me that my life is also like a river. With no clear path, somehow, I managed to follow your ways and meandered. Maybe that is why I am always heading to the ocean. Maybe that is why I'm attracted to dragons. And osprey, the original water dragon. During Chinese New Year celebrations, the street dragons meander in celebration of life and for hope that the new year will bring joy and prosperity. All meandering leads somewhere and sediments of all sorts come along with it. Each time the sediments come down through a rivers' meanders it eventually spills onto a plain. Not all sediment is rich like the Fertile Crescent.

The river travels to the ocean. I have thought that a river is like a daughter, like Persephone; and the ocean is her mother, like Demeter. Now, I wonder if the roles are reversed or if like all roles in relationships, they shift as they move through time. River daughters are taking care of their mother ocean. And the ocean then takes care of the rivers. Mysteries still remain in the deep ocean. Some believe they might be known to the rivers when they journey back as rain through the water cycle, believing that knowledge comes through transformation. The salmon may know these mysteries. Isn't it like a river to call the tide into its faraway places? So far away that even the vernal ponds dream of whales, and spring peepers call like the mighty roar of waves as they lay their eggs in the cedar waters' shade.

~ ~ ~

My Avon osprey, the pair that saved me last spring, were not here when I thought they should be. I loved finding them last year. Compared to the cell tower, I can sit in my car and clearly see them and the nest. It's on a human scale unlike the tower providing cell service to a vast area. They were on a mere wooden powerline pole. They were the early ones and their calls to each other were the best medicine. They finally came this year. Late like my cell tower osprey. Was I projecting that the male looked exhausted? If he had just arrived, he could have been flying for hundreds of miles over the last week. He arrived first, she arrived the next day. I saw them both on the powerline pole but it no longer had remnants of their nest they had used for several years.

Last year, I watched him vie for her favors by dropping sticks on the nest. Over the winter, just before the day I start looking for my cell tower osprey, I saw something so disturbing. The power company had put an angled cover on the top of their pole to protect the components on either end of the flat crosspiece. It was designed to stop the osprey from nesting there again. When my Avon osprey joined up, after their long journey from the south, they tried but could not add to the nest that used to winter over and they could not start another on their site. I could see where they tried. There were small branches caught here and there amongst the wires and cables. There were a lot of them at the base of the pole on the parking lot. Nothing stuck. Their attempts all failed.

They disappeared for days. I searched up and down Railroad Avenue. I'd go as far as Belmar, one town south, over the bridge and back. I searched through Avon streets near the old nest site looking for any flat sites where they might drop sticks successfully to build. I searched every day for two weeks. The only suitable surface I could find was the massive water tower nearest Bradley Beach, the town north of Avon. It's Bradley, Avon, and then Belmar. The eagles at the Bradley water tower had displaced the osprey that nested there the year before. They were still commanding that site. Eagles. I see them now and then hunting Bradley. Can you believe it? My mother would go, "Nu?"

The Avon osprey were gone.

~ ~ ~

Fog creates an immediate sense of intimacy with you, my river. Especially, in the early morning. Driving over the wetlands bridge to work, I look to my left to see the fog embrace your surface. The feeling my eyes take in reminds me of waking in bed and speaking to Lynn. Such comfort and easy intimacy. Swans often gather in large groups near my bulwarks when there's fog. Their white feathers a neon light.

~ ~ ~

I suppose I should talk to you the same way I would talk to those I love and miss; with the same desire to share what's been happening, knowing my words are heard by someone who gets all the nuances and context. That's what relationship history does for you.

I could talk to you as I would to the eagles across the way. I know the eagles see me better than I can see them. How much do you see?

All the reflections you provide could be a kind of talking. I know there is more than the mere telling of the place. For all these reflections I've come to look for take me beyond the reflections you capture on your waters.

~ ~ ~

Words report or describe. They share history and stories. They document. They can make you laugh or cry. They honor moments and commemorate. They have legal jobs and duties. They warn and remind.

I'm also aware that they may not capture what we were immersed in when using them to share our story. There's sometimes enough of whatever it is in some words to help us bring up the nap of the experience. Words are like sunlight on water. They may touch us deeply. They can sometimes be like a boat riding over the light. They convey us and we are also touched by the light as a leaf or piece of driftwood might be. Words, colors on canvasses, songs, may all come close to all that we want to share. No words can fly for months over the ocean like Wisdom. No words can build an osprey nest on a wooden powerline pole. No words can roll like the ripples over the surface of the water caused by a stone I plunk. They can't really tell anyone, least of all you, the impact of that stone.

Whenever I come by the bulwarks, often to plead, sometimes to just be, you are here. I don't often take notes. It's too much of a distraction.

Makes me feel removed from where I want to be. *'How many plovers on your mud? How many redwings swaying on the phragmites? How many herons were in that rookery?'* Counting and accounting does not allow me to be here. I know this. Yet, reporting bird populations as a citizen scientist might provide valuable information about bird populations. So, I count. Sometimes. But, I was just so involved in being here, I put down the pad and pen. I have no notes. I do not remember what all the deep good feeling was about. Something happened. Let's call it peace through osmosis.

~ ~ ~

The blessed unknown walk among us. Unknown to us, maybe even unknown to you, my river. And they are unknown to each other. But is it just that they walk? Could they be the fish that make the small bell sounds as their movements splash your surface? Could you be one of the sacred ones? Most of my life I have told others that I'm an ocean person. A beach person. That I ride waves. I body surf. Even more true, but I haven't said this to anyone, I'm a river person. You are my river. I have to wonder if all of us belong to a river in some way. If a spider's silk is a part of its mind, what am I to you and you to all who swim, fish and kayak in your waters? Eagles and osprey are part of your mind. They plunge and dive and fly away with their fish more than any angler I've seen here. What about the crabs I see, scrabbling from one muddy plug by the bulwarks to another? Your mind also has crabs and mud puckers and gurgles. What a mind! Sacred, and tidal. Muddy and flowing.

Some Jewish traditions talk about the concealed ones, the righteous men, the 36 who are dispersed throughout the world. Like the 36 righteous ones representing a higher connection to soul, you sustain the world. I think they include women and rivers. Unknown to us, unknown to each other and they also do not know they are one of the 36. If someone claims to be one of the Lamed-Vavnik, they are not.

The Lamed-Vavnik are connected to a great source of sacredness. You're connected to the ocean. And to me, that is the great source of sacredness I've known all my life. Every day, you may not know this, but every day it is possible you're in contact with one of the sacred ones. The possibility exists. I believe one of the 36 could be an osprey nesting near. What if one of the Lamed-Vavnik is the snapping turtle over there, sunning itself on the wet wood stuck on the sandbar?

Once I learned about the Lamed I knew the number of them might also be unknown. In Hebrew the letter lamed is 30 and vav is six. That's where the 36 comes from. But sacredness does not have a limit. I like to think that the Lamed-Vavnik is a door. Open the door and you see a blue dragon is also one of the sacred. Whale sharks swimming up the river, a sacred one.

In any given congregation of plovers, our piping plovers one of the most endangered shore birds, there might be a Lamed-Vavnik blown about by the wind, invisible against the sand it has for a nest.

~ ~ ~

I want to know my time here matters. What do you say to that, my river? You're tidal, right? The tide goes out and you're all mud. Is that what happens to us when our life is gone? I'd like to think that we're tidal too. It seems like a good way to be in the world. When I'm all mud, plugs that make giant sucking sounds when they're pulled because everything is a struggle, I could remind myself the water will come back and I will be fulfilled again. Or that my mentor will return and if she doesn't all that she's shared with me is a part of my water cycle.

    There's something anonymous about you even though you are right there, right there with wind painting your surface and the occasional fish breaking through or the sunnies running rivulets while the herons chase them. You keep the water cycle going. We are taught that life is movement. But stillness can also host life. Both movement and stillness are a part of your presence. The deceptive stillness is invoked in me even when the tide is moving your water.

~ ~ ~

You wouldn't say if you were anything special. By me saying you're a poor excuse for a river, which is how I've often described you, only to the uninitiated, only to those, I have not given you the respect all rivers should have. Whatever part of a river we come to, we should all know it's most likely a part of a large body of water with many phases and ways of being. I'm very familiar with your meanders by my wetlands. I know you widen out to a bowl and beyond to an opening where the boats go. Sharks have been known to wander in from the ocean. Whole schools of fish, especially the menhaden, have sought refuge in your waters. You are always more than I see. You just let me talk my fool head off all the time. You don't send any waves to sweep me under. Your reflections sometimes do give me pause. Is that how you hold your hand up? Is that how you say, '*Be still. Listen.*"? You might have noticed my easy willingness to talk to any and everything, even the phragmites. I have spoken to the phragmites fallen by the cold and ice, to the tufts catching the first March winds and those that obscure the path where we can ease our kayaks into your water. I do try to be quiet and speak with respect.

But somehow, I rarely have addressed you directly.

Everyone I meet here has a story about you, about something that they've seen in you or floating or on the sandbars you embrace.

You remind me, even by your neap silence, the space you hold between tides, your rest period, that stillness holds an opportunity for merging with our understanding of the themes that move through our life. Finally, I recognize how often the stories of Demeter and Persephone persist in speaking to me. I miss my mother so much. And I understand that when I'm near you the story is invoked within me. You, as well as me, are in relationship with your mother. Does your mother, like mine tends to do now, run with the herds across the tundra? Or play cards in an ongoing game of kalookie with more cards than you can hold?

I haven't asked you about the nights. The stars. The clouds coming down to your surface. Or how you experience a heavy rain when the osprey's observations are falling into you with each drop off their oily feathers.

    I'm sure that what I see is not all that there is of you. Currents run through you. Who knows what travels with them? Those smooth as mercury areas on your surface, another way you express yourself, possibly even a part of your evolving. Fish must continually pass beneath your surface unseen. Diving ducks must tickle your waters as they forage for eel grass. The low winds sometimes briefly, sometimes for hours, touch you. When I can see the winds touching your surface I'm reminded of the skimmers who come round late summer methodically tracing the waters near the bridge with their orange and black beaks. I noticed that they fly one behind the other and now I'm wondering if that's another form of cooperative hunting.

    The sounds I recognize as conversation from a human never come from you. I know, because I wait and listen, just as some who fish seem to listen for a response from their line in the water. It's silly. Possibly. I mean, there are times I feel that others, such as Grandmother, speak to me inside my head. She speaks to my inner hearing. That might be my most intimate, accepting self. For what I hear carries the weight of many realities. This is how I wait for you to speak to me as well.

    I have come here to plead quite often. I stand or sit on the worn and splintered wood of the bulwark, hoping I don't get a splinter in my ass as I plead for others, for everything connected the birds' wellbeing. I come here for my friends and family, and for myself. Never knew till now that asking on behalf of someone meant to be on their side. You are where I come to plead. On this side.

      Sometimes people will ask me what I've seen by you that day. They mean what birds or wildlife have I seen. I always know where to look for the eagle, and when the seasons are right, for the osprey. I don't tell them that sometimes I see the river stirred by the heron's pokes, or that the little fish came by sprinkling your surface with bell sounds. I hope they don't need me to tell them how you always catch the light. It would be nice if they see that on their own. Side by side with my yearning, I recognize that loss is pulled into the weave of your light. You have shown me, sometimes by the smooth slicks on your surface where I'd hope answers would form, that wishes fly into the clouds you reflect, not necessarily into the shapes I'd like.

~ ~ ~

I wanted to pronounce, 'Now in this time of legacy...' as if something magnificent was about to take place, like a jousting match for the princess' hand, or more apropos, a blue dragon about to walk to center stage where it will look at the waiting crowd along the shoreline, then slide its tail splashing the water between each sandbar so that it catches the sun and creates a rainbow spray. Then the dragon will project a moving image for us of the long voyage the dragons took to come to earth. Then it will show us the early days when they flew from one area to the next until they saw their first birds and love rippled through all of them like collective goosebumps. They knew they found home.

Instead of this show, a memory sailed into my heart-mind. It was the memory of my mother walking away from our apartment in Wayside after the guidance counselor called her about me. The counselor was asking permission to contact an out-of-state school I was interested in because my friend Joan went there. This call was a shock to my mother's system. It hurt her so much because my mother was in the middle of nowhere. That's what our suburb felt like to us. She didn't drive. There would be miles of walking before she might find a bus that wouldn't take her anywhere she'd know anyway. She was upset that I was considering leaving her. And I was totaled. I didn't know what kinds of feeling I was having but not one was good. Today, I understand the sense of being abandoned she must have felt. The isolation and the hole in her existence. It would have been the last straw after moving to nowhere from Newark. A widow with one child still at home to add context to her days. It is an awful feeling. I sometimes go through this even now for those I love who have died and seemingly taken with them ways I know the world and how to be in it. For the talks I sorely miss with them. And the card games. For my mentor. Still gone. For the osprey, not here yet.

In this time of legacy I want to help the birds because they touch every part of earth. I want to know that osprey will always return and the path of their migration will always be protected. We have seen so much loss of habitat that I know this is a

concern for many creatures. For the osprey, the management of the menhaden fishing industry is a key element for their survival. I am not going out of state to a college. I am not going to disappear into the suburbs. I'm standing here talking to my river. Rivers are daughters and mothers. Our veins are rivers. Our hearts the opening. Our minds are rivers, our thoughts the disturbances on the surface. I never did leave my mother. She left me. But I find her over and over again when I come here. For that, for the home you provide my osprey, for the beauty all around, your many voices, and for your good ear, I am grateful.
with deep respect and gratitude,
Leaping Lena's daughter

the conversation ~ 24

I wish my heart pumped clouds. Or that I could blow cloud rings and dance all day to the music of shade and hush, jumping in and out of the rings. 'Did I ever tell Mrs. Teale about the hush on my way to the new office?' A shaded, winding road that brought me into a place of joy. There were certain trees I'd wish a good morning. I'd call out to the people driving south on the Garden State Parkway, 'Welcome to the Jersey Shore.' And those driving North, I'd tell them to have a good day, play nice, and return home safe. The hush was before the Parkway overpass where the trees formed a canopy over the road. That's crown shyness in action. I'm sure I told her about that. I called it the hush because everything quieted within me. The shade was velvet. Peace seeped into every place in me that needed it on that stretch of the road. A group of pine trees were divided by a street on the left. The first group was the larger, the second group clearly once belonged to them. I'd say "Good morning" to the first group and "Hi kids!" to the smaller one. They were a part of a quiet joy that felt like all awareness was a slide on moss. Quiet, smooth, inviting shade. Hush.

liminal

It was official at three in the morning today, I couldn't sleep. Mrs. Teale was six hours away from my wetlands. Anticipation. Excitement. Memories. Three a.m. is a good time to review dreams and conversations. I could be wrong, but 3 a. m. is the time of liver in the acupuncture clock. It's a cleansing organ. The meridian is not the organ but it's the system of travel for this particular kind of energy. People have followed systems of energy for thousands of years. The Chinese associate times of day with each meridian. I have not read deeply enough but wonder if events, such as how and when a dragon will show up, might be a part of the meridian clock.

    When I finally gave up on sleep I started to recall the first encounters with Mrs. Teale. She called herself by many names, sometimes just signing emails with "Mrs. Marsh." I referred to her many ways as well, mostly calling her my marsh buddy because she and I both identified with salt marshes. Salt marshes call to me. This surprises me since I always thought of myself as an ocean person. Something in me reaches out to salt marshes whenever I'm go to mine or another salt marsh or when I see one driving by. Even when I see an image of one. I could dissolve into a salt marsh as if my experience of crown shyness was bridging the gap between me and the marsh. I feel no separation from this landscape.

    Mrs. Teale was an energy healer before she began traveling through the seasons with Mr. Teale. We became friends through a shamanic group. We shared journey experiences. We also got to the quick of things right off. She wrote me about the deep pains in her family life. Some pains push out on their own like nails release from old wood. She was working some of those nails loose when we first connected. Some days were easier than others she'd say. All relationships challenge the heart and can cause aches that are hard to ease. And family pains, whether love that was never there or betrayal, are difficult to overcome. They leave holes. And you know how the song goes, "We all have holes to fill." One hard day, cause nobody could express the heart pain as well as she could, I asked her if she would write a book and call it *Sucking Rocks and the Road to Being Embraced*. We all have to suck rocks sometimes. We are sometimes, as Elinor Wylie wrote "hard beset and we live by squeezing from a stone what little nourishment we get." Mrs. Teale texted back, "All I want is to cuddle. To feel someone's arm around me that knows how to generate the kind of love you can sink into like moss in deep shade. I want to slip through the umbrella of a Japanese maple and pretend that my world embraces me."

~ ~ ~

Mrs. Teale and I were prone to text banter. I used to do this with Virg and missed that play so dearly. Virg and I often texted about UFOs and weather. Nothing is better than weather texts. The UFOs, those we really experienced and those that were, upon discovery, industrial lights, had me peeing in my pants for the sheer clumsiness of my fingers and the interpretations that Virg would offer from my alphabet soup's poor excuse for a text showing up on her cell. One night through my kitchen window, I happened to catch an odd light move toward my next door neighbor's yard. Then it backed off. Then it came forward again. What are the odds I'd happen to catch this? Of course, I was texting Virg immediately. She offered I should duck when it came near, and to guard my thoughts. I offered that this was friggin' amazing. And then learned, the next morning, it was the kind of amazing caused by a neighbor's son operating his drone for the first time. Close call but no cigar and no close encounter.

Mrs. Teale and I would play a game we called Dead Woman's Poker. Played with a river card. Three eco topics that rip our hearts out and pull our souls out of their sockets. The river card was always Nolletquesset.

So the poker went like this – my hand: climate change, water pollution, big oil. River card. Her hand: acid rain, hunger, lead in drinking water. The river card. Her hand won the Dead Woman's Poker because she ended with the current disaster, lead in drinking water, we brought on our most vulnerable, including children in major cities suffering permanent brain damage from lead in their water. It just should not be.

Then we'd have to switch to Wild Woman Calls. We'd yell these. So, all caps if we were typing, all out yells if we were together or on the phone. This antidote to the Dead Woman's Poker hands called for invocations or any words that Dylan Thomas might say describes the "force that through the green fuse drives." You know, life giving, or as some might say, "To hell with it all, go for it".

We both needed an antidote to all the bad news those categories brought to our shores. I mean, sometimes it felt like unending waves of bad news.

The Wild Woman's Calls offered total release of our pent up anger, frustration, and fears. The root for this catharsis means to cleanse. We're cleaning up our act. Preparing the way. And then, we pour out energy into the skies. We weave in and out of each other's images, songs, and fragments of concerns. There were no rules, except to be all out.

~ ~ ~

I often talk to the dead. Especially, when I'm going on errands and alone in the car. And those times I'm overcome with missing my mother. I just go deeper than whatever that lower chakra is and yell, "MA!!!!!!!!!!!!!!!!!!!!!!!!!" because it brings me right in line with my pain. It's how I called her when I was a kid. "Ma." So, yes, one of my wild woman calls is calling for my mother. She's on the tundra with the herds of elk. What, my mother on the tundra? Well, I bet she's often playing cards with her friends. So, I have to yell loud enough to reach her. And when it's long and loud enough, I feel the connection. And the longing, the missing, the hole that can't be filled, eases up.

Truth is, I've also called out the names of friends that have passed. I don't spare the gods and goddesses my recriminations at all. And you should know, curse words work. Nonsensical words work well too. PUSHAPAPA, or YA-YA-YA-YA-YA!!!!! Or if your people have chants, I'm sure they would work as well. We all connect through sound.

~ ~ ~

I reminded Mrs. Teale about the journey experience where Virg was trying to tell me something. I've always been puzzled about what it was. I took a few guesses. I don't think I got it until this talk with Mrs. Teale. Virg was with the Crow Women. Crows have always been a part of my life. When Virg passed, I was moved to learn how much they meant to Virg as well. Recently, they've come to the little birdbath just outside my study window. What a joy, and an honor, to see them there. I love how large they are compared to the common criminals, like the sparrows, nuthatches, finches, and wrens that eat all the seeds and splash in the water or take dirt baths where the sandy soil just can't hold grass. Even the flickers and downies come round to splash and steal seed. Or the hoodlum gangs of starling and grackles taking turns to devour the suet around the front of the house.

    Crows have such great presence. The deep black sheen of their smooth velvet feathers could make you jealous. I remember when velvet was so popular. Now it seems old fashioned in clothing but so right for a young crow's crown. I'm always prone to jealousy of birds. It should be in the DSM. I wondered out loud about this on one of those meandering phone calls Mrs. Teale. I asked her if she thought the sudden appearance of crows was a wake-a-day connection to Virg in the journey-lands. Our calls with each other, where silence was okay, were often non-sequiturs that somehow all tied together even if they floated like fringe on a jacket in the wind.

    We talked about the shocker it would be for anyone who sounded the alarm about our world's ecosystems all in peril early on, to know where we were at today. I used to joke that I'd like to go back in time and show some of the mechanical marvels to the Egyptians. Just for "shits and grins" as my friend Barry might say. But even the thought of going back in time to tell Aldo Leopold what's going on is hard to take. He was already worried 72 years ago about the tearing asunder of our ecosystems. I am sometimes broken and unable to find hope knowing how bad it's been since his warning. "Mrs. Teale, look how long it took for everyone to wake up to this reality and take action. The time thing, goes so fast, doesn't it though?"

Mrs. Teale offered in response to my woefulness, "Yeah, new information, shifts in culture, take generations to absorb." And then she surprised me. "What if your feathers are part of the wake-up call?" I laughed, but she was serious. "Sometimes, we come upon a personal place in our path, whatever you want to call it. We come upon a boundary where we can step into a new place and turn around to look at where we were. It's like being on a border. Even as we are solidly in the world we built for ourselves we can see stepping over to a new place."

"You mean, we make a change? Or, do you mean, we can feel it but we have to step into it?" I replayed this whole conversation while waiting for her to arrive. I'm always waiting for someone. Waiting for my mentor. Wondering why did I only see the dragon that one time? Was that a delusion? No, it wasn't. All this corroborating information, some from an unknown source, some from my journey-lands, which many would find, at their most generous, interesting; and some from Virg's transcriptions of the Oracle's notes on dragons, all of this information countered the idea of it being a delusion. This was real, it happened and new information has surfaced to confirm. And I have to tell Mrs. Teale this, coming into my mind, like a fresh tide, almost daily. I've been getting these hits, sometimes on the *goosebump trail of acknowledgement* that our bodies use as confirmation.

"I mean this," Mrs. Teale had continued. "Feathers growing on your mid-section are something. They're real. The whole world is in peril. That too is real. We are experiencing a world-wide threat. In a sense, more people are working to change the ongoing environmental devastation while many are now aware that we are at a crucial juncture. It can go either way. And, isn't it interesting, that something odd and momentous has begun with you?"

She reminded me of a poet's words, "almost dark, almost dawn." We are all at a juncture in relationship to our world. Whether we want to be or not. Whether we are aware of it or not. Liminal. This was the word that Mrs. Teale used to describe where I was at with my feathers, where the world was at. Almost dark, almost dawn. I thought of Rachel's work over fifty years ago. Her warning was followed by so many others. If heeded then, it would have changed our course. But it wasn't and the projection is critical. Rachel's warning wasn't just followed by others, it was preceded by many. It was the daily knowledge of many people, many communities. But the warnings for the powerful mainstream culture were not enough. Things are so dire now that some say they see the cold night of doom on the horizon. There's climate change. That's the really big one right now. Habitat loss is a part of that. Rising seas threatening most coasts and the most vulnerable. Everything keeps getting subsumed under something more monumental, more frightening. Then we have many individuals and organizations waking up to this. Many working separately to stem the tide. If you step back, you can see some ecosystems being protected, some people talking about preserving so much of the world by this decade and that. People talking about preservation in slogans such as '30 by 30' meaning thirty percent of the United States protected by 2030. Almost dawn.

  "We are in the process of a rite of passage, a crucial moment. All of us are transitional," Mrs. Teale whispered. Then she started singing Marvin Gaye to me as if his words were riding her whispers. I just eased back into my car seat, closed my eyes and listened. "What's going on?," She repeated the phrase over and over, first deep and low, then she'd stretch the words until they morphed into Nina Simone's canticle of rounds in the raga she created with George Harrison's song My Sweet Lord. "Oh my lord. My sweeeeet looord. I really want to know you. I really want to know you lord. Oh my lord. My sweet looord. My, my sweet lord."

~ ~ ~

Almost dark. I've readied for the storms. Almost dawn. Now I can ready for the hope. I admit, sometimes hope is like a crowbar opening the crate. As some of their many jobs, my father and brother Lenny unloaded the boats at Port Newark. Sometimes they brought home "damaged" goods, sometimes they told us stories about the snakes on the banana boats and the rats that wore toolbelts. Crowbars lift many lids, maybe they can lift the lid holding hope down.

~ ~ ~

Walking to the river walks me to a better place. It is not a pilgrimage. But every step brings me closer to the water or mud; or both when the tide is twixt and tween. I've come here so often that whether I'm seeking solace or not, I find that my mood is lifted and I feel more centered. Virg liked it here. I've brought many to this place. Told them that just waiting here brings something special to see. But I know that there doesn't have to be a big event for me to find a deep pleasure here. I have found my home.

~ ~ ~

The river has a presence. I don't make formal introductions when I bring others here. But I think that I should. I will figure out how to do that. It feels rude not to acknowledge this relationship's importance to me and to many others. However we define it, we feel whole with family. I feel whole here. The river is my kin. Although, like many families not everyone always gets along. One time I was moved to sing everything I saw. The big, huge, blue heron was not happy with that. I apologized. It moved away. There were a lot of small birds on a spit across the way. I continued to sing to them. They stayed put. Maybe they couldn't hear me.

~ ~ ~

This land, as all of this country and continent, once belonged to many different groups of people. I feel a sense of belonging when I am here. It is humbling. My family, once immigrants, never had a chance to remain in relationship with their rivers. When I was younger, my relationship to the Jersey shore was something far less than the Lenape people who came here for generations to clam and fish. Some Lenape settled on the rich farmland here at the shore year round. I've met a few of their descendants who call themselves the Sand Hill Indians. My river's first known name is Lenape for "land of good." Nolletquesset, Land of Good. Home of the two rattling kingfishers. Home to the resident eagles for over 12 years. Home to the blue herons that show up for spring. And home to that red-tailed hawk hiding across the way. And that Cooper hawk that tried to get the kingfisher that time. And home to my heart. This river leads right to the ocean waves I like to ride. Maybe there's a path from here in my wetlands, through the streams in the ocean to the Lena River in Russia. I like to say that this is my mother's river. As Mercury is the messenger for the gods, maybe the Gulf Stream is the messenger of this river's connection to the land of good.

~ ~ ~

Every May 27th since I've known her, I would call my mentor to tell her it was Rachel's birthday. "Ah," she would say, "she reminded us that we were separated from our wisdom." I hadn't thought of that. Rachel's alarm was really a reminder, coming from yet another quarter of our world, that everything is connected. The hierarchical structure of the birds of prey put them in peril from the chemicals in our water affecting the fish they ate. This is how our country learned about DDT. Probably the same DDT was sprayed up and down our city blocks to control mosquitos. A friend told me how the kids on his block would run in and out of the spray because it was a summertime, fun activity. DDT was only a reminder that we can't tamper with the ecosystems without ripple effects. But the good that came from DDT, some would offer, wasn't tampering. It was tamping down on mosquitos. However imbalances are created, there is a negative result. The formation of the Environmental Protection Agency was set up to manage these concerns. My mentor would tell me, "The EPA has not connected us to our cultural knowledge." Even if their regulations were followed without all the tricky fixes that corporations tried and try to work their work-arounds to save money, without incorporating the shared knowledge of those that know the lands and cycles, how can anything work right? It's proven over and over again, knowledge of the areas and all in it, the ecos, is necessary. We have to work with and not outside of this wisdom. Law is not culture. Cultural wisdom has depth knowledge; and there's a much better chance that it accounts for all the pieces because it comes from a base of knowing what belongs. That's something we ought to respect. My mentor loved Rachel and knew her wisdom was from the sciences. Rachel Carson was vilified by the chemical industry who touted a different version of science. Yet Rachel is proven right and right again about the passage of toxins from one system to another. I love Rachel because she was able to show mainstream America the connection between DDT and the threat to our large predator birds, including our iconic bald eagle (fish thief though it may be).

My mentor would tell me I was a flooze because I would love this one and then that one. So many women to love. So many flowers in the spring, each my favorite. But the osprey, well, I think my love for them is always un-flooze-like. Although, I have come to love so many osprey, in person and through the cams I can access. I remember reading, "Abundance of wildlife is the norm." Now I know that abundance of love for wildlife is also the norm. You just have to head toward the river you love, or the field, or the community garden. Or even, just look for birds in the nearest piece of sky.

~ ~ ~

I remember the moment when I realized everything was connected. I used to hope I could help clean the oceans. My understanding grew as I did, which was along the same time many realized that ocean pollution, loss of habitat, so many species in danger of extinction, all of this shared a common source and was connected to how much is out of balance. Instead of scrubbing the ocean and rinsing it clean, I had to understand more about the imbalances. Too much of our progress and technology has been about extracting and commodifying nature for products without understanding, or at least, without paying attention to, our impact. And the truth is, that my understanding was part and parceling in the same kind of thinking. Ecos was the path toward understanding. The thingness of itself, Alan Watts might say. If our technologies and those who operate them are after objects or pieces of the earth, we are not seeing wholeness or paying respect to the ecosystems we're traipsing about. And we know this now through so many sources. We know about the rich mitochondrial connection that forests employ to protect themselves. We know the cycle of the salmon, the migration paths of the giant land herds or migrating birds; or the beloved path of the monarch butterfly across North America to its winter home in Mexico. We know where the whales go to sing and mate. We know the osprey rely upon the vast schools of menhaden, as do many industries that use the same fish. We know enough now to see wholeness.

Yet our industries too often work on parting and parceling this to bring our products to market. Eventually, this policy of separation creates problems we all feel. In ghettos, where they have often chosen to place waste treatment plants, the air is so bad that kids sometimes have to stay home from school. Poor people suffer the most immediate, harmful consequences of pollution and climate change. And our wildlife, right along with them. But none of us are immune. Toxic waste goes downstream to all of us. Down to my river, down to the Land of Good.

~ ~ ~

Waves tell you where they've been not where they're going. Sometimes their tracings on the beach seem like echoes because each successive wave of high tide leaves a trace wrack line. You learn to read about the ocean's reach while beachcombing. I can't say the same for dragons. But it might be I have to refine my detection skills. There might be more evidence of their appearances in my life than I can consciously recall. I'd like to know what brought a dragon into my skull. I can guess that the incident on 95 in Connecticut was the main cause but were there also mitigating factors? Some unknown or strange attractor that provided a pathway for one to curl inside my skull? I should do a survey to see if there are others like me. Do all dragons curl up and assure you everything will be all right when making first contact? Did they slip from one reality into my physical world or were there worlds within my skull? It's all speculation. I'd even speculate that both could be true. And there could be many more paths they can follow and cross. Pablo Neruda wrote about toes locked in a shoe. Perhaps my toes also have contact with other realms. I would not want to keep dragons stuck in my sneakers all day long. I think I'm stepping over and into other realms all the time. This would mean that other realms may be stepping over and crossing into my realm all the time as well.

~ ~ ~

Clearly, my mother withheld dragon information from me. She also never told me about osprey. She never once came close to a sex talk with me. And learning about my period was a totally unexpected wake up call. Was she a bad parent? The only time I ever saw her take a walk was for raw clams in Asbury Park. Who knows what that might mean? My relationships with land and water have been broken or disrupted. The generations I come from might have had a long-term relationship with place. I don't know that history. My mother didn't either. The story I do know is only two generations old. But, my mother does hold another connection to a river for me; and not in name only. Although, Lena, ought to mean 'heart of the good.' She certainly brought me summer and summer was the gateway for me toward osprey, water dragon, and Nolletquesset.

~ ~ ~

Virg was trying to tell me that she was my crow sister. Were then crows suddenly appearing in my day world no coincidence? You may find this foolish, but I find that synchs, synchronicities, or meaningful connections happen all the time. I pay attention because when they happen I feel like I just got caught in a spring shower of the Tao. Virg and I, we're connected in the wake-a-day world through crows. One day I will dance with the Crow Women as she does now. When Virg threw a clot and her life was hanging in the balance, all of us at the hospital, this was around 1 am, meditated or sent healing. We did this as a group. I went on a spontaneous journey. I saw Virg fly off with the crows. I didn't tell anyone about this except Lynn. When Virg was flying away I remember looking up to the sky and yelling questions up to her. She was on her way to the journey-lands. She hollered back, and that wasn't easy because she always spoke so softly, that she couldn't fly with so many questions on her.

    Crows would hardly stoop to be considered mere messengers. They're more of a paradigm shifting velvet twilight gliding yakker. They recognize good and evil. They remember human faces and those that have been bad actors should watch out. Crows will peck them into order. They unite friends. Or, I should say, they reunite friends. They dance the danceless dance that keeps the world turning. Even water dragons move aside or fly away to give crows their air space. Virg was trying to tell me how simply cool beans it was to be a Crow Woman. Cool beans. Cool, velvet crows.

like a blessing

One directive from my mentor always stuck with me. Never stop asking questions. She wasn't as likely to say that there's no such thing as a stupid question. Now and then, with a smile, she would say to me, "Now, that is a stupid question." Only because I would ask questions that seemed as if I just arrived from the void. She wanted me to remember who I was even if I couldn't quite settle on who I was at the time. She objected to finite thinking, posing dualities, and artificial manipulation of facts that squash the horizon. About finite thinking, she would say, "If you know the end, why would you head in that direction?" About posing dualities, she'd say something like, "If either-or went up a hill, who cares what they fetched?" And 'squashing the horizon', this meant that if you could think like a genuine poet of the haiku, using nature or what comes natural to you in your images, then it's incumbent on you to open yourself to new understandings. Don't be false. If it's not there, share the unknown. Don'ts squash the horizon. The poem itself should be an awakening. From unaware to aware. That was the goal. But also, she believed in community. All efforts should keep in mind the community. She meant people, yes, but she meant, and this would not be apparent to people-centered people, that all beings were members of the community. You could only belong if you had compassion for all beings, all wildlife, the land and waters. She made no distinctions between community members. She made it clear that you needed to put time into belonging. If you didn't grow up in a community that respected nature you could work your way into it. She did say this a few times, almost like a gesundheit when you sneeze, like a blessing, "Laugh, cry, and then work."

~ ~ ~

The last time I saw a dragon is easy to remember because it curled inside my skull as traffic sped by on I95. I saw other dragons in the journey-lands with the Old Woman. But they were not specifically visiting me. I remember the sense of safety the dragon offered. I have felt that at different times in my life. After visiting my family in Nevada. That always feels like a balm or a shot of B12 and I feel like I'm shored up against loneliness for a few months. I have not figured out what this loneliness is all about. There are people in my life but the emptiness comes round like a siren song threatening to drown me. Well, it doesn't just threaten, it pulls me off the ship, off the known world. Let me tell you, terra firma is a very good thing. And it brings me, however I come by it, a sense of safety. What is the danger I'm feeling? Is the loneliness, the emptiness, a threat? After all, a warm hello, a 'just checking on you' call from a friend, or a dragon curled inside my skull removes all of that in an instant. Even emptiness, which sounds like something too slippery to distance yourself from, is gone. Scientists know the truth to that lie called empty space. It's got stuff in it. Dragons must know about space because they travelled through it a long ways to reach Earth and their beloved birds. And one of their descendants, or possibly an original traveler, curled inside my skull. I am grateful for that experience. I am also able to appreciate what I did experience now and I long to have the dragon in my life again.

~ ~ ~

Everyone knows you can hide an awful lot of something inside your own skull. If you've noticed any dragons curled up in the corner of your head or home, or if they are very bold, in your living spaces, you might understand, this is no ordinary time. This is the time to engage with community and help Earth. Start with a monarch butterfly. Start with a sparrow. Start now. This is the time.

~ ~ ~

I hope these stories comes through as 'a just checking on you call from a friend.' And that you'll go to the nearest wetlands, or open your door and listen for birds. Everything around you is nature but for some it's helpful if someone points out the birds, the cicadas' summer tunes, the spring peepers. You may have gotten busy, you may have not noticed. You have had difficulties and are struggling. When you can, open your door and listen. Look. Shadows are nature too. All of what we produce, alter, and enjoy, is nature. Wildlife, flowers and animals, are somehow seen by the world as separate from us. Many of us know this is not so. We recognize our kin. I do. It's my hope that if you've been separated from nature, that you can see, hear, and feel the bond again. Many cultures have language that only know this way. They do not see any separation from them and Earth and all wildlife. Their words and living, their planning, and doing are connected to the body, air and great spirits of this world. Their shadows too.

It is my dream that you feel the solace nature brings; that you feel the sense of belonging and your place as a part of the whole living world. You have kin that fly and swim; relations that grow in the ground, on the ground and reach to the sky. Leaves on the trees that try to make them sail. Information pulled from context is coming at you like an enormous haboob, rolling toward you and taking over the horizon. That is why you might feel afraid and lonely. You might not even see the sparrows' shadows on the ground or crows flying overhead. Yes, we need our own kind, our relations, but if they are not there, you have to know that you are loved and you are not alone. And if they are there, join the chorus of all beings with them. Just open the door. The Earth and sky are waiting to rejoice with you.

~ ~ ~

There were more notes on the blue dragon that I had saved so as to savor. This blue dragon wrote as if it stood apart from its kind. "They fail miserably all the time." I didn't know what that meant but I could guess they tried a few homes before they found Earth and our birds. The blue dragon wrote that, "They leave streams of joy, the lasting effect of rainbow spray, the curry of moments." And my blessing day, when one curled inside my head, reminds me that their history is fraught with pain. But they searched for a new home and reacted with joy when they saw birds. If there was a Big Bang and all particles and pieces of materials were flung far and wide, then maybe our stardust shares something in common with the dragon's home world. Maybe, birds that navigate thousands of miles during their annual migrations, have, after all, a common ancestor with dragons. Dragons might have found their way here because they were heading toward a home that was built into the fabric of their being. They love Earth. They may appreciate it more than many of us humans. The vast majority of us have not yet gotten the message, we have to take care of our home. This is the time. Dragons know it because they've so recently, in their timeline, found sanctuary here. They were almost disappeared many times in many worlds. They know that one of the names for this time is the Age of Extinction. They've become adept at moving between many realities. They have an innate wisdom borne from being attached to nature like a mother to a child. They know a thing or two about making a stand and showing their love. They're not just gliding on bird dreams. They're building momentum. The creative force of imagination is something all particle physicists should know in addition to gravity and the electro-magnetic field. There are seen and unseen worlds. They are connected. It is possible that bird songs are the connective tissue and dragons have learned to travel on nature's morning choir.

what must be shared, call them songs

I beg your indulgence for the songs that follow, each one like a piece of moss that lifted off the ground, as some mosses do, but remain a part of the landscape I want to share.

June 3 - I know for now that the work can begin again. Everything unfolds from a question laid humbly on the ground or one that flies in a gentle breeze from your lips. I believe I started this way but nothing is clean cut or direct. Sometimes I am on this path and sometimes doubts create shade. In and out, forward and backward. Same as time in the wake-a-day world where time is the weaver. Here, time is a part of the path no more than a stone or a fallen feather.

~ ~ ~

Familiar beauty
like my cat Stoner's exquisite eye makeup.
I feel the same intimacy when I look at the sky.
beauty is kin.

~ ~ ~

No need to go to the journey-lands. I saw a young eagle learning its new grace soar through the air like a middleweight champion. I got into my car, buckled up and did a K-turn heading up the little rise in the park toward the exit when I glanced at my clock. 7:11 pm. I laughed because this time often comes paired with special moments. I asked Lenny if there was any way to make a buck on the numbers other than the Pick-3 lottery which pays no better than a bookie. Nothing he could think of.

~ ~ ~
When do songs become cantos?
~ ~ ~

My friend LN, who so often reminds me of my mentor, shared this in an email -
"This morning, I read these lines from the beginning of a poem by WS Merwin:
> The words have been used
> for so many things
> how can they speak now

and it made me think of words as live beings - servants for good or ill - and if they react to their placement and the purpose of their use?
Using words gently may change a life."

~ ~ ~

We leave stones at the grave
to give weight to our memories
and hold onto the love that
lingers through time and mistakes.

~ ~ ~

There is a river in Yakutia with her name.
In the winter it is a road
so people are not isolated by the season.
They are able to float down the Lena again in May.

~ ~ ~

There are several ways to travel a river,
to accept memory,
to move down a long stretch of grief
which has no measure of time or distance.
Nobody really knows this road too well.
Memories of it dissipate.
They may return from the mind's grey bends

when everything is moving.
Right now you notice that everything is different
and that the river remains.

~ ~ ~

Let your heart, loneliness, and whatever else speaks to you, move you to the work. If you don't let them sing you will be lost forever in a whirlpool.

~ ~ ~

I knew early on there would not be a knight. Who wants one anyway? They just clank about and need oiling. Yet, something in me always had thoughts of rescue. Whether it was to rescue others, this was the subject of many fantasies, or to be rescued, the idea was there. Was it vestigial? A Hollywood implant? Birds use half a brain to cross oceans while the other half sleeps and dreams. I did not expect a dragon to curl up inside my head. Now that it had, I have to note that it was softer than I would have expected. It was empathic. And it came when I was scared. What I want from the other half of my brain, is to fly on the back of a pelagic bird or tag onto the dragon's tail as it rides an osprey's dream.

~ ~ ~

Our words move in the air. Prayers, like the cantos of falling feathers, are sounds that may change with the light. The wind navigates around obstacles or creates kettles of ideas flying beneath the wings of turkey vultures. Why, with or without ambition, do our dreams travel to meet other dreams? A consensus might form. The will of guardians can move the weight of agreement toward action. These days, there's reasons for many different ways to work toward restoration and stewardship. It's not only the vast migration of people and wildlife through time, it's that long-held customs have been broken. Those who recognize the pieces, know they need to be picked up and put back in place.

~ ~ ~

Some birds never touch or fly over land more than one third of their life. This is not true for osprey although they will fly over open water. I have waited for them hoping to belong to their group. I do not eat fish. Osprey, also known as sea eagles, river hawks, fish hawks, even water dragon, mostly eat fish. I was hoping that I was becoming an osprey. If I did, then eating fish would not be a problem. I came to believe for a while that half of my brain was unknown to the other half where I move around in the world of people. Mammals keep guard with their awake half. Would my brain allow me to be in different worlds? Could I be living two lives at one time, tickled by the quantum entanglement? One half in the world of migrating osprey faithful to my nest and mate. One half waiting for their return while trying to navigate the world of people.

~ ~ ~

A raga weaves sounds so that you are moved on waves and spirals. The song that seems without end takes you everywhere. You forget who you are and then you belong to the song. W. S. Merwin's *Elegy for a Walnut Tree* shares his relationship with the tree through time and seasons, his absences and leavings. He ends the poem "and you were the way I saw the world." Watching the osprey nests high up on telephone poles

and cell towers are the way I see the world. The skies
are more beautiful each year.
~ ~ ~
I regret logging the ospreys' return.
Now I see the skies and feel something is missing until
they're back.
~ ~ ~
Hope is like a comet
that leaves its orbit
eclipsed
by remembering
waters once teamed with lobsters
whales migrated
without being hunted.
~ ~ ~
When rivers gain personhood
and are given the rights of people,
the dispossessed will know home as a compass point.
~ ~ ~
Be the light.
Let it wick off your body
dissipate in the air
join the wind
touch the night
rise in the morning
open with the day.
Be the light.
~ ~ ~
You ask what the air tasted like when I was fifteen.
Smiley had taken a turn under.
My father was dead.
Me and my mother spent a year exiled in the suburbs.

> I listened to Jean Shepherd until the early hours.
> He recited a recipe for root beer scallion soup.
> It tasted like the air.

~ ~ ~

Were it not for shadows, there would be no beauty. ~ Jun'ichirō Tanizaki

~ ~ ~

I cried through the window hoping my tears would stop her leaving. Years later I learned that my mother left to watch movies in New York. The rain didn't stop her either. When I see Hiroshige's rain I remember my tears. He was known as the 'poet of rain' for showing so many people on errands, heads bent from the insistence of the rain and their determination to continue. You can feel the dampness. Some memories come on the same angles and rain down in my head. I once dreamt that I discovered hundreds of Hiroshige woodblocks. The art was in the lines and scenes he created. The colors bring them life. Blocks of my wetlands journal filter into my words here. I sing the lines that capture my soul but your memories will add different colors than mine. I now look through the window and hope my words reach you.

~ ~ ~

And then the wave came, but it wasn't water. The journey was unexpected as all I was going to do was to thank my Grandmother. She called or pulled me near and asked me to describe the bowl or opening over the dry marsh. what do you see? I see the opening to the ocean, I see the marsh. Yes, that is right. But the opening is more. And then a wave came. And what came to shore, as waves will leave things they bring from across the world, was my future. It's close, the dream.

~ ~ ~

The saltmarsh elder guards the bulwarks.
Its lance-shaped leaves ready to protect.
But it does not do a good job against the wind and weather

~ ~ ~

Like wood in salty air my hair is turning gray.

~ ~ ~

All things are possible with water, even the desert. I must go down to the sea again, but first I'll stop by the river, where the invasive phragmites surround the bulwarks. You can see the river through their fringe. Sometimes it's just a thin line of water. Sediment from upriver has made all of us, and the osprey, contend with mud. Nobody cares to dredge and allow the deep pools for the fish. My thoughts are like the invasive phragmites. Loren Eiseley wrote that "If there is magic on this planet, it is contained in water." For sure. I'd add, it's also contained in birds, and, of course, mud. Didn't we come from mud? Who can remember? I sound like my mother. Her belly looked like a whoopie cushion when she was in the tub. I remember patting it to make splashes when I got in with her.

up the creek

I went down to the wetlands very early the morning of the day before Mrs. Teale was to come. I was so aware that I was waiting for a day to pass and that wasn't living. I could even hear Mrs. T say that to me. So, I dragged my lazybones down to the river. If nothing else, I could share the news with the river and all that were listening that Mrs. T was coming to visit. But when I got there, I debated whether to get out of the car or just stay putskie. Laziness comes in many forms. As much as I loved being there, that morning, it was a debate whether to get out of the car or just sit. I opened my car window and felt a beautiful breeze. In fact, it was so enticing that I got out of the car and headed to the bulwarks to have a sitzkie there. Laziness abides even when I think I'm moving freely and following my heart (I know this because I have to feel a fierceness to know I'm pulled by something positive. Until, at least, I've relaxed into my own rhythm. But I know I'm not there yet.) Something about the wind was enough to pull me off my butt and got me going.

  The county works people had left a pallet along the left side of the parking lot. The porta-john was new so I suspect the pallet was from that delivery. I was heading back home after a brief hello to the river and osprey. A wind caressed me open a memory. It was like a vision. But it was a memory from when I was a kid and not one I ever recalled, not the most magical part of it at least, before. How is that even possible? I knew Shark River when I was a kid. I was at this river long before and never connected the memory to it until now.

~ ~ ~

I was with two summertime kids. Please don't ask me their names 'cause I don't remember. One was a boy, he had to be older. He was taller. And I think it was his sister who was also with us. We were dropped off at a nearby park. I'm guessing, as often happened in the summer, much to my dismay, that someone said 'Oh, I bet they'll have a great time playing together.' I hated being forced to play with anyone in the summer especially because I had my haunts, the beach, the arcade and either or both with Maryann, my best summer buddy.

When I was a kid, I rarely ventured farther inland when I was down the shore than two or three blocks to the store on Newark Avenue in Bradley Beach. Only then because my mother sent me to the S&S Market for a few items that Morris carried. He had pickles in wooden barrels. Gathering them into the containers was my favorite form of fishing. Going to a park was not even something I did that often when I was home in Newark. The smell of the soil and trees drives up your nose in the summer the same way wasabi does now or some of the pickling spices did back then. I didn't like it but I don't know that I could have figured that out to say so. I was stuck there with them when their mother dropped us off and said she'd pick us up in a few hours. Next thing I recall was sliding down a small hill to a creek. And there she was, our boat, also known as a pallet. We didn't hesitate to get on it and see how far the creek could take us. I found a great branch, the boy found another and his sister just sat down on the front of the pallet, ignoring the splinters sticking up like wet bangs and waited for us to go. The water was rusty. It was never deep, no more than five or six inches I'd guess. But I remember viewing all of it, the water, the banks of mud, with tremendous suspicion. The only water I ever knew was the ocean. Or, the polluted Fletcher Lake. No rust at either place and no mud for sure. Other than the bathtub in Newark - we only took showers in the summertime in Bradley - I'd say I could count my personal knowledge of bodies of water on one hand. But I knew a thing or two about rowing and I was quite aware, even at that young age, that we were up the creek without a paddle. Branches are rarely good substitutes. But it's what I had and I remember being glad I had at least that. I remember the boy wanted to be the captain of the ship. I wasn't giving up my limb no way, no how, but he fended off the main blocks to our passage and I kept a wary eye on everything else with my branch at the ready.

  Just for now, I'm going to give the boy a name. If he reads this and wants to claim ownership, I'll be glad to swap his name out. Dennis turned out to be more adventurous then me. His sister, let's call her Callie, was just fine sitting at the front of the pallet hugging her knees. The smells that assaulted me, rotting vegetation by the water, the bugs, all made me yearn to be back at the beach. Thunder and lightning were better than this. Then came this bug skating on the water. Legs like thick hairs made them cover more distance than I'd have guessed until I saw them move. They really creeped me out. Yuck. Nothing like that in the ocean. Not even on polluted Fletcher Lake. I'm guessing these bugs liked the deep woods' shade. Maybe their feet would fry on sunny, polluted water.

It was hot. My clothes felt sticky. The water skaters gliding all over every inch of water also made the rusty colored creek less appealing than sweat and goo. I stayed as much put on the pallet as possible. Honestly, when we finally snagged, but good, as my mom would've said, and I was only slightly impaled by a thumb-sized branch bit sticking out of the main branch that snagged us, I was done with the creek. Thankfully, Dennis agreed. The water took us as far as we could go. It remained for us to get up a muddy embankment with no sure hand or footholds. More mud. More yuck as far as I could tell. My idea of the outdoors never included the woods. This introduction wasn't blessed with any kind of fun. Of course, I have since come to love mud. Who knew?

    Dennis and Callie scrambled up the mud wall faster than me. I still hung onto the hope of keeping all the dry spots, or if not dry, clean spots, on my fingers. It made climbing slower. The moist grass was at first a relief but the squish from each step of my sneakers proved mentally challenging and affected my walking. I moved so slowly because I was sure something was going to seep out of my shoes with each step. I created more mud as I went along. My steps made that amazing gastrointestinal suction sound that plungers will do when working a clog in the tub. I fully expected to see a gliders' leg to reach past the rim of my sneaker and gain access to the world above the creek. And then, who knows what might happen if they could run across fields as quickly as they covered the surface of the water.

As I recall, I kept walking. Dennis and his sister found ways to chase each other like those white butterflies tracing a double helix in the air. Until they stopped. And they stopped short. When I caught up to them, we were all standing at the edge of a clearing. The grass was as short as Dennis' Marine haircut. The arch of trees surrounding this area offered some shade, except at the opening where we found ourselves.

We weren't alone.

Where to begin? There was a gathering of all kinds of people, all colors, ages, but mostly older people. There were also animals, just sitting in this area, among them. Lord knows there were bugs too. It was still early in the day. Some birds were filtering into and out of the trees as if they were part of the gentle breeze. I remember that breeze because it cooled me and dried my tee shirt. Everyone there sat in half circles like the ancient Greek theatres. Each half circle got smaller and smaller as they approached the deepest part of the opening that we were looking into. There, at the head of the whole shebang, stood an old woman.

Honestly, I don't know how I could have forgotten this part of that whole creek adventure. Have pallet, will travel. That memory came to me in the past, but not the part about the Old Woman, for that's who I now knew her to be, the Old Woman. She was talking to everyone and all of them, birds, animals, people, and I imagine, bugs alike, seemed to be listening to her.

My summertime friends remained quiet too. That was something different for them. The dappled light offered no camouflage as we drew closer. The Old Woman saw us and indicated that we should come close and sit down just by the use of her fingers held together opening and closing them to her palm. It worked. Without a word amongst us, we joined the group. Then I heard the old woman speak. She said that there were dragons among us. Everyone seemed delighted to hear this. They all looked to their left and right, ahead and back. Everyone was searching for dragons. My friends and I just sat there, too self-conscious to look anyplace except straight at the Old Woman.

    She snagged my eye with her gaze and before I knew it I followed her lead and looked up at the trees. Nearly every point on each leaf seemed to have something attached. My eyes were really good then but I just didn't believe what I was seeing. Same kind of feeling I remember once when I caught that catfish in Fletcher Lake. My line was so taught I figured it was caught up on something. You couldn't see past the surface of that water. But when I kept turning my wooden H-shaped fishing line holder over and over to reel in the hook I nearly came face to face with a catfish. It was gigantic. Had to weigh at least five pounds. It felt more like a thousand. What I saw on the tips of leaves seemed just as unreal. Little dragons, all different colors. They seemed soft. They were small. I swear they were smiling back at the Old Woman.

the Old Woman talks

"Long ago there was an ancestral link we all shared. Many of you remember, many have forgotten. We are here today because all of us are called together by something within. When you want, I invite you to look to the treetops. We have more friends up there. We also have friends flying about and slipping into the trees. We are here, those seen and unseen, to share our presence with each other. To remember each other. To honor our connections and the ways we move about in the many realities. We know this together, everything starts from a feeling. It may not have a name but it calls to us. That is why we are here. When our world's balance is disturbed, a thousand calls reach toward the skies and waters drawing our attention. We are sometimes called from far away and even far from our kind.

If you ask why, you will get many answers. Our friends up in the trees, connected to us from long ago as well, once travelled from even further away to be with us, to love our world, especially, as you know, the birds. They remind us that our world, like the one they came from, needs our attention, needs harmony, needs the love they bring to be seen and felt by all. The work ahead is big and long. But all work must first start with celebration."

Sounds arose from the gathering. There were those gazing up and many touching each other with affection and playfulness. The Old Woman waited for the wave of congeniality to wash over everyone. And then she spoke again.

"We will have a treasure hunt. Our friends, the dragons, when young, shed scales. All of us are to form groups and gather these scales. Some will have writing on them. Some will serve as windows and telescopes so that you can see the world as they do. As you may know, many have spoken about old texts and missing pages that are written on these young dragon scales. The search begins here and will spread all over the world from the words you share with your kin."

She paused and said, "First, we will listen to the morning songs of the birds. When they quiet, we can begin our search. The work of loving the world into the good begins with the search. We will know when to come together again, as we knew today."

There was some quiet discussion among all at the gathering. A sense of peace seemed to come through to me standing in the back. The words 'dragon scales' echoed in my mind. I have skipped many thin shells on the surface of the ocean. They were nearly as clear as glass but had a texture like ice. Perfect skipping shells were prized. I'd only see them now and then. I stood there wondering if they were baby dragon scales. Imagine, counting how many times a baby dragon scale will skip over the water.

As if anticipating concern about the frailty of these scales, the Old Woman spoke and said that baby dragons lose the scales as they fly across the skies clinging to their mothers and fathers, who themselves are holding tight to bird's dreams from one dream to another, from one reality to another. They shed these scales as they grow. All of this, at that time, seemed to make sense even though she was talking about dragons. It also seemed exotic, although I didn't have the means to understand that at the time, so it registered as something off but on enough that I accepted it.

    The Old Woman continued, "There is a tale, and many believe its truth, that a blue dragon's writings have been written on the scales. Find them and you have found one of our greatest myths and brought it to all of us. The blue dragon's words are considered greater than the mysteries the oldest trees have held in their rings, greater than the magnetic codes of migration held in the deepest places of our birds' eyes. These pages are as renowned as all the mysteries that Gaia is said to hold, equal in stature to the memories of water; and a part of the immortal songs of the dragons themselves who are said to have ridden the dreams of far flung galaxies before they came to Earth. I believe it possible that many can find missing scales that carry this blue dragon's tale. As you move through the world, sewing the search with love and mystery, remember the winds that lift the birds to the skies touch everything and everyone. If the blue dragon's words are not on the scales you find, they may be in the wind where only sacred listening will reveal them."

~ ~ ~

Since I was made aware of her, I have always felt like I'd like to know the Old Woman better. Turns out I have known her all my life. A wind brought all these memories back. There is so much we don't know about the elements. Science impresses with its move toward greater understanding. But I also recall that different ways of knowing unveil different realities; and that one reality without the others can be barren. Were it not for this wind teasing me out of the car, I may never have remembered this long time ago experience that links all of my life to the Old Woman. And to dragons.

The gathering of all in the park ended when someone stood up from the group, it was an old woman also, and today, as I recall her, she had a familiar face. She said, "When our purposes are merged, imbalances shift toward the good." With those words, all quietly, seamlessly dispersed, many whiffling through the grasses looking for baby dragon scales as they went. Many, with a steady purpose it seemed, but moving on a wave of quiet joy, even a sense of contentment, as they followed some path that only they knew. The Old Woman turned toward the deeper woods. Even with her back to the crowd I could pick her out among the many figures also entering the woods. She wears her soul like a shawl.

~ ~ ~

I've been going down to the river for a long time. But it was longer than I could have known until this memory opened again in me. I have been at this river since I was a kid. I'm not the first person wondering how we forget the magic of the world when we were young. I think that sometimes many of us are writing about ways we love the world so that we can remember what we once knew; that we loved the world and want to protect it, that there is magic in just being in nature. And we always belonged. Turns out, it was truer than I thought, there are several ways to travel down a river.

i ask all the time

I ask my cat Molly all the time, "When did you first realize you're an animal?" Cats. If they deign to answer, you might get love in the form of a rub by, that's when they walk by and deliberately touch you (of course, nothing a cat does is by accident, everything is deliberate), or the droll look which is always interpreted by each cat "owner" based upon the weakest places in our psyches. Molly knows where the doorways are to my guilt and give-in. She just looks at me, and I'm done for. So, as with everything, cats and their looks are always open to interpretation. You can never be sure and that's how they like it. You learn their language. They will not learn yours. I know I'm almost always in trouble from those looks and I'm never sure what I did to deserve them.

But the real question, if I'm interpreting that look correctly in this instance, is, when did I forget I was an animal? When did I forget that I am earth, air, water and fire? I have to say, it is elemental. I am elemental. We all are.

The best part of language is silence. Among people, facial expressions or gestures, however one makes them - with arms, legs, elbows, eyebrows - are the true syntax of conversing. The pauses, the spaces between sounds, jam packed with meaning. Why is that? I asked Virg this question once. She said it's because we are reaching further back into our brain's development where we learned to communicate and that was more body than sound, more gesture than phrase. She said when we first communicated it was with short sounds, each one cupped in silence. I remember she added, because she knew I was addicted to this candy, "You know, like peanut butter covered by chocolate." And she continued, because we were once, long ago and in a land far, far away, English majors, "And when we are taken back, so to speak, or as Chaucer would say, 'Sooth for to sayn,' we're on a genuine pilgrimage to our ancestral lives. There, right there, is where we are connected to the life force."

    I asked my mentor the same question. "There is no one answer but when we pose the question and wait in quiet, we should respect what comes to us." She also believed that standing still and listening were all a part of language. She once told me that is why she learned that trees and mountains talk. She stood by them. And one day she heard them. She had learned to listen. Mrs. Teale said she learned something similar by crisscrossing the country with Mr. Teale. They both noticed the natural boundaries of sound and silence when they were in the woods or at the shore. There is always talking going on, she told me. And "silence should be known by so many names because it is always different depending upon context."

    I know I might have mentioned this before, but languages are disappearing because lives and peoples, their cultures, are being absorbed by the more powerful cultures cutting into their worlds. The deepest wound this causes is to the connective tissue and knowledge base that people have to the land. Think of it like the tissue that you see when you peel a hard-boiled egg. Without catching that thin tissue just right, you can't easily peel the egg. Language is that tenuous and continuous element that helps to hold the world together. It is remarkable for its place as matrix, mother and home to the living but also keeper of the wisdom and home to our ancestors and their store of knowledge; and if we're fortunate, home to our future relatives.

There are people designated as the keepers of their language. There are people who also understand the language of birds. And those who can recognize hundreds of bird songs. All of these languages and songs hold my hope for the world. May they always be heard; may they always be sung.

the council of all beings

Mrs. Teale pulled into the parking lot in her rental. I could see her face from where I leaned against the weathered wooden rail at the grand entrance to my wetlands. The entrance was merely the space between two sections of rail fencing but the access to my wetlands is what made it grand. She was laughing and it was contagious so I also began to laugh. She parked, she laughed getting out of the car and walking to me and I laughed walking to her. And then we hugged, a bumpy hug at first because we continued to laugh. It had been too long I can tell you. Way too long. And then we embraced and really held each other close and then the tears and then more laughs. No words the whole time.

~ ~ ~

Mrs. Teale and I spoke about the word 'liminal' weeks before her arrival. I've always loved that word. She had said it's because it's about discovery, that something is just over the next hill or roll in the road and you'll soon see it coming into view. "It's hope," she said. Hope. I agreed. Then I told her about this story, turns out she knew it also but neither of us could remember the name or who wrote it. About kids running around and playing in their idyllic neighborhoods where just breathing the air filled them with joy. Life was a sweet, happy, daily dream. But now and then one of them would go missing. Each kid soon learned that would also be their fate. And it added a momentary note of sadness, uncertainty to their lives. They would be born, they were told. And when you're born, you go to Earth. The story was really about how we all come from a place of soul. That our journey here is such that we forget that we came from soul. Joy is always a reminder of that place. When we become embodied, this story, and many philosophies seem to say, we forget our beginnings.

I have a different idea of our original connection to the great spirit. It's in everything here. When we recognize our place in nature, we are connecting to the great spirit. Our journey never separated us from soul because Earth has always been our home and starting place. Maybe all the work of the many groups and people around the world toward restoring, stewarding and preserving our home, maybe all of this is liminal. And we're on the cusp of remembering who we are and our connection to spirit; and our many layered relationship to Earth.

But when she was right here with me I had to bring up liminal again. "I'm just so struck by that word." She listened and then she said, "It's not always about the jump or the stepping over onto a different landscape. Most often the boundary is internal and can get absorbed into our unconscious so quickly as to not wake us up when we approach it or even step over. But there will always then be something whispering in our heads, some thought or sound that doesn't take shape as an action but will create a calling, a yearning, that maybe we do, maybe we do not, know how to satisfy."

"I guess that's right. There is something calling to me and it feels like it's from far away. I thought it was the osprey. And it might be. But now I'm wondering if it's many voices, and even other things I can't know to name."

~ ~ ~

"Look, yesserlegs!" Mrs. Teale spotted some lesser yellowlegs. I told her that I started calling them yesserlegs by mistake. The name stuck. And I noticed that spoonerisms abound when memory hazards are around. We were trying to imagine what it was like to have such long legs, a long beak and still be able to fly. We agreed that their beaks alone would make flying awkward. They make such sweet sounds, a lot like the killdeer but softer. Mrs. T said, "Maybe they ease into the air on their own songs." Now, you're talking. That's what I thought too, now that she said it. So many people have opposed anthropomorphizing because they feel it leads to harming wildlife. I'm not so sure. Maybe that was once true. Today, I think the more ways we can find to identify with the wild, the greater people can find ways to love our natural world, the wildlife, the plants, trees. And that's the hook, right? If you love something, you'll protect it, respect it.

    Mrs. T and I talked about the news we've both heard of some rivers gaining personhood. "It's a good thing." She agreed. And then she riffed on it, "Perhaps the river flows into otter territory and becomes half otter. You've told me about half dragons and half otters, yes? What about the river? Now that it's got legal rights it might also be seen in the fullness of our imaginations for capabilities and sensitivities beyond our utilitarian default thinking. So, you could be half you and half river. Or I could see a raft of otters charm the dragons into the water, into their curls and slides down banks; onto their backs into the floating armadas of the joyful creatures with the densest fur. And they love shellfish, which the banks of this river offer in abundance. What could be more joyful? Half otters, half river dragons."

    "Right, the mussels are the blue/black borders of the river's banks. Plenty of otter food to go around. And dragons could slide into otter dreams."

~ ~ ~

We sat down to talk and I broke open a small cooler pack with the snacks and drinks I had prepared. I had a roll-up blanket pack in my car so that we could have a picnic. It's something I usually didn't do but I will stop everything for a feast, and this was a special day. I had goat and sheep cheeses, almond crackers, salty kalamata olives, shelled hard boiled eggs (no salt for them, so the olives had to step up); sun tea, and my ever present hotnot tea, which was a splash of goat's milk with stevia and hot water; something I developed because I would otherwise drink strong black tea all day and night. She declined a sip of the hotnot and opted for the dirty lemonade I made. A family secret that can't be shared at this time, but so refreshing.

"So", she said to me, "what is that look on your face? What is going on?" I had to tell her. Once she stopped using contractions I knew I had to come clean even if I didn't know where or how to begin. Somehow, I managed to share the memory of the Old Woman and the gathering in the woods from so many years ago. "From, really," she said, "the start of your being." She reminded me that I never had a formal ceremony, as many do, into my teenage years. She said the river was my initiation. But the gathering, well, that was something else she noted. "I'd say, that was a council. In fact, a council of all beings."

A council of all beings. I let that phrase sink in. Mrs. T reminded me about what happens when you touch a sugar cube to the very top of a steaming hot demitasse. Slowly, the demitasse climbs up the cube. "Remember?" She paused. "Remember, one of your favorite analogies? You've been coming here every day. You're the cube." I was listening and smiling. But also I remembered about the soul story. And wondered out loud if this is how we remember our long ago connections to the great spirit in all life, by happy accidents, by steeping, or by following a path that calls us. Sometimes, by sheer, dumb luck. She said, "Maybe most often we don't even know we're on a path until something opens and we go, 'Ah.' Little pockets of awakening. Especially for those of us who have not been schooled by our elders with long-held knowledge."

~ ~ ~

I shared more details from my memory of the gathering in the woods. Many might not see the dragons on the tips of leaves. I had to follow the Old Woman's lead. At first I saw the sky through the spaces the leaves created. They were like celestial windows. But she was showing us the dragons and also, I believe, a way toward other realms; some of which may be visible in certain states or frames of mind; some that may seem imaginary until you are shown a path.

~ ~ ~

Mrs. T suggested that our blanket and foods, our talk, was an open invitation for all council members to join us. She even squared her shoulders and shifted them back in preparation for making a formal announcement. An invitation as it turned out. She opened the meeting, using her deeper, more formal voice, I've heard her many voices over the years, and announced, "We humbly ask for your participation and communing." She moved our picnic to another realm. I understood what was happening. It was now ceremony. I followed her and tried to bring a sense of solemnity into my voice while feeling quite humble. After all, this was the eagle's airspace, this was where I would often depart for my journey-lands, this was a sacred place for me, and this was the river's home and the birthplace of my osprey. It would have felt like a lot of responsibility if Mrs. T hadn't winked and also brought a level of fun. So, I added, "We want to join you and leave space to embrace all that we join and those who join us."

~ ~ ~

Mrs. T knows my heart. Even so I felt a little shy when I shared that I'd like to invite the Old Woman too. She went, "Of course. Agency. We have that and she would love it." And then I also just had to stand and at first I felt like a kid, and then something happened and it felt as if something from the sky and something from the earth decided to come through me and fill me with a sense of 'I own this.' I don't know how else to express it. I felt I had to project the sureness of my belief and wish. So, I went from feeling awkward to feeling that this was high play and high time. It was also high tide and time to own these words, "I'm inviting all women who want to participate, whether in body or spirt or by heart-proxy, to join us. Especially older woman. For too long, the sounds of our voices, our songs and concerns, have not been heard." Mrs. T added, "We belong." And I added, "And the dragons belong. The osprey. The wetlands. All our lands and waters."

 Mrs. T and I were solemn and smiling. She stood up and encouraged me, by a sweeping gesture of her long, elegant arm, to include the river. "Let me introduce you all to Nolletquesset, provider of clams, home to wandering winter seals, and the occasional dog shark. The river of good."

the jump

As we walked toward the bulwarks I spotted the eagle in a pine tree on my side of the river. No sooner had I pointed her out to Mrs. T, she flew past the stream of river coming in with the tide. You could see that the mud flats were breached by the incoming water and slowly disappearing. I shared my memory of seeing one of the eagles drink for the first time, remembering how she took three or four steps. Now that is really something to watch, I told Mrs. T, as I mimicked the eagle's walk, pretending to hold up layers and layers of clothing so that they don't get muddy and bogged down with water. I demonstrated. I bent over with my elbows sticking out and my hands hanging down by my knees grasping imaginary layers. "They get so bogged down." I acted as if I were hoisting them up. I made a face as if the mud and weight of my skirts were such a chore. Then showed how they walk across the mud, swinging one leg around and then the other.

      We watched the eagle take off with more wing beats than I would have thought needed to soar into the oaks just below where her empty nest was. Without taking my eyes off her, I said, "Imagine being across a river from each other and being able to see each other so clearly as if we were just across a dinner table."

We stood at the bulwarks and watched the river. Mrs. T was wearing a long, flowing beach top. I'm not sure exactly what it covered. When she lifted her arms, the material, all soft, blurry pastel colors, opened like a wing. It was enchanting and moved my mind to recalling something Mrs. T once told me. She had said that I am on the border of one reality and another, on the brink, in the liminal rite of passage. I'm not sure how to dress for such occasions but I loved what she had on. It flowed and was a perfect blend for the day, for the slight wind that curled around my shoulders and the late summer sun. I had on my very special, all occasion cargo shorts with pockets for everything except a cell phone. After years of pocket starvation, myself, and many I know, discovered that we can buy men's clothes and have an abundance of pockets. You can never have enough pockets. `Not exactly like squirrels and some birds who hide their acorns, but I still can have trouble locating whatever it is I thought so important that it needed its own pocket. My motto, I did not actually have a motto for any length of time, but currently, my motto was, as Mrs. T put it, "Be prepared for takeoff." And so, like many of my fine feathered friends, my pockets, in lieu of my genetic shapeshifting, would hopefully help me to prepare. Or, as Mrs. T just said, I can have "little pockets of awakening."

    I wasn't quite there yet. Although a sense of urgency was building. Before I knew it my body told me that it was time to go. I moved a few steps back from the bulwarks and looked toward the cell tower.

My osprey were not there. But something of them was in me. Something that called from me to them and them to me with a little dragon spin on it to boot.

    We both noticed a movement on the water. It was a hooded merganser right across from us where there usually is a sandbar. It took off with a quick splash before heading toward the bowl of the river. Yesterday, the sky was filled with the mergansers' sound. Today, we could hear the water break open from the merganser's feet. All the beauty here, the wise trees, the birds that grab onto the reeds, it is my paradise and I felt doubly happy to share it with Mrs. T.. I told her that I planned to seed bomb milkweed in paradise again when the cold weather comes. The parks people won't allow an official planting.

    Looking through a veil of time across the river, I remembered how persistent our grey days in winter felt.

~ ~ ~

I looked at Mrs. Teale who had her eyes closed as she was absorbing the joy from the sun. Then, with plenty of room for takeoff, I started running toward the bulwark. I could see the water covered the broken areas of the tops of the planks, but a few edges remained backed by the phragmites. The mighty phragmites try all the time to stop the flow of the river. But this is Nolletquesset and it flows from here to the ocean, it threads through to the Gulf Stream. It touches my mother's namesake river, the Lena. I called out as loud as I could "I AM WATER DRAGON!" and then I leapt over the bulwark, and cannonballed into the deep river. Thank the gods it was high tide. When I broke back to the surface I could see Mrs. T running toward the bulwarks. She was yelling something, but I wasn't quite sure. I was amazed how well she cleared the rough top of the bulwarks and then I heard her, "I AM MARSH HAWK!" Of course she's Marsh Hawk. Of course. All this time, my friend, with the extraordinary powers to really hear me, because she has hearing like an owl. She has always been my marsh buddy, she's always been Marsh Hawk.

~ ~ ~

Mrs. Teale climbed out of the water first. She had to leave and she knew I had to stay a while to stand in the place that launched a new turn in my becoming. She called out to me once she knew my ears cleared the surface. "So, what else do tomboys transform into?" I just smiled and she smiled in return. Joy rose like the tide and pulled me into a place I never wanted to leave. I am water dragon.

when mrs. t leaves

"I don't want you missing me when I'm gone. You should write a book. It'll keep you out of trouble. Call it, 'Nolletquesset, skies and reflections from around the bend.' That way I don't miss you either, knowing you're happily engaged, and we'll see each other before I go north with the spring. The days will be longer then and we'll work on making summer come sooner." She continued as she took my face in her hands, and tickled me around my cheeks with her fingers, "The mornings are getting darker but soon both morning and day get their act together, and hope begins to send out its tendrils."

~ ~ ~

"You know what?" she added, "I've been thinking about what you told me, wondering what Virg was trying to tell you. Virg was trying to tell you that the dream world and the waking world have paths that cross back and forth. All the time. The way a flower is held by the stamen is how the dream world holds our world." She winked at me knowing that my spirits might flag when she left. "Sink into that and feast." It wasn't tough love. She always managed to bring poetic love and cohesion and continuity. Sometimes, I'll tell you, I think we were also connected by some kind of stream.

~ ~ ~

With Mrs. T leaving I went through some of my strategies for bucking up. One I no longer needed since I left that miserable job. But, I was reminded that I missed and should visit my two friends that would see me on the way to work, the Brazilians. They are beautiful sycamores, and these two in particular always seemed to be celebrating so they reminded me of the Carnival festival in Brazil. They also reminded me of the imbolic and it is connected to celebrating the approach of the season, for me the season of return. Their branches stretched toward the sky as if they were doing their morning qigong. They're bold, saucy. I call them each Brazil and greeted them every morning with "Hi, Brazil!" The smaller one is by the traffic light before I turned left, just two blocks from the job. It's beauty shines through its leaves, even when they turn with the weather. The biggest one, gay and most festive is nearer to the job, and was my last roadside sanctuary and support. It helped me buck up so the nasties' foul mental spray could not touch me. We said hello every work morning. When I first learned about osprey I read they migrate to Brazil and the newbies stay there for their first full year of life before returning to their birthplace. Not all go as far as Brazil. For me, these sycamores, the country Brazil, and my migrating osprey are forever linked. However long it takes them to return, I will be waiting for them through the hollow bone of winter. I know their parents will return to the nest just as spring begins. As I'm ageing I'm getting more sentimental and I think about dying and wondering if anything I've done in my life continues into the evolving seasons. When my osprey leave I'm reminded of a deep wish that I carry. I'd like my friends to hold this place, this waiting space for me when I die. It is a big wish knowing how busy everyone is, how pulled in so many directions and affections. Part of who I am will always be at the bulwarks waiting for the osprey. It would just be good to have some company now and then.

~ ~ ~

The river's central stream across me was moving fast. The tide was leaving and big mud would soon be in front of me. But past that by the ripps area and beyond, a range of river is always in view. I heard the green heron cry out. It flew with a lot of athleticism; small gazelle-like jumps in the air as it pumped across. Solid, graceful. It drew my eyes across the way where I spotted a few red-wings on the tall grasses. The movement of birds always takes my thoughts away from me and flies off with them. I'm sure birds dream of flying when they're sleeping. Flying is that good. We sometimes dream of flying but we'll analyze all the joy out of it. Dragons recognize the beauty of birds and love all the elements they dwell and move through. That means, they love everything. Sooner or later, birds, people, even the sometimes cocky Mrs. T, touch everything, even the contours of the dream world.

~ ~ ~

Mrs. T told me, "We are sisters. Here and now. But I think we always have been. The only thing I don't know is if I'll be a Crow Woman when I move permanently to the journey-lands or if some other group will call me. I'm sure that's a time to explore. As is now, but it's definitely different." She paused as her gaze seemed to gather me in. "I know this, you are my sister," she tapped my forehead, "even if you are weird." She took off in her rental but left me in mystery with a knowing smile. I might add how annoying those knowing smiles can be when you're not in the know. But if you love someone, and I loved Mrs. T, then you're going to end up accepting mystery. Maybe you'll even love it.

~ ~ ~

Evening was slipping on.

belonging

I've figured out where I need to spend time to steep with the stuff of my soul. I rigged it so that I don't have to travel far. I mean, I'm taking an awful lot of credit for falling in love with osprey when I know the river has something to do with it. Not to mention my mother bringing me to summer. The beings, many of the non-human variety in my life, including the elusive river otters, and some special humans, including my absent mentor, are strands in my braid. It's not too tight these days. My head and heart are cinched up within reach of each other. I needed guidance. My life is a weave of many strands, always getting braided up and undone. Same as everyone else. Something sent out a tendril from the wetlands and I was fortunate enough to find it and stand at the bulwarks where I reeled it into my life. Then I looked at the skies, pulled in the air and found that my outbreath completed the connection.

  Believe it or not, I used to worry that my heart wasn't big enough to hold all the love. Now I know the truth because the ocean opened a place inside so that I can remember all that I'm connected to and engaged with, even if I don't know what it's like to turn with a school of fish or finish off my flight by slipping into a tree. I know that I have kin I've never met. Some of them have fins, some have feathers and some are rivers in Russia where my family probably relied on the guidance of a shaman and knew the familiar rhythm of seasons.

  And then there's this, how often we can all be stopped by a familiar chorus of doom? A writer asked "What do you do when the places you love become unreachable?" She was talking about the places in Colorado where her familiar access was no longer, because of the great fires out west. Her question echoes in what I know and what I fear. What do you do when the seasons are no longer a rhythm you recognize? Or when another species is placed on the endangered species list or worse, the list is too long, and this has happened, and a species couldn't be placed on the list? What do you do when you learn, as we all did recently, that our world lost three billion birds over the course of a lifetime? My heart aches. There is no communal ritual to mourn these losses; many of us are taking this blow to our guts in silence. The projections for the next fifty years are even worse. My braid does not come undone but I know that every thread pulled into its weave is fragile and ephemeral. Ephemerals return if you hold the place for them. Bird populations can return if we do the work of stewarding our home which overlaps their habitats. We took a path way back when. Birds flew, we walked. We covered ground together and now sky. Our fates were never separate although many of us might not have seen it that way.

~ ~ ~

They added things up and scientists cannot account for all the unaccountable weight in the universe. This leads them to believe there is more than meets their many ways of looking. People find it astonishing that the Eskimos have so many words for snow. But they never ask why. There are simply different kinds of snow and if you lived where snow was everywhere you'd need lots of ways to describe it. Each word holds a different meaning. Each may provide information, or save you. I hope to learn more about my wetlands. I'd like to know more about the mud and sandbars, the spring crabs, the odd semipalmated plovers that move as if they're in a kabuki play. I'd like to know more about the egrets that perch and light up the evergreen trees along the river and their cousins, the honking, sometimes dilapidated looking herons that stalk the edges across the way; and the gulls that only move quickly when the eagle soars. All make up my spirit home just down the block from where I sleep. The unaccountable weight is dark matter, it's the sounds you can't identify, it's the movements that shimmer with grace like the lace of sunlight on the surface of the water. The unaccountable weight is the spirit of place, the soul of home, the redwings hold on the tips of the tallest weeds. The unaccountable weight is the journey you took while standing your ground, at your special spot, but for the nearly imperceptible rocking that shed your old skin.

~ ~ ~

There's no singular tradition whose rails I learned to walk between, or whose ceremonies I enact to touch those that have come before me. Like so many, I have had to find my own ways. I was open to the influence of many teachers and traditions. Life moved through me like the wind. My heart beats faster when I come to my river. I hope everyone can find a place they love, where you can stand and just be, listen, watch, take it in and become a part of it. Sound is a powerful way the wetlands invokes its presence within. I might not recognize the sound, but I steep in it. How many heartbeats am I hearing, and not recognizing any, when I stand at the bulwarks? I have felt love and solace here. And I transformed the dross of the tired, disruptive energies of people who've lost their kindness in a haze of office politics into a deep peace. I've been here to listen to the tide calling the river out to the sea and when the river calls for its waters to return. I know part of what I'm hearing includes the sound of the heron's quiet breathing as it stalks the small fish. I'm hearing the kingfisher rattle its call across the river to its mate. In the retiring summer days, I listen to the geese inhale one last touch of the river's air as they lift and move together across the western skies. The sounds at Nolletquesset include the heartbeats of the eagles and osprey and their thin faint calls. All that comes here from far away or just up river, the crabs that move on the mud in early spring, all the late summer skimmers, add their sounds. Many strands, some caws, some claws touching the dry oaks and pines, some wings, some splashes and ripples, some waves pushed by the winds and shaped by the river, all ride up into my being. Every shift in tone comes through my core.

~ ~ ~

Touch an ocean wave or a ripple in a stream and you are connecting with the entire world's network of vital energy. You always were a part of the currents that move our spirits and create thermals that lift birds high in the skies. Awareness of such things is an act of joining. I simply fell in love and everything that love can be, sometimes passion, sometimes comfort or companion, has framed all that I shared. There are so many threads that weave into our lives. Please know this, we are the ones that determine the value of the many threads we choose to weave. I've found some and I'm open to more. I'm open to the wind, to the sounds of the wetlands and birds that visit. Somewhere in the vibrations that make up their voices I know we've touched each other, you and I. People you love are connected through birds and skies and winds and trailing echoes of our heart's beat as it joins the flow of water. I am honored by the presence, even the absence, of many beings in my life.

~ ~ ~

There are pristine wild lands. The highest designation for these lands is called wilderness. Where the wild lives. Moving gyres of wind, rivers of flowers unfolding, unpredictable weather, raw, open spaces; dangerous animals; birds sailing through canyons; chaos edging around the calm; untamed nature. Like many, I was unfamiliar with these places and have felt so far from them. Yet wilderness shaped who I am. The wild gave birth to my soul. My mother didn't tell me this but I know she would recognize its truth. I believe that being by the river brings back the distant pieces of my wildness that migrated, or was forced out or moved someplace against its will. Some parts of my wild soul were lost in transition from one generation to another. I want to bring the pieces together. Maybe one piece is a small poem written on a dragon's scale. Whether it's a sewing circle in the journey-lands or in the basement of a church, stitching the pieces of sky and water together, recognizing the lands and waters that nurtured my kin, opening to my connection to the wild, all came together in me because I belong here and I found a place that I love. The many paths I have found brings each place in my life in touch with the other. I belong here, I always have. I just haven't always known it.

~ ~ ~

The beauty of the fleeting moments at the river touches me like a wind. The grasses move like silk blown by the angels, a kettle of vultures towers above the pines near a quiet corner of summer and I look up at the skies framed by their turning.

~ ~ ~

There are so many things to learn about osprey. Do you learn them first or first become one? I have to figure it out. I'll send up my questions to the skies the way I did when I was a kid sending messages up the kite string. The changing tides remind me of all that I'm connected to even if I don't know what it's like to migrate, or work with the wind to get back to my nest, or dive after a fish. They have a quiet rhythm, perhaps muffled by the feathers I'm growing but when I come to the wetlands I am in the song.

~ ~ ~

There was a slight chill. How quickly does the phragmites fall to the cold. My right hand moved to hold my midsection. It's a habit prompted by the feathers layering on my body. I feel the feathers through my tee shirt or sometimes just slide my hand up and rest them on the feathers. So, lower than Napoleon's stance but when I caught myself doing this I had to laugh. How many women freely lay a hand on any part of the front of their body in public? And there I was, the last stand at the bulwarks for the day. And what a day it was. I looked at the place in the trees across the way that one of the eagles just entered. I must have been there two, three minutes longer. As I turned to leave, a small sedan pulled up and this young fellow stepped out of the car. I called to him to let him know the eagle was right across the way. "Cool." But as he started to walk toward the gateless gate at the entrance, the eagle took off, slow but steady. We were both watching as it lifted into a spiral pattern and soared, circling higher and higher. And then it moved over my neighborhood. The young guy and I spoke briefly before he went on his way. I recognized him as someone like me, who loves the river and this wetlands area in particular, which so few in my neighborhood seem to know.

~ ~ ~

For the first time I saw a bat flying over the river. I was there late. The last light lingered along with me. The rest of the day ran off to the west where I looked to see my osprey's tower. The sky was awash with burnt orange. Darkness will soon be down.

~ ~ ~

As I headed to my car, I was reminded of more sounds and voices that made up my Nolletquesset. The Old Woman, the dragons, and who knows how many there are, half or whole; my mentor and the conversations I had with her sometimes drifting into my focus. "Wisdom flies across a vast ocean most of her life but she returns to give birth to another generation." I caught myself nodding 'Yes."

the end for now

afterword

Inspired by actual events. *bird dreams, riding hope* is a mosaic; a weave of many forms and realities. The humans I write about are created from the many ways I have known them or dream of knowing them. My depictions of them are creations and therefore not bio at all but a way to weave in the many facets of our beings through the multiple ways we may have or would have or might have known each other. Inspired by love, deep and abiding friendship and the quilt of memory.

many thanks

I have to offer many thanks and a humbling gratitude that words will not ever convey as well as I'd like to many who have shown me the path and walked down the road with me or offered to when I was ready. I'm grateful and moved to the deepest admiration for Lorraine Niemela, my real life mentor. She tickles my mind and opens so many paths, windows and doors for me that I never knew existed. I walked with Merry Brennan and Pat Heaney down many of the paths leading to these sharings and I'm very grateful for their presence in my life. I know the journey continues too, which is the sweet part of it all. Thanks too to Ryan Borbely for support with the cover design and bridging the technical highway to my porch. Some of the love shared in the book, woven with magic and mystery, is for people I know and have known. Always remembering, always weaving you into my days. And for the osprey and wetlands, the winds, the dragon, I am only possible because of you.

Made in United States
North Haven, CT
13 June 2022